Rhonda Browing White's finely written debut novel brav~~~~
of modern Appalachia, mountainto~
is no simple polemic. White center:
Jasper and Romie, a couple whose l
We root for them as they struggle th
Romie learns, and White shows us t

— **Marlin Barton**, award-winning a ... ... *Pasture Art*

"A poignant, powerful, necessary story of the men and women who work vineyards, forests, and mines they will never own. Moment by moment the writing is incandescent, heartfelt, authentic, full of grace."

— **Robert M. Olmstead**, author of nationally acclaimed *Coal Black Horse* and *Savage Country*

"Men go into dank, dark, dangerous coal mines to win food for their tables and the respect of their fellows. Rhonda Browning White knows this world, and that of the women who cope with the effects: disease, injury, addiction, death. With the inevitability and closing shock of Greek tragedy, she illuminates the joys and agonies of an Appalachian family who face narrowing choices brought about by their own actions. *Filling the Big Empty* is a modern classic of Appalachian literature."

— **Valerie Nieman**, author of *To the Bones* and *In the Lonely Backwater*

"Rhonda Browning White's novel starts with its characters confronting the ravages of mountaintop removal mining and ends with them tackling a chemical spill that poisons their county's municipal water. The author uses this apocalyptic world to explore, with empathy and in a limpid style, the daily struggle of miners, opioid addiction, the importance of family as well as the joys, demands, and challenges of friendship. A captivating and thought-provoking story which leaves us with hope in the face of tragedy."

— **Vinod Busjeet**, author of *Silent Winds, Dry Seas*

Filling the Big Empty tells the story of a haunted people: haunted by a toxic landscape left in the wake of a callous coal industry; haunted by the addictions and struggles of their friends and families. And yet, it is also the story of a people who find a way to bend, no matter how dark the skies, toward hope.

— **Andrew K. Clark**, author of *Where Dark Things Grow*

In her wrenching and moving debut novel *Filling the Big Empty*, Rhonda Browning White bears plangent tribute to a struggling young Appalachian couple and the love that sustains them. Alternately tragic and inspiring, the novel also speaks eloquently to an array of interconnected societal issues--mountaintop-removal mining, opioid addiction, and the quest to save one's family and home from the ravages of corporate greed--while credibly carving a path to redemption.

— **Eric Giroux**, author of *Zodiac Pets* and *Ring On Deli*

Filling the Big Empty paints a vivid picture of life around modern-day Appalachian coal fields. Miners are grateful for the money they make while simultaneously fearing the day it's snatched away, either in the seconds it takes for a mine roof to collapse on them, or in the years the coal ravages their bodies and their lungs. On the backdrop of mountains millennia old, two young couples experience life, death, treachery, fear, betrayal, hope, and discovery. Rhonda Browning White cuts no corners in exposing the desires to leave the mountains, and the inexplicable draw to return to them.

— **M. Lynne Squires**, author of *Letters to My Son*

FILLING
THE BIG EMPTY

A Novel

Rhonda Browning White

REDHAWK
PUBLICATIONS

FILLING THE BIG EMPTY

Copyright © 2024 Rhonda Browning White

ISBN: 978-1-959346-53-1 (Paperback)

Library of Congress Control Number: 2024938459

Any references to historical events, real people, or real places are used fictitiously. Names, characters, and places are products of the author's imagination.

Book design: Robert T Canipe
Cover Design: Patty Thompson
Author Photo: Rebecca Browning Gray
Cover Art: "Romie & Jasper at Endless Point, New River Gorge, WV" by bitkizzy

Printed in the United States of America.

First printing 2024.

SCAN ME

Redhawk Publications
Catawba Valley Community College Press
2550 Hwy 70 SE
Hickory NC 28602
https://redhawkpublications.com

For Jacob, forever My Little Heart.

Portions of this novel previously published in slightly different form:

"Chapter One: Romie" first appeared as "Bondservant" in *Qu Literary Journal.*

"Chapter Four: Jasper" first appeared as "A Big Empty" in *Bellevue Literary Review.*

"Chapter One: Romie" and "Chapter Four: Jasper" also appeared as "Bondservant" and "A Big Empty," respectively, in *The Lightness of Water & Other Stories* by Rhonda Browning White, published by Press 53, October 2019.

The author is grateful to these publishers and their generous editors (especially Kevin Morgan Watson at Press 53), as well as their discerning readers, for believing in her work.

CHAPTER ONE

ROMIE

These mountains are killing me—killing all of us—though I know it's in self-defense. Getting away from here is all I can think about as I step off the bathroom scale, skim my jeans over my pelvic bones, take up the slack inch of denim with a safety pin. Another pound slid off me this week, even though I shoveled the last of an orange-glazed Bundt cake into my mouth yesterday. Missy's momma baked the cake for Paw, but my father-in-law wouldn't eat it, sent it home for Jasper and me to share. Paw won't eat much of anything these days. He went from mining to logging when coal dust sucked the air from his lungs, then from logging to sitting on the couch when his Crohn's disease turned to cancer and his body started dissolving. Like mine seems to be doing.

My ribs look more like a washboard now than four years ago in high school when they nicknamed me Bony Romie. Maybe I have Crohn's, too. It's wiping out half the mountain, what ones don't die of cancer or black lung. The GI doc in Bluefield told Paw he'd called the CDC down in Atlanta, told them they should start tracking it. Said it wasn't normal for Crohn's to nest in an area like it had in Stump Branch. Paw and the doctor think it has something to do with the coal mines— something they're pumping into the ground, or something they're pumping out—probably the same thing that's causing the grass to burn up and the fish to swell and lay on the riverbanks like wall-eyed shovel heads.

The smell of sweet cornbread baking wafts into the bedroom, and my mouth waters, but I don't care to eat. Food sometimes turns against me these days, causes a quick rush of nausea. It always passes, though. Paw told Jasper the same thing happened to him right before he was diagnosed.

I put away the pink Myrtle Beach 2012 t-shirt from our last

vacation, pull down one of Jasper's bulky West Virginia Mountaineers sweatshirts instead. It'll hide my ribs and the little swollen paunch that's shown up low on my belly.

"Anybody home?" Jasper calls from the living room. Our trailer trembles when he slams the front door behind him, and I massage the dull ache building behind my temples.

I snatch the notice about the mountaintop-removal-mining protest from the dresser, shove it into the drawer before Jasper sees it. I hate the anti-MTR meetings and protests. The things they say about what's happening to the land and to us who live here scare me, give me nightmares even.

Yet I can't seem to stay away.

The woman who invited me to my first meeting in the back bay of Walker's Garage told me that what I didn't know could kill me. Since then, I haven't missed a meeting. I want to learn everything they're teaching, see firsthand the changes taking place in the people of Stump Branch.

I've seen a dozen locals become spies or environmental activists in a matter of weeks. Men and women I've known my whole life have turned into scientists who show us soil and water samples, toxicology reports, easily pronouncing six-syllable words and reading long lists of deadly chemicals—and one of those men never finished high school. Funny how staring at death makes people smarter.

I shove worry to the back of my mind, smooth my hair, and make myself smile, then head down our short hallway. "There's my man." I lean in to peck a kiss on Jasper's lips, the only part of him besides his eyeballs that isn't pitch black. "Did the nightshift treat you all right?"

Jasper nods, sets his lunch bucket on the vinyl runner by the door, slides out of his coal-stained twill coat. "I smell cornbread." His blue eyes light like propane flames, their brightness intensified by the mask of coal dirt surrounding them.

"Can't have brown beans without it," I say.

"Mmm, lady! I'd marry you again if you weren't already mine."

I swat at him. "Get cleaned up. Cornbread'll be done in a jiffy." I turn off the warming flame beneath the pan and spoon potatoes fried with onions into a blue-speckled bowl. "Might want to bring in your work boots off the porch, set them in the tub. We're supposed to get a skiff of snow later this morning."

"Too early for snow. I ain't ready for it, yet." From the bathroom down the hall, Jasper's voice echoes as if he is still deep inside the mine. "You check on Daddy after work yesterday?"

"I did." I add a thick pat of golden butter to the fried potatoes, the same thing I made for my father-in-law yesterday, and I think of the man's yellowing, wary eyes. Paw—I've always called him Paw instead of Daddy, out of respect for my own daddy who died when I was twelve— Paw's sliding downhill fast. It isn't just his sickness, either. His mind ain't acting right. He's not himself, and I worry he's up to something. A no-good sort of something.

A long pause settles between us before Jasper asks the heavy question I know will follow. "He send any more Oxy home with you?"

"On the bedroom dresser." I set the table, stand by the kitchen window, and watch the morning sunrise illuminate the miles of flat, beige scab that used to be a cloud-grazing piney mountain. I unclench my teeth and work my aching jaw.

Ten minutes later when Jasper pads out of the bathroom bare-chested, barefoot, and smelling of soap, I slide the pone of steaming cornbread onto the table. "Want milk for dunking?"

"Heck yeah." He flashes his white smile, and just like that, my icy mood melts.

Jasper picks up a slab of cornbread, slathers it with butter, takes a big bite, and talks around it. "How many pills did he send this time?"

I look out the window again, listen to the harsh wind whistle past the windowpane. No deep folds of mountain, no heavy forest out there anymore to hedge us in, protect us. "Didn't count 'em." I break off a piece of cornbread, crumble it between my fingers, watch the grains sprinkle onto the plate. "Felt like too many." I dust my hands together and take a long swig of milk to wash away the bitterness on my tongue.

"You'll wish you had more, the day comes you ever need to sell 'em."

I thump down my glass hard enough to make my fork jump. "Dammit, Jasper, you been dying since the day you walked into that mine. I'm tired of you always planning for the day you don't come home." I stand, rake my food into the garbage can, and run scalding water over the plate.

"Don't be like that," Jasper says. "Sit down, honey. Eat."

"Not in the mood for cornbread," I say.

"Want me to make you a sandwich? Peanut butter is my specialty."

"I'm not hungry." I dry the plate, and I startle when Jasper breathes into my hair, slides his arms around me, pulls me back against his chest. I rest there, let his warmth seep into me.

"We talked about this when I started working for Prospect. You know the chances I got of coming home in a box."

I know. Oh, yes, I know. Roof bolting is about the most dangerous job an underground miner can do. It also pays the most.

Jasper nuzzles my neck and whispers in my ear as his hands move lower on my stomach. "Babies cost money, and if we want a little Grodin some day, I need to stick around there a while."

I squeeze his hands, slide them a bit higher. How I ache for a baby in the hollow of my belly, pray day and night for a child. A selfish prayer, premature, but one that, if God will answer, might help Jasper see the sense in leaving this place. Stump Branch might cradle Grodin family land, but it's no longer the place for Jasper and me to start our family. The land is sick, the people are sick, and now I'm feeling sickly, too.

I turn around in Jasper's arms, look up into his once-smooth face, now lined and creased a decade beyond its twenty-two years. "You promised you'd quit in five years."

He nods, and a trickle of water sluices from a light-brown curl, skims his neck, and slides onto his chest. "Still got part of one to go."

"We could get out now, Jasper, go to North Carolina. Plenty of textile jobs down there. Construction jobs."

"You ain't got no reason to worry about me spending a lifetime underground. I can't stick around there no longer than six or seven years, anyhow."

"Six or seven years! You mean you'd stay longer?"

"We're less than a year from tearing into the last big coal seam on the property. After that, no more underground mining. Prospect's doing everything above-ground. MTR mining all the way. I'm the last of a dying breed, baby." He grins.

"Jasper, nobody says you got to stick out the full five you'd promised. Besides, Stinson didn't keep his word, neither. You still ain't got no medical card. You have to beg for a day off and lie to take one."

He tilts his head, touches his lips to mine, and electricity snaps between us. I flatten my hands on his chest, push him away. "Finish eating and get some sleep. I have to run into town. I'll check on Paw again while I'm out. I believe he's supposed to see the doc again tomorrow. He thinks he can drive, but I want to make sure."

Jasper eases onto the straight-backed chair awkwardly, gingerly, like an old man.

"Your back bothering you again?" I ask.

"Not too bad. Big slab of roof fell today." He lifts his palms heavenward. "Had my hands up just so, caught the edge and shoved it to the side before it crushed Jimbo. I might have twisted wrong." He rolls a shoulder, arches, then digs his spoon into the beans. "Say Paw's going again tomorrow? Didn't he just go a few days ago for that scope?"

I take a deep breath, let it out slowly, quietly. "They go more often

when it gets to end-stage." I watch him carefully, but he won't look at me.
"The doctor called and said the big polyp he took out last week showed
more cancer. Said Paw needs to have another ten or twelve inches cut out
of there, but your daddy won't hear of it. Said no more knife."

"No more knife," Jasper echoes, pushing food around his plate.

"I'm sorry, Jasper. I know you hate talking about these things."

"So . . . what's Daddy gonna do?"

I watch my husband for a moment. He wouldn't want me to
candy-coat the truth. "He told the doc to double up on his pills if he
would, but no more cutting."

Jasper chews slowly, puts down his spoon and looks up at me.

I hold up my hand, stop him before he can speak. "He needs
them pills himself, Jasper. You know he's got to be hurting."

"Ain't like I'm taking anything he ain't offering. His idea to skim
off the bottles, not mine." He breaks off another wedge of cornbread,
dunks it into the milk. "He don't take half of what they prescribe for
him, anyhow. Said if he took Oxy at the rate the doctor pushed it on
him, he'd O.D. in an hour."

I turn away before I wipe my eyes, so Jasper won't see.

"Besides," he says, "I told him he ever needs them back, I got
them right here, and I'll come running. Told him I'd never sell them,
anyhow. They're yours for when—"

"For when you die! Hell yes, I know that!" My eyes feel like
they're on fire, and I look toward the door. I want to be away from this
room, from this house, from this place.

Jasper shrugs, bites off the sopping cornbread, swallows with
hardly a chew. "It's the only life-insurance policy we got."

I blink hard, his words stinging me like a slap to the face. I yank
Jasper's good hunting jacket from the coat tree by the door, shove my
arms into it, and push the cuffs over my wrists. "I'll try to be back before
you leave," I say.

Then Jasper's words circle through my head again. *Caught the edge and shoved it to the side before it crushed Jimbo.* My Lord.

I speak a bit softer. "You pulling a twelve again? What time you go in?" He doesn't answer, and when I turn, Jasper's eyes catch me, hold me in the way that hurts my heart.

"Baby, come here." He holds out an arm, and before I know it, I'm wrapped up inside him, he's wrapped inside me.

With the groceries bought, the electric bill dropped off, and what's left of Jasper's check deposited, I head back up the mountain toward the Grodin homeplace, almost wishing it wasn't my day off work. Not that I like calling sick folk who can't afford their medical bills to remind them a turnover to collections is looming, but it sure beats watching Paw die.

The Grand Cherokee rocks like a boat among waves as I try to straddle the ruts and climb the ridge toward Paw's place. I peer into the skeletal tree-line as the afternoon sun begins to sink, but I find no colorful fall leaves, no late green shoots, no encouragement that spring will follow winter, will ever come again to Stump Branch.

As I near the top, I slow and steer the Jeep to hug the inside of the narrow road, my stomach fisting in anticipation of meeting one of the monstrous coal trucks that race up and down the ridge all hours of the day and night. Since Prospect Mining opened in '98, each year someone has died either in a head-on collision or from being run over the steep embankment by a coal truck. Prospect always pays the fines, but they've never lost a court case, and no family has ever received a settlement for loss of life. My fingers ache from gripping the wheel too tight, and I flex them, telling myself that maybe tonight I will paint my nails for Jasper, telling myself anything to get dying off my mind.

I let out a pent-up breath when I round the blind turn without meeting a coal truck. A jarring blast from the mine a mile and a half away further stretches my nerves, and I grit my teeth as loose dirt and rubble tumble from the steep shale bank above onto the Jeep's roof and hood.

You can't ever have anything nice around here.

Topping the knoll, I gaze out the passenger window at the bleak desolation below. Another big gray slurry pond—nearly the size of a lake—burbles and pops where once a field of Queen Anne's lace, wild strawberries, and morning glories ambled over the ground beside the creek branch this place was named for. Nearly seven years have passed since they dug the pond, and not a weed nor blade of grass grows within a hundred yards of it. Poison slop. Full of arsenic, copper, selenium, and other chemicals I can't yet pronounce, but have heard named at the anti-MTR coalition meetings. I study the pie charts they show us, and I always pay special attention to the one depicting water quality, where the chemicals cover all but a blue sliver of the pie. A pond can't hold in that kind of misery for long. Nothing can.

After the turn-off toward Paw's place, the Jeep travels a smoother road along the man's well-tended drive. I pull alongside his mailbox, reach out the window and retrieve a handful of doctor bills, insurance notices, and the same anti-MTR flyer that was in my mailbox yesterday. Paw hasn't been outside since my last visit.

The house hasn't changed much since the first time Jasper brought me home to meet his folks six years ago, right after he'd gotten his driver's license. The white clapboards don't look as proud now that coal dust stains the crevices, and though Paw usually keeps up with the ditch lilies Momma Grodin planted the year before she died, he hasn't cut them back this fall, and they lie like heaps of wilted broomstraw along the edge of the porch.

Paw doesn't come to the door as he usually does when I drive up, so I jump out of the Jeep and mount the steps two at a time. He could be in the bathroom, I tell myself, trying to banish bad thoughts.

I knock at the door, three quick raps. "Paw?" I open the door without waiting, knowing my father-in-law's front door has never been locked. As easy to lock the boogeyman in as out, he says. May as well let him come and go as he pleases.

"Paw?" A rush of heat wraps around me, nearly takes my breath, and I cross the wooden floor and check the thermostat. Eighty-five. "Where are you, Paw?"

"Be out in a minute." His voice sounds strangled, and he rattles a wet cough.

Bathroom. I drop the mail on the coffee table, shed Jasper's coat and lower the thermostat to seventy-three. "It's hotter than Hades in here, Paw. You got the chills or something?"

The toilet flushes, followed by running water at the sink, then Paw emerges. "I've been a little chilly, yeah."

I suck in a breath. His face has grayed overnight, and his eyes have sunk so deeply into their orbits that he looks like the plastic Halloween skull I put on our front porch last week. He offers a strained smile and walks cautiously down the center of the wide hallway, as if barefoot on broken glass.

I rush to his side. "Paw, my Lord, why didn't you call me?" Once a foot taller than me, Paw now walks with a stoop, and he levels his hollow gaze with my stare. "You look a mess," I say. It's an understatement.

Paw grins around his grimace, and his watery eyes make me want to cry.

"Ain't nothing you can do for me, doll baby," he says. "If they was, I'd tell you." He pecks a hot, dry kiss on my cheek. "'Sides, I'm getting along just fine for an old feller."

When I slide an arm around Paw's back, his spine presses against my arm through my sweatshirt. He feels so light I think I could carry him on my hip, like a baby. "Let's rest a bit, why don't we?" I say. He leans on me as I lead him to his recliner and help him sit. "Can I get you anything? Drink of water? Coffee?"

He lifts a bent finger and points toward the kitchen. "Just put on a pot about six hours ago. Ought to be stout by now. Black. No sugar, sugar." He grins at his joke, but his lips are thin and tight, and another cough bubbles in his throat.

"Want me to take you to the hospital, Paw?"

"No. Next time I come out of this holler, it'll be in a box."

I can't stifle a groan. "Great. Now you and Jasper are both talking that foolishness." I fill two mugs, add a spoonful of powdered creamer to mine, carry them into the living room.

"What's got Jasper dying today?" Paw asks.

"Slab of roof fell while he was bolting. I swear, Paw, between worrying about him and you, and the blasting that goes on all hours of the day and night, I ain't had a solid night of sleep in a month."

Paw's gaze settles on the fluorescent pink flyer that came in the mail. "Reach me that thing."

I curse myself for not throwing it in the trash before he saw it. "Aw, you know it's another piece of propaganda. They're right, of course, those protesters. But it ain't doing no good, and it only serves to stir up trouble and hurt feelings."

He grunts, and I don't know if he's agreeing or disagreeing. I push to find out. "Need to take their fight to Charleston, or maybe Washington. Only making people feel bad who have to earn a living in that mine. Ain't like the men's got a choice."

"Everbody's got a choice." He sips the steaming brew, sets his mug on the side table. "They got a right to protest, and what they're saying is the truth, Romie. Prospect Mining is killing all of us, what ones are working in the mines, and what ones ain't." He stares off for a moment, then speaks softly to the air. "I've had enough of it."

He turns and fixes me with a serious stare. "Jasper don't know you go to them anti-MTR meetings, does he?"

His question catches me off guard, and I wonder how he knows, who might have told him. "No, sir. I've only been to a couple. I just wanted to see what they were about."

"You ought to go to all of 'em. Don't miss nary a one." He points again at the flyer.

I hand the stack of mail to Paw, taking care to shuffle the flyer to the bottom. His words sound foreign to me. He's long supported the miners, worked the mines himself in the years when men only went underground, gouged deep to get the coal instead of decapitating mountains. Used to say underground mining might not be the best way to treat Mother Nature, but it sure beat chopping off her head like Prospect has started doing now.

Paw's glistening eyes rove the hot-pink page, then he lays the flyer on the table, sips again from his coffee mug. "They're going about it all wrong." He stares silently at the dark TV for a full minute. Then he turns to me. "Say you'll help me, if I need it?"

I wipe the dampness from my forehead, wish I'd worn my t-shirt instead of Jasper's sweatshirt. "Think you ought to go to the hospital, after all? Let's get you a bag together." I stand and head toward my father-in-law's bedroom.

"Sit down. I told you I ain't going to no hospital." He stares at me in a hard way that tells me not to argue. "I want your word that you'll carry out my last wishes."

My throat clogs. I try to think of a joke, something funny to lighten his mood, but the words won't come. Momma Grodin's old cuckoo clock sounds from the kitchen, as if telling me it's time to listen, time to do what Paw wants me to do while time is left. "Of course I will, Paw," I whisper. "You know that."

He points. "Reach me that Bible."

I lift the worn, oxblood Bible from its place on the center of the coffee table, offer it to Paw.

He puts on his bifocals with trembling hands, then opens the leather-bound text to the last pages. "Let me read you something."

I try not to look surprised, but it's hard. I know Paw reads the Bible, believes in the Lord above, but he's never preached to anyone, always says a man must find God on his own terms, and that he can find Him anywhere.

"The Book of Revelation," Paw says, "eleventh chapter, verse eighteen . . . 'The nations were angry, and your wrath came, as did the time for the dead to be judged, and to give your bondservants the prophets their reward, as well as to the saints, and those who fear your name, to the small and the great; and to destroy those who destroy the earth.'" A wet cough gurgles its way out of Paw's chest, and he snatches a tissue from the side table, closes his Bible.

He composes himself, and when he looks at me, his eyes are puddled. "You get that, Romie? '. . . to destroy those who destroy the earth.'"

I start to nod but shake my head. "I get it, Paw. I think."

"I want to be a bondservant."

Dread slops over me like smothering slurry, and I ache to have Jasper here to hold my hand, to pull me to fresh air. "I don't . . . what are you saying?"

Paw dabs at a watering eye with the tissue, points toward the coat closet by the front door. "You done give me your word. Now look in there. On the floor."

I stand, and my feet feel heavy, like they're stuck to the carpet. "What do you mean? About being a bondservant? How does that work?"

He points again toward the coat closet but doesn't speak.

I think he must have taken some OxyContin that's made him loopy, and that's a good thing. He surely needs it. I open the dark wooden closet door and stare at the strange thing on the floor. I step closer, realize it's a hunting vest that stands rigid, rust-colored sticks of dynamite holding it erect. My knees want to buckle. "Paw." The word comes out on a half-breath.

"Destroy those who destroy the earth."

I kneel in front of the closet. "No."

"What time's Jasper go in tonight? Five?"

"No, Paw."

"Look at me, Romie."

I turn my head a bit, but my stare won't leave the hunting vest.

"All I need is for you to drive me up there."

"People will die, Paw! You will die. We have friends at that mine. *Jasper* could be in that mine!" I finally turn to meet his gaze.

His smile comes easier now; his face is peaceful. "I'm already dead, doll baby. Only a matter of timing."

It's a struggle, but I manage to hold back a sob.

"Jasper will be going in soon, won't he? I could go into the mine this evening at shift change, during their meeting," he says. "They always meet in that old office trailer near the entrance. Either way, won't be a soul underground, 'cept me." He holds out his palms like Jesus on the cross. "You take me up there, go interrupt the meeting to see Jasper, tell him loud and clear something's wrong with me."

I shake my head to clear the cobwebs—can he really be saying these things?

"Say it loud, so the others will hear. Tell them you came straightaway to get help . . . phone's out, so you couldn't call for an ambulance."

Paw lets his hand fall between his recliner and the end table, and when he lifts it again, he holds up the phone line he's cut, so I can see its frayed edges. He gives me a white-lipped grin. "I'll mosey down past the equipment bays while you've got their attention. You and Jasper will be off the ridge before I let her blow. The ones atop the ground'll shudder and shake, but they won't be hurt none."

He wipes his mouth with the back of his hand. "The shafts will collapse . . . mining equipment will blow all to pieces. It'll cost more to wade through the EPA and OSHA paperwork and replace all that equipment than it will to shut her down. They'll clear out of here." Fresh pink blooms on his pasty cheeks.

My racing heartbeat slows, and I chew on a fingernail. It can't be that easy, can it? Jasper won't have a job, a place to work. If he's unemployed, we'll have to leave the state for work, won't we? Get out of here. Have a baby in a place where the water isn't chemical soup.

"It's my dying wish." Another cough breaks from his chest, and this time red dots spot the tissue.

I lurch toward Paw, wrap him in my arms.

"All you need to do is give me a ride," he whispers.

After a moment, he pushes me away from him, holds me at arm's length. "They done killed more'n five hunnerd mountains in this state and four times that in people. Somebody's got to show them we ain't gonna take it no more." He shakes his head. "They poisoned me." He pokes a finger at my stomach. "And they're poisoning you. You, and Jasper, and everybody else in Stump Branch."

I look down at the concave void just below my ribs, and I imagine a mound there in its place, a swollen womb full of Jasper's child. I dry my wet face on my sleeve. "Don't you want to talk to Jasper about this first?"

Paw shakes his head, and tears slip out again. "That'd hurt worse—hurt me and him both." He looks away, wipes his sunken cheeks. "It's better this way, he don't know." He motions toward the small table by the front door with a shaky hand. "There's two more stock bottles of OxyContin sittin' there, both plumb full. Ought to be enough to buy a new start in Carolina. You can go to nursing school, like you've been wanting to do."

I follow the direction his fingertip points, look at the big, white, square bottles. Has to be more than a hundred pills in each, a dollar a milligram. Thousands of dollars pressed into little blue tablets.

Paw pats my hand, rubs away the dampness on my cheek with his thumb. "I done laid out my UMWA life policy on the bed, ready for you and Jasper to take to the lawyer. Ain't much, but it'll help. There won't be no funeral, nothing left to bury."

I squeeze his hand. "I know you think you've thought this through, but them mine owners won't shut down. They'll just lop off another mountain on down the road. Jasper's already said that's their next plan. And that life insurance policy—it won't pay for suicide."

Paw waves his hands, and his voice comes out in agitated wheezes. "I'm sick, Romie. They'll say Oxy stunned me ... old man wasn't thinking right. He got confused ... went to the mines ... thought he still worked there." He swallows against the gurgle in his throat. "That much dynamite ... all the methane that builds up around there ... they'll never even know I blew the place. What's left of that hollowed-out mountain ... it will be gone. Insurance will pay, you bet. It's the United Mine Workers Union."

"They'll fight it. You know they'll fight it. Insurance companies don't care about us."

Paw's bushy eyebrows lift, and again I'm struck by how gaunt his face has become.

"Prospect'll make 'em pay. You think they want word to get out? That one of their own blowed up a mine . . . on purpose? That miners are turning against the mines?" He clears his throat. "No, they'll want to cover it up ... quick as they can ... money's the best way to do that. They think money'll shut up anybody."

I grind my teeth, shake my head. "Paw, this is your sickness talking. I'm taking you to the doctor." I stand and offer him my hand, but he waves it away. Instead, his gnarled hands grip the armrests, and he thrusts himself forward, upright.

"Get my jacket."

I take a deep breath. *Finally, he's thinking right.* I return to the closet by the door and pull out Paw's flannel coat, averting my sight from the hunting jacket.

Hunched forward, Paw eases toward the door. "Not that one." He points at the hunting vest. "That one."

"Humor me, Paw. Put this on." I hold open the flannel coat, guide Paw's long arms into the sleeves.

"Humor *me*, now." He jerks his head toward the open closet.

"Get it."

It's not a bad idea to get the dangerous thing out of the house. I can set it over the hill and send Jasper to take it apart later. I pick up the heavy vest, surprised that it takes both hands to lift it. I look toward Paw, but he's headed out the door, trusting me to do as he said. I slide the vest onto one arm, and then I see the two medicine bottles. I look toward the ceiling. Would it do any good to pray? I heft the vest against my hip, and my hand trembles when I pick up the large bottles and slip them into Jasper's deep coat pocket. I hurry out the door to steady Paw as he ambles down the porch steps.

When we reach the Jeep, I set the hunting vest on the ground, help Paw climb inside, and start to close the door.

He grabs my arm and tilts his head toward the vest. "I'll take that."

"Bumpy as this road is, we'll blow to Kingdom Come before we get off the mountain."

"Who's the master blaster here? I've hauled dynamite around most of my life. It won't blow unless somebody blows it." He reaches out his hands, and his voice is stern. "I said I'll take that."

I peer into the bone-dry woods on the other side of the driveway. I've never disrespected my father-in-law. Never spoken a harsh word to him. He and Jasper's mother treated me like their own child from the first time I stepped into their home.

My shoulders sag as I lift the awkward vest, ignoring Paw's outstretched hands, and place it on the floorboard at his feet. I close the door, walk around the Jeep, and slide behind the wheel.

The pills clatter inside the bottles in my pocket, and Paw looks at me and smiles. "Good girl," he says, his voice hoarse. "I hate it's come to this. Shame you two got to sell them pills to make a life, but the Good Lord always provides, don't He?" He clears his throat, sinks backward into the seat and sighs. "I'm looking forward to meeting Him."

I press my lips together to keep from cursing. "Hope you know we're going to the hospital."

I glance toward Paw, but he won't look at me, keeps his gaze on the homeplace as I head down the graveled drive.

"Last time I'll be seeing this place."

"Don't say that."

"Romie, I won't last another day or two. I don't want to die in no hospital."

"You can stay with Jasper and me." I reach the end of the drive, brake, and the digital clock on the dashboard reads 4:44. The numbers seem like a message; one I can't decipher. I turn to look at Paw. "I'll take care of you."

"No pride in that. I'm a strong enough man. Still got one more job to do."

I look out across the rutted road, once smooth blacktop, now fractured into a million pieces by the overburdened trucks hauling out tons of mountain soul. Beyond that, what was once the rising mountain where I picked blackberries, chewed teaberry leaves, and made love to Jasper among blooming dogwoods is now low-lying, scarred craters—sterile, desolate, and barren. No place to live. No place to birth a baby. Only a place for dying. A place for destroying those who destroy this good earth.

I take Paw's hand in mine, kiss it, let him go. I hold tightly to the wheel, turn onto the road and drive toward the mine.

"I love you like a daughter, Romie. You're a real good girl. Thank you for doing this."

"I ain't doing nothing but taking you to see Jasper, let him talk some sense into your head. Lord knows I can't."

Paw's fist slams the dashboard, and I flinch.

"I told you I don't want Jasper in on this." Red-tinted saliva flies from his lip, and he wipes his mouth on the back of his hand, glares out the window.

"When you brought me in, you brought Jasper in." Another blast at the mine causes the Jeep to vibrate, and I grip the wheel tighter, shoot a sideways glance at the hunting vest standing in the floorboard between Paw's feet. "You sure that thing won't blow?"

"Got to light the fuse, first." Paw pulls an old Zippo lighter from his pocket, flips open the metal lid.

"For God's sake, Paw! Put that thing away."

Paw shoves the lighter into his coat pocket, speaks with a soft voice full of hurt. "I would never lay harm to you. You ought to know that."

I reach the entrance, drive past the Prospect Mining sign. I want to throw up, rid my stomach of the nerves writhing like snakes inside it.

Paw touches my arm. "Stop here and let me out." His voice warbles, and he clears his throat. "By the time you get to the trailer, I'll be at the equipment bay entrance. You get Jasper, and y'all get off this mountain. I figure it'll take me a good fifteen minutes to get to her first belly. That's where I'll . . . you know . . . let her blow."

I set my jaw, press the gas pedal, and cut the wheel, slinging red-dog gravel and coal dirt in an arc across the wide parking area as I drive toward the office trailer. "I'll do no such thing. I'm going to get Jasper, all right, but only so's he can straighten you out. You're going to sit right here while I do it, you hear me?" I turn off the Jeep and snatch the keys from the ignition. "If you can look your son in the eye and convince him to go along with this fool idea of yours, I'll stand with you on it. But I won't let you put this burden on my shoulders to carry alone."

I step out, turn, and glare at Paw. "You staying put?"

I want him to say *no*. Want him to sling that heavy vest onto his shoulder, march like the soldier he'd once been into that mine, defend his family, defend this land, even at the cost of what few days he's got left. My face grows hot, fired by coals of shame smoldering inside me.

Paw's lower lip thrusts outward, and he reaches into the floorboard, tries to lift the heavy vest onto his lap.

I hold my breath.

Paw grunts and strains. "Help me put this thing on."

I look skyward, blinking hard and fast. Overhead, a lone, red-shouldered hawk screeches, searches the gray mine in lonesome circles, moves on. I look again at my father-in-law, wonder if maybe I should do this God-awful thing that he asks of me. "Paw?"

Another rattling cough shakes his body. He lets the vest fall against the floor, leans back to catch his breath. He presses his steel-blue lips together, stares straight ahead, won't look at me.

Ahead of us sits the trailer, and I know Jasper's in there, know this is the place where he spends his nights and part of his days making a living for us, making a life for us, and in a way I can't pretend to understand, he likes mining coal. How can I take that away from him?

Paw drops his head, stares at hands curled like dead leaves in his lap. He sniffs and turns to me, lets out a long, jagged breath. "Useless," he whispers.

I climb back into the Jeep, pull out a handful of fast-food napkins from the console, and offer them to Paw. When he won't take them, I put all but one in his lap and dab the blood-tinged spittle from the corner of his mouth. "This ain't the way you want to go out of this world, Paw. You're too good for that kind of destruction."

He looks out the window, surveying the wasted mountain. "I'm a foolish old man." His chin quivers.

"No. No, you're not."

A wet cough rattles Paw's body, and I turn my face away. "What say we go, before the men come out of that trailer?"

He picks up a napkin with a trembling hand and swabs his damp face as I start the Jeep and turn it around.

I wipe my eyes as I drive past the Prospect Mining sign.

Paw stares out the window toward the eight-mile fissure where once stood a mountain. He reaches over, pats my hand where it grips the gearshift. He lets out a ragged sigh, turns his ashen face toward mine. "You done the right thing."

I try to smile at him but can't. "It ought to feel like it then, oughtn't it?" I glance at the rust-colored dynamite, push away second thoughts, and drive down the broken road toward home.

CHAPTER TWO

JASPER

"Oh no you don't," Jimbo says to me. "Move outta my seat, Jasper."

I already know it's Jimbo's turn to drive, but I love messing with him almost as much as he loves manning this lowriding mantrip. If he could get by with it, he'd probably try driving this heavy crawler, made for taking us deep into the mine, out on Highway 19, though he's got sense enough know he'd get squashed pancake-flat by the first coal truck to come roaring up behind him.

I climb out, then slide into the second row of the mantrip's metal seats and adjust the self-rescue kit strapped to my waist, making room for Nelson and Cleavon to sit alongside me. Stinson yells from the mouth of the mine for the others to hurry, and soon everyone but Darius has climbed on board.

"Where are you, D?" Stinson yells again. "Darius! Get your lazy black ass in here, or you're gonna walk the five miles to the face."

My jaw tightens, and the air thickens around us. I hate talk like that, but whatcha gonna say to the boss man who holds your livelihood in his hands? I duck my chin into my coat collar, hating even more that I don't have the guts—or the money—to speak up and tell Stinson to shut his prejudiced pie hole. I sometimes get mad, wondering why Darius doesn't pound him, shut him up himself for that kind of talk, but then I feel bad for thinking that, for thinking D has any more influence than the rest of us to right said wrongs. Can't none us make the kind of money Prospect pays us anywhere else, so we keep our heads down and our traps shut and let Stinson say whatever he wants.

Cleavon's bony elbow meets my ribs, and his whisper is loud enough for everyone but Stinson to hear. "Stinson's a peeping Tom racist." We all look at him, and he shrugs. "If he wasn't spying, how would he know what color Darius's ass is?"

Jimbo grins, leans back, and speaks out of the side of his mouth. "Awww, Cleav, it don't matter none. We're all black underground."

Everyone laughs, though a little uncomfortably, and the tension dissipates, but then Stinson bellows again.

"Darius! Time is money!" Stinson stomps the ground with a steel-toed boot. "If you are one ton—" he says and shoves a thick finger into the air, "*one measly ton—*lighter than yesterday's load, you're fired. You hear me, boy?"

Darius, a man still built like the high-school linebacker he once was, lopes from the men's room rubbing his nose, heads toward us, and slides low into the front seat beside Jimbo. He loudly sniffs a couple of times, and I know he's already coked up. Jimbo glances at me over his shoulder and cocks an eyebrow, then he turns back to the controls, and the mantrip lurches forward. As we enter the mine, we turn on our headlamps, and our glow pierces the gloom and reflects off the bright-white limestone we've sprayed over the walls to tamp down the coal dust.

Five minutes into the half-hour ride to the face, the good-natured ribbing has subsided, and we've grown quiet. Beside me, Nelson's breathing grows slow and steady, and his whiskered chin rests against his chest as he dozes. I shut my eyes, too, thinking I'll take advantage of the peace to take a little snooze before work begins.

And then Darius yells at Jimbo. "That as fast as you can go, boy?"

Nelson's head jerks up, and we blink at each other like startled does in the auras of one another's headlamps.

"I'm at the three-quarter mark now," Jimbo says.

"That's what I'm talking 'bout! Let's go! Full speed ahead!"

Nelson elbows me again, this time by accident, as he pulls up the collar of his mining coat over his ears. The deeper we go, the colder it gets, and even at five or six miles an hour (our mantrip can only go eleven), the moving air will chill your bones. Jimbo speeds up, and I'm guessing we're going about eight or nine miles an hour now. Slow, it might seem on the outside, but on a mantrip going downgrade, that's a pretty good clip. These heavy slugs can't stop on a dime. When I hear Nelson's teeth chatter near my ear, I'm glad I got stuck in the middle.

"We got to make up lost time, boy!" Darius yells again. "Hammer down!"

"Can't go any faster, man," Jimbo says. I can't see his face, but I know the tightness of his tone, know he's not happy about being pushed past a safe speed into the frigid air.

"You can and you will." Darius leans over, puts his giant-sized hand over Jimbo's smaller one and pushes the throttle forward. "You heard Stinson. Time is money."

The mantrip picks up speed, and though our path is straight, on the twelve-percent downgrade to the face, we all know this ain't safe. One piece of fallen slate in our pathway, one big chunk of coal, and we're airborne. I look around, and the men are exchanging glances, but not one of them says aloud this ain't okay.

Laramie's overgrown gray mustache twitches, and he finally speaks up in his slow drawl. "We a-heading down, now. Might oughta ease up on the power. I've heard tell these brakes give out now and then."

Darius whips around on his seat. "I don't think I asked you, old man." He glares at Laramie, then at a couple more men in turn. I stare at the back of Jimbo's hardhat, won't meet Darius's stare. You can't reason with him when he's like this, and he's too big and too mean to pick a fight with. I ain't chicken, but I ain't stupid, either.

The mantrip's whine slows as Jimbo eases off the throttle, and Darius leans over, pushes Jimbo's hand forward again. In the glow of my headlamp, I see the muscle in Jimbo's jaw flex.

"Stop it," Jimbo says, easing back on the throttle. "It's not safe—"

"Don't *tell* me what's safe. I was mining coal when you's cutting teeth. If you can't drive like I tell you, get outta my way, and I'll drive." Darius grabs the brake lever, jerks it back hard, and the mantrip locks up, skids sideways, too heavy to stop quickly on the downgrade leading into the slope mine.

I grab the back of Jimbo's seat as Nelson's body falls against me, and the backend of the mantrip thunks against the wall.

Jimbo manages to straighten it up, get it under control, but not before Laramie flies off the back end, rolls a few yards and lands in a heap near the wall.

Darius's hooting laughter echoes off the walls. "Aw, man. That was righteous!"

"Stop it, D!" Cleavon glares at the big man. "You coulda killed us. Crazy mother—"

"Let me out!" I shove Cleavon. "Laramie's hurt."

Cleavon catches himself before he falls off the mantrip. He follows me, with Preacher on his heels, the three of us stooped forward beneath the low slate ceiling, hustling toward Laramie, who's lying flat on his back, gasping.

"You okay, man?" I ask.

Cleavon kneels beside Laramie's head, pops open his self-rescue device, puts the oxygen mask to Laramie's face. "Breathe."

Laramie makes sucking sounds, then soon he's taking in deep gulps of air. After a moment, he pushes the mask away, holds out his arms. "Help me up."

"You sure?" I grip one of Laramie's elbows, and Cleavon takes the other.

"Just knocked the breath outta me. I'm all right." Laramie gets up slowly, pulls his arms away from us.

I'm not convinced he's as fine as he's pretending to be, especially when he limps toward the mantrip. Preacher catches up to him, puts an arm around his waist, but Laramie pushes him away.

"Hurry up, old man!" Darius says. "You heard what the boss said. I can't be getting fired. I done told y'all my baby momma's pregnant. I need dis job."

I scowl at him, don't say what I'm thinking, don't say if he'd buy condoms instead of coke, he wouldn't have a money problem.

"You coulda killed us," Laramie says, his deep voice rumbling off the wall. "You need this job so bad; you better hope I don't report you to Stinson."

"Stinson's the least of our worries." Darius nods his head toward me. "Better hope Jasper don't tell his old lady."

I look up as Darius snorts a laugh out of his broad nose. "What are you talking about?"

"Shut up," Jimbo says.

"What are you talking about, D?" I say again, louder.

"Your wife," Darius says. "She bring the tree huggers down on our heads, she gets wind of a fender-bender in here." He slides into the driver's seat, side-eyes me and smirks. "Don't act like you all innocent."

I stare at him, try to figure out if he's gone crazy, or if he's too high to think straight. "What the hell are you talking about?"

"I said shut *up!*" Jimbo stalks around behind the mantrip, slides out a crowbar from the back of the machine, wallops Darius a good one across the shoulders—not enough to do damage, but enough to hurt, to let Darius know he means business. "Get outta my seat. You want to get to the face, you let me drive. Ain't none of us getting in this thing with you behind the wheel."

Darius jumps up, reaches for the crowbar, but Preacher and I rush him, push him toward the wall.

"Settle down," Preacher says. "He didn't hit you hard. A man like you can take a whack."

Darius relaxes beneath my grip, and when I look up at him, he's glaring toward Jimbo. He points a finger. "I'll stomp you into a mud puddle, little man. Don't let me catch you alone."

"Yeah? You're lucky a crowbar is all I'm carrying. Next time it'll be a gun."

Darius lunges forward, taking Preacher and me with him. "That right?" he shouts.

"Hey!" I yell. "Y'all calm down, and let's get to the face and get some coal loaded, or we'll all be on the welfare line in the morning."

Preacher and I grip Darius until he quits straining against us, then we lead him toward the mantrip, where everyone else is waiting. The back bench is empty, and Preacher points toward it. "You get in the middle, D. Gonna hem you in till y'all calm down."

I want to ask Darius what he meant by Romie bringing down the tree huggers on our heads, but now's not the time. Besides, I know he's sky-high and strung tight right now, and whatever he says will probably make me whop him harder with the crowbar than Jimbo did.

Fifteen or so minutes later, Jimbo stops the mantrip, and everyone but him slides out of the low-slung benches. He backs up the mantrip a couple hundred yards toward the entrance, where it'll sit until we need it again. The rest of us stand hunched over as Preacher closes his eyes, says a prayer to bless our work and safety. After his "Amen," he takes ahold of the square metal control box and fires up the continuous miner that reminds me of a giant-sized turning screw, lets it warm up. I cover and uncover my headlamp with my hand, make the light flash to signal Preacher, make sure he sees me. When he gives me a two-fingered wave, I walk in front of the massive machine's rotating drum, its cutter heads ready to rip into the solid seam and tear out the coal. I grip a steel poker in both hands, stab it into the roof, checking for loose slate as I work my way back toward Preacher, and when I'm sure we're safe, I give him a thumbs up and hustle out of the way. The huge machine grinds forward, and I figure I've got about ten minutes before Jimbo and I need to start pinning the roof.

I head toward where Jimbo parked the mantrip, meet him halfway. "What was Darius blowing on about—about Romie?"

Jimbo shakes his head, won't look me in the eye. "He's just blitzed."

"That was more than just blitzed. Tell me."

He stops walking, and I know there's trouble. "I hoped she'd be the one to tell you."

"What?" He's slow to answer, and my jaw tightens. I want to shake whatever it is out of him.

"Aww, somebody's running their mouth, told about how Romie's going to them anti-MTR meetings down at Walker's Garage."

"What? Who would say—when would she even have time—there ain't no way."

Jimbo studies the ground, rolls a pebble of coal under the toe of his boot, doesn't speak.

"You know Romie wouldn't—"

"Missy's seen her coming outta there, too."

My breath leaves me. Why in God's name would my wife do such a thing? Why would she go against Prospect, go against the very company that feeds us?

And then I know. I *know-know*. I know her mindset as if it were my own. But it's not my own. It's as far from what I believe as right is from wrong. Romie wants this mine shut down, so we'll have to leave Stump Branch.

"Hey!" Preacher shouts. "I need a roof bolter up here!"

Jimbo claps a hand on my shoulder, pushes me toward the face. "Sorry, bud. I hate to be the one to tell you."

My brain grinds louder than the roaring crunch of the continuous miner. Jimbo and I walk alongside its conveyor belt, and I watch the broken chunks of coal it's carrying out of the heart of the mountain. When Preacher shuts down the machine, I almost wish he'd left it on, let its raucous noise fill my head instead of the anger grating there. I glance around me, wonder who else knows. I yank open the snaps on my coat to let the heat escape before I burn up.

Jimbo drives the first round of bolts, and I wedge the heavy support posts against the roof. I stab at the overhead, break loose a few chunks of slate, and we go again. Ten minutes later, we're done —too long since we're already behind schedule—and Preacher fires up the miner again.

I roll my head to stretch the muscles strung tight in my neck, and when Hippie puts a hand on my shoulder, I lurch, part of me ready for a fight.

"Sorry, dude." Hippie, the stringy-haired, day-shift roof bolter, holds up his hands in surrender, and behind his prescription safety goggles, his eyes look like they belong to a bug. "Scared you, huh." He jerks a thumb over his shoulder. "Redd needs you at the UCB."

"What are you doing here, man?" I ask. We've already traded shifts back at the surface command trailer. He should be home by now.

Hippie shrugs, looks past me, reaches for my tamping rod. "Got called back in."

He heads toward Preacher, and I stand dumbfounded for a full minute before I move. Why would Stinson call in Hippie to do my job, when I'm already here, already working?

I head toward the long tunnel made of heavy plastic sheeting that directs airflow and helps keep coal dust and the stinkdamp methane gas away from us, and it dawns on me that Stinson probably got wind of Romie working with the protesters. Pressure builds in my head, and I try to think of what to tell him, how to say I didn't know until minutes ago that she's doing this thing, how to explain why she's against what we do. Romie don't appreciate mining. She don't understand where I'm coming from, how this is my family legacy, how it's something to be proud of, this digging out the buried sunshine that lights up our world, keeps all of America bright and warm.

I slip through the plastic fly into the makeshift office known as Underground Command base—UCB—which is little more than a few rectangular folding tables covered with maps and papers, rolls of plastic standing against a limestone-dusted wall, plus the battery-operated phone that's our wireless communication to surface command. Nelson looks up from his metal folding chair when I walk in, and he drops the pen he's holding, stands, and walks out past me without looking at me.

This is bad. Real bad. I am in serious trouble here.

Redd Truby, our UCB shift boss, quickly shifts some papers on his desk, covering a page that's filled with some kind of doodles like rows of daisies or something. He gathers himself and stands, motions toward the yellow plastic phone box, his long horse-face grim. "Stinson called. Wants you on the outgoing load."

I lick my lips with a dry tongue before I speak. "What's going on? Why's Hippie here?"

Redd picks up a sheaf of papers, looks at me over his bifocals, shakes his head in a hangdog way. "I'm to tell you Stinson needs you. That's all I know to say." The handheld wireless crackles, and Redd picks it up. "Go," he says into it.

"Loaded up. Heading out," Darius's voice says from the receiver.

"Hold up a sec. Got a hitchhiker for you. He's on the way." Redd puts down the wireless and nods toward the plastic fly. "Better catch your ride. Darius won't wait." He looks at the papers in his hand, turns his back to me, and walks away.

By the time we reach the surface, fists are pounding inside my head, and my hands are sweaty despite the chilly ride. Darius hardly slows down for me to get out, and I half-climb, half-fall out of my seat, and though I know I'm hustling toward the trailer, my boots might as well be cinder blocks.

Stinson steps out the trailer door onto the small wooden porch, the lines on the sides of his mouth drawn so tight he looks like a wooden puppet. He runs his fingers across his well-oiled hair, then rests his hands on the banister, leans over.

He's not even going to let me come inside. He's going to fire me right here. *Oh, Romie, what have you done to me?*

"Jasper," Stinson says, his voice low and gravely. "Your wife called."

The pounding in my head grows louder, and I wonder if I even heard him right, but then he's shaking his head, and I try to head off what I know is coming next.

"Sir, she doesn't understand—she's just worried—"

"It's your daddy, Jasper."

My mind struggles to jump tracks, to latch on to what he's saying. *My daddy?*

It must be the pills. Daddy didn't keep enough Oxy, and now Romie can't find where I hid the stash. She probably needs to take some pills to him to stop his hurting.

She was right. I got too greedy, and now Daddy's in pain.

"Reckon I need to go check on him?" I ask.

Stinson's face twists up, he squints, and his lips pucker like he's bit a lemon. I swear I can hear him swallow from here where I stand down below him.

"I'm sorry, son." He shakes his head. "He's gone. Died just a bit ago."

Stinson's words suck the air right out of me.

My chest heaves, and I look back towards the mouth of the mine. I think of that first day I followed my daddy into its darkness, how he laughed when he told me that we all end up underground sooner or later. I wish he were here to laugh again now. I wish I were still in the mine now, pinning the roof over my head, keeping the earth from crashing down around me.

CHAPTER THREE

ROMIE

Gravel crunches as Jasper pulls into Paw's long, sloped driveway, and I stand with one hand on the doorknob until I hear his bootsteps hit the porch, afraid if I open the door too soon, I'll bust out of the house, run right past him, run until I can't run no more.

He crosses the porch, not stopping to take off his mining boots, and I swing wide the door. I fall into his arms, fall apart. I can't believe I've lasted this long.

He holds me for a time, then he unwraps my arms from around him, takes me by the shoulders, moves me aside. "He's in the bedroom?"

"Yeah."

I follow him through the living room and kitchen, down the hallway, then stand in the doorway as he sits on the side of the bed, taking Paw's gnarled hands into his own. I'm struck by the blue paleness of Paw's hands against the coal-darkened blackness of Jasper's, and the crazy thought strikes me that this would make a pretty picture. I shudder.

"How long?" Jasper asks, his voice thick.

I glance at the bedside alarm clock. "About an hour ago." Paw's hands are now smudged with coal, and I know he would like it, be proud of this reminder of the hard labor he used to do underground.

Jasper's lips flatten into a line. "You shoulda called me."

"I called as soon as I could, as soon as he took his last—"

"*Before!* You shoulda called me before he breathed his last."

I nod, shake my head, nod again. He's right. I should have called. But if I'd left Paw's side for even a second—

"I could have been here with him. I had the right to be here." His voice is clotted, and I know he's trying not to cry.

"I—I'm sorry. It happened so fast. I didn't know . . . ."

He smooths Paw's wispy hair over the crown of his head, leans forward, kisses his forehead, his cheeks.

I backstep into the hallway, give them this private moment, my chest squeezing hold of the sob it wants to turn loose. When I compose myself, I step back into Paw's bedroom, speak as softly as I can. "He didn't say much, wouldn't hardly talk. Asked me to read a little Bible to him, so I did. I was careful to check the concordance, choose verses about hope and heaven. He'd doze a bit, then jerk awake. He nodded when I asked if he was hurting, so I gave him an Oxy, same as today when you were here, same as yesterday. I got him to slurp a little broth . . .." My throat clogs up, and I can't say any more. Four days now, I've fed Paw broth, ice chips, and hope, one teaspoon at a time. It's all he could swallow.

Tires chew and spin on the slight incline of the gravel driveway, and headlights splash across the lamp-lit bedroom wall. I cross the room to peer out the window at the white van gleaming in the moonlight. It's hard to breathe, hard to speak, but I somehow manage. "They're here."

Jasper's eyes widen. "Hospice? That's the coroner? You already called? They said we could take all the time we need!"

My hands tremble, and I squeeze them together, try to make them hold still. "I thought—I didn't know—" I let out a breath that sounds impatient, though it's anything but that. "Stinson said it'd take you an hour or so, that you were already at the face. I was afraid . . .."

And there it is—the truth. I was afraid. Terrified. My father-in-law, the man who is—was—as close to a father as I have known since childhood, lying here dead. And me alone with him as night fell.

Jasper leans over, rests his body across Paw's, presses his cheek against Paw's silent chest. It's the saddest thing I've ever seen. I cover my face and bawl.

"The hospice nurse said two or three weeks." Jasper paces from the kitchen to the living room and back again. "Two or three weeks. It hasn't been but a couple of days." His stare pierces into me, accusing me in a way I've never seen, don't understand. "Why was it only a few days?"

I put the glass I've washed on the drain board, dry my hands. "She said it could be any time, Jasper."

He holds up two fingers toward my face. "She said *two weeks*."

I don't know how to respond, how to answer him. He was there when the nurse said Paw might live another two or three weeks, but that he could go at any time. He was there when she said to keep him comfortable, warm, dry. He was there when she said to talk to him, to keep in mind that Paw could hear and understand everything we say, even if he couldn't respond. Jasper was there, but then he left and went back to work. He checked in every day, sure. Ate the dinners I fixed right here in Paw's kitchen, sat by Paw's bedside, even slept on his couch all day yesterday, before going home to get clean work clothes for the nightshift.

I missed work to take care of Paw, but Jasper didn't.

"Two weeks!" he shouts.

Tears. Wailing. The silent sobbing of a broken heart. I expected any of these, even all of these, but the last thing I expected was my husband's anger.

"Jasper," I say softly, not wanting the two men in Paw's bedroom to overhear us. I try to get the words right, try to comfort him, explain to him without hurting him. "I held his hand. He reached for me, and I held his hand. He closed his eyes. I held his hand the whole time. Right until his last breath." My voice hitches, and I swallow hard. "He didn't die alone."

"And he would have if you'd called me? That's what you're saying?"

"Maybe. I don't know. I—I'm sorry. It happened so fast. He went fast." I want to tell him it was merciful, a blessing when Paw's suffering ended, but Jasper's back stiffens, so I stay quiet.

He crosses his arms, stares out Paw's kitchen window.

My hands need something to do besides rub at my burning eyes, so I turn to the sink, pour out the cup of now-tepid beef broth, dump the glass of mostly melted ice chips down the drain.

From Paw's bedroom, a metallic sound ratchets and clicks into place, and though it's a racket I've never heard before, I know it's the clatter of the gurney being raised, the gurney holding Paw's lifeless body, the gurney that will bear him out of here, taking with him a piece of our hearts. I can't stand by and watch him leave, watch as he, too, abandons me.

"Ready?" One of the men from the funeral home asks the other from down the hallway.

I cover my ears with my hands, unable to hear this, unable to watch this, and I run from the kitchen, out the front door, down the steps, to the steep bank at the edge of Paw's front yard. My stomach clenches, and I wrap my arms around my middle, bend, and heave over the bank.

The cold November wind ices the wetness on my cheeks, and I shiver. Despite its wicked bite, it soothes me, this frigid chill that reminds me I'm still alive. I suck in deep gulps of the wintry air.

Behind me, I hear the *thunk-thunk-thunk* of the gurney wheels as they bring Paw down the steps, and I do not turn toward him. I don't want to see however it is they have covered him—white sheet or black body bag—a veil to hide his lifeless face from us.

The van door opens, and after a moment, it closes, and behind me, soft murmurs, footsteps coming closer.

"Ma'am," the attendant says softly. "I'll need you to sign this."

I take the clipboard from his hand, and it's then I realize how very young he looks, younger even than I am, and I wonder how he came by this job where he sees so much death, and how he can bear it.

"You're his daughter, yes?"

I want to nod, to say *yes* with a strong voice, but I am not his daughter. I am no one's daughter, not anymore. I shake my head.

The peach-faced young man appears confused, and I look toward the homeplace, where Jasper stands, arms limp at his side, staring wide-eyed at the back of the white van.

"That his son?" he asks.

This time I nod.

"Then he'll need to sign." He purses his lips, reaches for the metal clipboard. "Next of kin . . . you know." He slips the pen from my hand, and he walks toward Jasper.

I'm so very tired, exhausted, drained. I sit down hard, and the frozen grass crunches beneath me. I stare out toward the treeline, and at the weed-filled, overturned earth where the garden thrives in summer. I recall plucking ripe tomatoes from the heavy vines at Momma Grodin's side, and how she'd slip a hand into her apron pocket, pull out a tiny blue saltshaker, and we'd bite into the season's first red tomatoes, juice running down our chins. I know Paw must be so glad to see her again.

The van starts up, pulls out the long driveway, and soon it's out of sight. I bury my face in my knees.

Jasper squats down beside me, puts his hand on my back. I look up, and his face is wet. I lean into him, and he folds me in his arms, and we cry.

We pull apart when headlights flood the air around us, and he turns, and I see Missy's car over his shoulder, as she pulls into the driveway behind our salt-covered Grand Cherokee.

Jasper turns to me. "You call her, too?"

I sniffle and nod.

He stands, squeezes his eyes shut, and his hands form fists. When he looks at me, his whole face is rock hard. "You call her, but you don't call me? Who else did you call first? Who else did you put in front of me?"

"Jasper, I called you! I called her *after* I called you. I called hospice *after* I called you—like I was supposed to do, like they told us to do. Hospice called the coroner, not me. Then I called Missy. I needed someone to come. I didn't want to be—"

"You didn't want to be here. That's it. You don't want to be here. You're always one foot out the door, ain't you, Romie. You're always ready to run away." He huffs out his anger on a cloudy breath, looks toward Missy, shakes his head and stalks toward the house.

Missy heads toward me, but stops and turns toward Jasper, then looks back at me. She holds out her palms.

I stand and dust the frozen seat of my pants as Missy walks up. She hugs me, and I am glad I don't cry.

She tilts her head toward the house. "He's not doing well, is he?"

Her question seems ignorant to me, insensitive. Who in their right mind could be doing well at a time like this? I don't answer.

"He seems mighty angry."

So that's what she meant—not that Jasper should be doing *well*, but that he should be—what? Sobbing? Having a breakdown? Maybe he should. Lord knows I could have one right now. I allow a nod.

Missy looks at the night sky, and for the first time, I see how clear it is, how the stars appear brighter than normal, as if we're closer to God than usual. It seems wrong, all wrong, because this feels more like hell than heaven.

"They say anger is one of the stages of grief," Missy says.

I know she's trying to be helpful, but I want her to shut up. I want her not to be here, which is crazy since I'm the one called her to come. "I need to get out of here," I say.

Missy blows on her hands to warm them, rubs them together, then shoves them into the deep pockets of her coat. "No."

"What?"

"No." She drops her head as she looks at me, and she pushes away hair that falls over her eye. "You have to stay with Jasper. You can't run away from this, Romie." She nods toward the house. "He needs you right now . . . and you need him." She links her arm in mine, half-pulls, half-guides me toward Paw's front porch—no longer Paw's front porch, because Paw is no longer here. I feel his absence, his abandonment of this place, his abandonment of *me*, as Missy guides me up the steps and into the house.

"Jasper," she calls out to the empty living room.

He appears from the hallway, rubbing his eyes with the heels of his now-clean hands, and he crosses the kitchen and walks into the living room, into Missy's outstretched arms.

"I'm so sorry, honey," she says. "So sorry."

Jasper's eyes are closed as he hugs her, and when he opens them, he looks at me, then looks away. It feels like a slap, and my breath catches in my throat. I don't know what I have done to him, what I have done to deserve this. I was here when he wasn't. I didn't leave.

"He's better off," Missy says as she releases my husband. "He's no longer hurting. He's at peace now."

My stomach roils again at these tired platitudes that mean nothing at all, just a bunch of words to fill air that's too empty now that Paw is gone. How many more times will we have to hear them before this is over? I want to disappear, stay gone until it's all over and done.

"What can I do to help?" Missy looks around the living room, then stoops to pick up the newspaper lying on the couch. She folds it, places it on the coffee table. She turns to me, studies me for a minute. "You two want to head on home? Let me straighten up around here? I can lock up afterward."

I nod, but Jasper shakes his head. "I ain't ready to leave just yet." He glances toward me. "You can go, if you want."

I look toward the front door, want to run out, jump into our Jeep, go home, and take a long, hot shower, wash the dying off me. "No." I fix Jasper in my stare for a moment, some kind of answer to an unspoken challenge, then turn to Missy. "I'd like to straighten up Paw's bedroom before I go."

"You sure?" Missy's eyebrows raise, telling me she's giving me an out, and I should take it. "I can clean up in there."

I shake my head. "I've got it."

"Well . . ." Missy looks around again. "There must be something I can do. Someone I can call?"

I motion toward the end table by Paw's recliner. "The address book there by the phone. There's a list in it, people Paw wanted us to call when . . . people he wanted us to tell. You can call them if you will." A grin tries to play on my lips when I think of Paw holding up the phone cord that he'd cut some weeks ago. I'd replaced it the same night.

She picks up the red book filled with Momma Grodin's handwriting, then reaches for the phone. I block her arm. "If you don't mind, would you do it from your house? I can't—I don't think I can stand hearing you say it over and over." My throat tightens again, and I try to clear it. "Besides, we could probably use a little time here to ourselves."

"Okay." Missy gives me a funny look, as if I don't trust her.

"Just tell them we'll let them know more after we make arrangements."

"Sure you don't need my help here?"

I meet Jasper's eyes. "Jasper can help me, if I need it." I hold out my hand toward him, and he stares at it like it's a snake that might bite him, and just when I'm sure he's not going to take it, when I'm sure he's went inside himself to some place I can't go, he reaches out his hand.

CHAPTER FOUR

JASPER

Romie and I haven't talked since we left our West Virginia homeplace over two hours ago, both of us teary-eyed, too afraid to put words into the space already overfull of emotion. Every now and then, I hear Romie sniffle in the seat beside me, and she'll squeeze my knee, or I'll squeeze hers. It's the only way to say what we feel. It surprises me then that she speaks when we're partway through East River Mountain Tunnel.

"Look at them cracks," she says. "You think it's even safe to drive through here?"

I register her words and peer out the Jeep window at the long, zigzagged cracks between the bricks that hold the land away from us. "I feel safe," I say. And I almost do. Five years of underground mining taught me to seek a measure of calm in the disquiet of trespassing the belly of the earth. There's always danger, sure—men get crushed in roof-falls, die in methane fires and explosions, breathe silica and coal dust that seizes up their lungs—but we got to keep the lights on somehow, don't we? Need coal to do that. Still, Romie says it's time everybody admits that tearing apart a mountain can kill you. She says violence done to the land can never come to a good end.

That's why we're leaving.

I reach out a hand and lay it on the soft mound of Romie's belly, as if I can protect this life inside of her that is part mine. She lifts my hand, kisses my palm, and places it again over her womb as we leave the tunnel and drive into morning brightness.

Romie miscarried her first baby. We learned she was pregnant with that one on the day of Daddy's funeral, but we should have suspected it sooner, as Romie had been sick a while. She had it in her head that she had Crohn's disease, like my daddy. I have to admit, I worried about that, too, her not eating much, sick to her stomach, losing weight—just like Daddy started out. Even when she fainted next to Daddy's casket, I never thought *baby*. People faint at funerals, don't they? Grief, stress, exhaustion. Lord knows, she'd worn herself down those last days Daddy was alive, cleaning him, changing him, feeding him ice chips or broth with a teaspoon. She hardly slept.

It was Momma's oldest friend, Bessie Harmon, who held Romie's head in her lap right there on the floor of the funeral home, looked up at me with a smile and said, "You don't know, do you? She's with child." Everyone in Stump Branch knows Bessie to be some kind of seer, but if she knew then that Romie's baby wouldn't live but another four months, she didn't let on.

The doctor said there was no explanation they could find for the late miscarriage, but Romie blamed it on the land. Said the land was poison land, that it was poisoned by mountaintop removal mining and the mine owners. Said if we keep on killing the land, the land has no choice but to kill us right back. I can't tell you how it hurt to hear her say those things.

Romie said Daddy felt that way about the land, too, and that hurt even worse. After he died, when she told me about him wanting to blow up the mine where I worked, it shook me. My daddy loved mining. Or used to, before they started lopping off the mountains. Over thirty years he worked underground. Went from shoveling coal into a rail-cart to watching it gouged out with a continuous miner and dumped onto conveyor belts. I seen his face the first time he saw the dragline megaexcavator shearing off the head of Kayton Mountain. Looked like he'd get sick.

Made me feel sickly, too, watching the monster that stands taller than Lady Liberty eat two-hundred-forty tons of mountain in every bite, two bites a minute. *Progress*, they call it. Progress that puts thousands of underground miners like me out of work. Progress that changes the land forever. Progress that pumps sickness into the water supply, kills fish and deer and daddies and babies.

It was Daddy's plan for me and Romie to pack up and head to North Carolina. Romie said we needed to get out of the West Virginia mountains before the coal companies flatten them all, before the mountains bury us in return. I could hardly bear it when Daddy agreed with her. It felt like a message from beyond, then, when we learned on the first anniversary of Daddy's death that Romie was pregnant again. I knew right then that no matter how much I love underground coal mining, we had to leave.

By the time we drive through Mount Airy, we're breathing easier, talking easier. We plan how to decorate the nursery, and I tell Romie I want to do it in Flintstones, put a big old Pebbles and a Bam-Bam holding a club on the wall over the crib. Romie looks horrified, and I goose her kneecap, feel a thrill in my chest when she giggles. I'm excited at the chance for a fresh start, but I still feel the cord of the mountains pulling at me every time I look in the rearview mirror. I stare ahead and make myself look towards what will be.

Three weeks into my new job, I still ain't used to working in the Greensboro heat. I take off my hardhat, wipe the sweat and red dirt from my forehead and look toward the treeline, thirsty for shade. My first gig with the Billings Construction crew is to build a home improvement warehouse, one of them big-box stores that eats up acres of land. Two of the men I work with are from West Virginia, and the owner Mack Billings used to spend summers with his grandparents up in Fairmont. He took a liking to me right away, said he'd hire more West Virginia boys if they'd come down here. Said we're the best workers he's got, 'cause we know hard labor, and we know hard times, and we ain't afraid to earn our pay.

I'm calling it, all right. I'm on my second t-shirt today—first one was dripping wet by ten-thirty—and it's not even lunchtime. Leveling footers for concrete under the Carolina sun makes underground mining in the chilly darkness seem like a pleasant memory, so I know the heat must be affecting my mind.

Mack landed a contract to build two of the big stores, one each on opposite sides of Greensboro, and he said that'll keep us tied up for nearly a year, though there's a short break in between he'll try to fill. That's security like I've never had. We've got good insurance that even covers our families, so Romie and I don't have to worry about paying the hospital when she has the baby.

There's other good benefits, too. Mack graduated Chapel Hill, and he's all about his men getting an education. He told all of us that if we get our EMT license, he'll pay for the classes, plus he'll up our pay seventy-five cents on the hour. Only three months to graduate, so that's a deal I'm taking. Mack said it makes us safer workers, and it lowers company insurance, too.

Romie loves the idea. "I'll study your books alongside you, Jasper," she says, tossing aside another empty cardboard box. She's done most of the unpacking herself while I work, which is just as well, since she's particular about where everything goes. *Nesting*, Mack called it. "If we study together," Romie says, "when the baby's born and I go to nursing school, I'll have a jumpstart on the other students."

I think it's a fine plan, and before long, we're discussing aortas and hemophiliacs at the dinner table.

The whole thing seems funny to me, and I tell Bucky and Mack about it over lunch. Mack runs a hand through his bristle-brush red hair, looks at me with that squint he gets when he ain't sure about something, and he tells me to be careful about letting Romie get smarter than me. I ask him what he means.

"You can't let your woman pass you by, Jasper. Got to stay one step ahead of her. Be smarter, be stronger, keep her under control."

I have to laugh. He don't know Romie like I know Romie. There ain't no keeping that woman under control.

Mack watches me a full minute; then he puts a hand on my shoulder. "Tell you what," he says, "why don't we go to B.G. McGee's on Saturday, grab a burger and a beer, and watch the Tarheels beat the Mountaineers."

"I'll be there," I say. "And we'll drink a cold one and watch the Mountaineers whup the Tarheels then clean up the field with their carcasses."

Saturday rolls around, and I'm surprised at the way Mack's tongue loosens after he downs a few. He starts talking about women, admits he's fresh out of his second marriage by only a few months.

"Married Satan's spawn the first time," Mack says. "The other one wasn't bad, at first, but then she got above me." He lifts an eyebrow, a warning.

"How do you mean?"

"It's what I was talking about the other day." He draws the last from his bottle of beer, throws up a meaty hand for the bartender to bring him another. "She was—is—an attorney."

I let out a whistle, then laugh. "That had to hurt."

Mack laughs, too. "It could have. She was fair, though, seeing as how I put her through law school. You know that mirrored-glass building on Eugene Street? That's her law firm. I built it for her. She took that, I kept the house." He swabs at a puddle of ketchup with a french fry, downs it, then looks at me straight-faced. "Be careful is all I'm saying."

"Not sure I understand."

"Romie wants to go to nursing school. You work construction." He lifts his bottle, as if in a toast. "Reputable business, no doubt. It's done me well." He pulls a swig from his beer. "I got a degree in engineering, studied a little business along the way, decided I'd start my own company. Had my degree before she had hers. But while I was working, starting my business, building us a house, throwing up stores and condos and law firms, she was getting smarter. Too good for me. Next thing I know, she's marrying a judge. Someone who understands her, she said, who can relate to her." His voice goes up an octave at this last, and I press my lips together to keep from grinning.

I take a drink and think about Mack's words; then I square my shoulders. Mack don't know us. He don't know what Romie's done for me, for Daddy. He don't know she's the one who took Daddy's OxyContin to Jimbo's house that night and made the trade for the stack of cash that brought us here. She wouldn't let me risk losing my job, said if she got caught, they wouldn't be as hard on a pregnant woman.

Mack's eyebrows raise, and I realize I'm looking at him harder than I mean to. "That won't happen to us," I say. "We've been through a lot together. We're having a baby."

He lifts his beer again, this time towards mine, and our bottles ring together. "Congratulations, man. I wish you all the best in the world."

Romie and I decide we'll call our baby girl Mariah Jane when she's born, name her after our deceased mothers. I pray each night she'll be born healthy, with my blue eyes and Romie's pout of a mouth. We've been here three months, and Romie spends her days now shopping for miniature dresses, applying to nursing programs, and reading used textbooks so she can get ahead before school starts in the fall. "The baby's going to eat up a lot of my time, Jasper," she says, "so I want to learn all I can while I have some peace and quiet."

I ain't forgot what Mack said, and he'd remind me of it, if I did. I pay attention to what Romie reads and what she says, and I keep some of the books she's read in my truck nowadays. I read history and Hemingway during lunch break, work on my own education, so we can stay on level ground.

It takes no time to finish the first home-improvement store, and Mack gets us a contract on a new spread of condominiums on the far end of Wendover. Our second day on the new site, Bucky calls in sick, and Mack points me toward his new Cat 568 Forest Machine. "Looks like you're clearing today."

My jaw drops. I've driven dozers before, but not a forest machine, and I've never cleared land. Mack had let me play on it one day shortly after he bought it, raising and lowering the boom, opening and closing the grapple claw with a joystick that moved as easily as the yard-sale Atari I'd played with growing up.

Now he spreads the blueprints across the picnic table in front of the small trailer that serves as our portable office, and he jabs a thick finger at the overlapping circles that indicate trees. "All these trees have to go," he says. He shields his eyes from the morning sun and points far left of the trailer, where packed yellow dirt gives way to scrub brush and several acres of loblolly pine. "Start at the far end there. Get as much as you can cleared by lunch, moving back this way."

I smile when I fire up the 568. *Killdozer*, Bucky calls it, after some old movie he'd seen where machinery goes wild and kills people. Killdozer rumbles beneath me, and as I shift gears, raise the boom, and swing, my grin grows broader. I throw a thumbs-up Mack's way, and I see him laugh, but can't hear him. With an easy flick of my wrist, Killdozer moves forward, not in a lurch like the D9T dozer I sometimes drive, but smooth, like we're rolling on glass, not rocky dirt. "This here's power!" I yell.

In under a minute, I've crossed the expanse of yellow, reached the treeline, and there I bring Killdozer to a rest. I look back over my shoulder, but Mack's moved on to other things, pointing and ordering the crew around the site. I take a deep breath, raise the boom, and open the grapple. I've seen this done before, know how to fell a tree with a boom—start halfway up to keep from getting your head conked—but now it's here in front of me, acres of sweet-smelling timber. It's my hand on the joystick. It's my job.

I think of Daddy and swallow against the knot that comes in my throat. He'd like this sun-colored piece of equipment, like to crawl up in here with me, see how easily Killdozer maneuvers. I manage the controls, simple to do, open the grapple, and the metal claw grabs the first pine midway up the trunk. I startle at how easily the tree shatters, quicker and smoother than snapping my fingers. It's about a seventy-footer, and just like that, it's split in half.

My heart beats faster than I've known it to for a while, and I pick up the top of the tree, swing the boom to the side and start my stack. Back to what's left of the tree, I maneuver the grapple to the base of the pine, snap it off like I'd break a toothpick, one quick and easy motion, lift it to lie alongside the treetop. I glance at my watch. Less than a minute.

I figure sixty trees an hour, give or take. Four hours later, I've cleared at least an acre. When I climb down off Killdozer, my hands tingle from the vibration of the joysticks. I don't want to look behind me, at where I've been, what I've done, but I have to count the stacks, survey the damage.

Standing beside the 568, I feel small, but I shrink to puny when I walk to the last stack of trees I made, see the oaks and maples and pines smashed into splintered haystacks jutting twenty or so feet in the air. I turn away, and my eyes find the bare ground where I've been. Crater-size holes pockmark the dirt where root-bases once sunk deep. Scrub brush lies bent and flattened where Killdozer—and I—left tracks.

I think of the waste back home that once was Kayton Mountain, and my stomach knots up. I close my eyes, try to imagine the condominiums from the drawing on the wall in Mack's office trailer, the playground area with the wooden jungle gym where kids will laugh someday soon. This here's nothing like what's been done to Kayton and hundreds of other mountains where I'm from. This here's hardly any harm at all.

A week passes, and on Wednesday night Mack calls me at home to tell me that Bucky has gone to jail and lost his job. Busted selling a bale of weed—I didn't even know marijuana came in bales—so he's making me full-time operator of Killdozer. I'll get Bucky's company truck, too.

Hours after I should be sleeping, I lay awake and think of Bucky's arrest and how, without the grace of God, Romie could be in jail, too, serving a term a whole lot longer than Bucky will get. Felony offense, selling even a couple Oxy capsules. Romie sold nearly six hundred. Then Jimbo turned right around, sold them to Weasel—*middleman,* he liked the term—so he could have gone down, too.

"You worrying about your friend from work?" Romie turns toward me beneath the covers.

"Yeah."

She somehow reads my mind and lets out a breath that tickles my ear. "What's done is done, Jasper. Ain't no danger in it, now. Nobody's coming for us. We're hundreds of miles and four or five months past that kind of trouble."

I mumble, not sure if I agree with her, or not. If Weasel were to get busted, point a finger at Jimbo, then Jimbo tell where he got the pills . . . but Jimbo wouldn't do that to us. I don't think.

"I know that don't make it right," she whispers, "but it's nothing to worry over now."

"I wasn't worrying about that," I say. "I was thinking about who's gonna do my job, if I'm doing Bucky's."

She knows I'm lying, and her lips find mine before I can tell another untruth.

I hear the screech of the lunch whistle over Killdozer's groan, and I drop the tree I've cleared and shut off the engine right where the forest machine sits. I step down off the dozer and pull on a clean t-shirt, and that's when I hear it—a howling mewl unlike anything I've ever heard. It sends a chill skittering across the back of my neck. I shake off the shudder and stand still, trying to situate the source. It comes again, more of a squeal this time, from the tall stack of broken trees to my right.

My workboots are quiet as I step across the soft ground, lunge over Killdozer's ruts in the rain-damp soil, maneuver around broken knee-high stumps I've yet to tear out. The sweet, pungent scent of fresh pine resin and maple sap fills the air, and on the breeze, I catch a whiff of the bitter whang of diesel fuel.

The animalistic whimpering grows louder, but when a fallen branch snaps beneath my footfall, it silences. I wonder if I've trapped a cat in the pile of broken trees, except the sound doesn't quite sound like a cat . . . or a squirrel, or a bird, or any small animal I've heard before. Two yards ahead of me, a low blur of movement in a pine bough catches my eye, and I hold my breath as I step alongside the shattered crown of a loblolly pine to find the source.

The scrambling movement grows more frantic as I draw near, and again the pained howl erupts, tensing me all over. Small branches crack beneath my boots, and the long fringe of pine needles on the ground in front of me stop moving. I cautiously push them aside, startled to see a smoke-colored rabbit nearly the size of a housecat. The panicked rabbit sees or senses me, lets out a pitiful squeal and furiously digs at the ground in an effort to escape. One of the heavy pine limbs has fallen across the rabbit's hind-parts, pinning it to the ground.

"Shhhh," I whisper. "Be still. I'm here to help you." I squat near the rabbit, reach carefully around its head, and grasp the scruff, holding it with one hand while I lift the limb with the other, push it to the side.

The rabbit squeals again, a terrified sound that sends a shiver across my scalp. I hold the creature aloft, and he's badly mangled. He twists in an effort to escape, and his hind legs dangle uselessly, his innards begin to slip loose. I look away, bury my face in my shoulder.

I know what I have to do.

I slide my hands together around the rabbit's warm neck, close my eyes and give a quick twist, hear the soft crunch I feel between my fingers and thumbs. Daddy would call this a mountain-mercy killing. The breeze turns cold. It will soon rain.

I hammer the ground with heel of my boot, carve out a trough where I can bury the rabbit, and that's when I see them. Seven kits. Only two have their eyes open. The limp rabbit I hold was a momma.

I lay her in the trough, and resentment tightens my jaw. I stand, stomp the ground like a temperamental child. Why me? I look at the kits again, each no bigger than my palm. I can't bear wringing their little necks—they're so tiny I'd have to do it with my fingertips. I stare at the momma in the furrow. It would be a slow, cruel death to bury the babies alive with their momma. They have to be killed, first.

As I kneel and scoop loose soil over the momma rabbit, I push away the memory of the fistful of dirt I crumbled over Daddy's casket. Fury I can't account for surges through me, and I stand and smack dirt from my hands, look again at the seven kits. Romie's voice speaks in my head—*if we keep on killing the land, the land will have no choice but to kill us right back.*

That works both ways, don't it? Daddy died of Crohn's and cancer caused by the poisoned land. So if the land kills us. . ..

I let out a low scream as I stomp my boot-heel into the nest of kits, quickly snuffing their little lives. "You killed my daddy, and you killed Romie's first baby!" I curse the land, tromp at the earth, kick dirt over the rusty, fur-smeared ground, then drag the pine bough to cover my sin. I turn my face to the overcast sky and growl through my teeth like a madman.

I unpocket the key to Killdozer, skip lunch with the guys in the office trailer, stride instead directly back to the machine. No sane man could have an appetite after what I've done.

I brutally attack the trees with Killdozer, grunting and shouting each time I snap one in half. The branches of a tall elm become arms reaching for the sky, and I grasp it in the middle with the grapple, right where I think its heart should be, and I split it in half. It feels good, like the land deserves what I'm doing to it. Soon my rage burns off, and I start to feel sick again. I look behind me at the long row of tree-stacks waiting to be fed to the chipper—more trees than I've ever cleared in an hour—each stack standing higher than Killdozer and me. Tracks and ruts and splintered stumps mark where I've been, and I pause and look around at the woods I've destroyed. Soon, this will all be asphalt.

I drive the dozer between two of the tall stacks, out of sight of the office trailer and the half-dozen men roving the ground in the distance. I climb down and sit on the ground behind the leafy crown of a fallen maple. I hide my face in my knees and cry.

A big empty part of me aches to talk to Daddy one more time, to ask him if what I'm doing is right or wrong. After a few minutes, I climb back onto Killdozer, take a swig of water, and spit it onto the ground. I'm proud of the paycheck I'm earning, of how well I take care of my family, but when I look around me at the trees I've slaughtered, I'm ashamed. I can't do this much longer.

As I work the last three hours of my shift, my head churns with memories and stories and new ideas, and when I head back to the office trailer to punch out, I've decided it's the last day I'll drive Killdozer. Mack ain't around for me to tell him, so I head home, grateful for the start of cleansing rain, for the heavy traffic that allows me more time to think.

I'll talk to Mack in the morning and tell him I'll accept the pay cut that comes with the step-down. I'll go back to where I started, digging footers again, laying block, building something, instead of tearing things apart. I can't wait to tell Romie.

At the first red traffic light, I remember to turn on my cell phone, in case Romie's called for me to pick up milk or bread or cat food on the way home. Before traffic even starts moving again, the phone chimes again and again and again with messages, and I know something's wrong. I pull into the first parking lot I come to, hit the speaker button on my cell.

"Jasper, call me as soon as you can." It's Romie.

The next message is also from her. "Something's wrong, Jasper. If I don't hear back from you in ten minutes, I'm going ahead to the hospital."

I let the phone fall into the seat beside me as the third message starts to play, and I punch the gas, cutting into traffic, ignoring the blaring horn from the black Chevy I've nearly sideswiped.

"Jasper, I'm in the ER at Women's Hospital. It's the baby." There's a sob in her throat, and I match it with one of my own. "Get here as quick as you can."

I drive too fast, too dangerous, Romie's words sounding again in my head. *If we keep on killing the land, the land will have no choice but to kill us right back.* I have done this to her, I think. Part of me knows I haven't caused anything to happen to her or the baby, but another part of me thinks that maybe I have.

There's an empty parking spot in front of the emergency room entrance, and I jump out of the truck and sprint through the hospital's automatic doors. The moon-faced nurse acts as if she's been expecting me, as if she knows who I am, who I'm here to see. I'm surprised when she leads me past the rooms made of green curtains and down a hallway, where she stops beside a private hospital room, holds open the door. She places her hand on my shoulder and looks at me, her eyes sorrowful, and my mouth goes dry.

Inside the dimly lit room, Romie looks small in the hospital bed, and when she looks up at me, she's crying. She holds out a hand, and I take it, sit on the bed beside her, and hold her in my arms while we weep.

The next morning, I help Romie pull on her blouse, wishing I'd thought to go home while she slept to get her a fresh one. The maternity top now hangs in soft folds across her middle. We sit side-by-side on the hospital bed, while we wait for the nurse to complete paperwork and come for us. I stroke Romie's hand.

"I want to go home, Jasper," she says.

"I know, baby. Not long now."

She grips my hand, stops its movement. "Home. Back home. I want to go back to West Virginia."

Back home. Her words strike a familiar ache in me, a throb, like a toothache I've probed with my tongue.

There is no home to return to, no empty house where we began married life together, and we've rented out the homeplace where I was raised for another year. We sold our trailer and little plot of land to a young couple more rooted than us when we left Stump Branch.

Again, it is as if she pulls thoughts from my head. "I don't want to go back to Stump Branch."

I wonder if this is her way of running, of leaving behind all the bad that has happened. "Where would we go?"

"Morgantown. Maybe Huntington. Or Shepherdstown." Her shoulder lifts and drops. "A place where there's a good nursing school."

I stare at our hands nestled together, hers smaller than mine, softer, yet somehow much stronger.

Her voice drops to a whisper. "I don't want to do this again, Jasper. No more trying for babies."

She is fraught, upset, grieving. It will pass.

"We don't have to think about that right now. The doctor said to wait six months, get your strength back."

Romie shakes her head, and hair falls over one red-rimmed eye. "No more." Her voice comes stronger, louder. "No more."

I suck in the sadness, the hopelessness in her voice, swallow it down where it tightens like a fist, hard and cold in my stomach. "Okay. No more."

Daddy once told me the greatest joy of a man's life was a walk through the woods with his child. There will be no child for me. *No woods, either.* No coal mining. No slaying trees. No babies. No more. My scalp prickles.

I try to imagine what the future holds, where Romie and I will live—just the two of us, no child to bring us joy in old age. Where will I work? What will I do with the rest of my days? I close my eyes, but I can't picture anything at all, can't see what lies ahead, only see blackness like I found in the belly of the earth. There's a void there, a nothingness, a big empty so powerful I still taste its icy bitterness in my mouth.

CHAPTER FIVE

ROMIE

It isn't the switchback turns and vertical inclines making my stomach quiver. These curves and swells are as familiar to me as my own face. I've been driving and riding on roads worse than this one since I was born into these West Virginia mountains, and though I've got no real love for Stump Branch, it feels good to again be swaddled inside these mountains. No, it's seeing Missy again that has me dry-mouthed and nauseous.

For reasons I don't understand, Missy took offense when Jasper and I packed up and headed to North Carolina. At first, I thought it was because she missed us. I mean, the four of us have been running around together since high school, and we stood as witnesses at each other's weddings.

Jimbo finally told Jasper that Missy'd felt betrayed when we moved away. She had it in her head that the four of us would grow old together, side by side. She and I married our high-school sweethearts only two weeks apart, so I reckon we were supposed to have babies at the same time, carpool together as football moms, follow each other to the grave. Well . . . the baby thing didn't work out so well for me, did it? And any wife in her right mind ought to jump at the chance to get her man out of the coal mines, right? Missy ought to be happier for us.

The road follows the ever-flowing creek branch—Stump Branch—down a short way, before we again head up the next steep incline, then we top the wooded knoll that levels out into a straight stretch in front of Missy and Jimbo's new place. Jimbo shoos away the butterflies flitting in my belly when he bolts out the front door and heads toward us, waving his arms in the air and whooping like a crazy man. "Well by God! If it ain't about time! We thought you'd outgrown your old buddies." He yells loud enough to be heard the next ridge over, and I giggle.

Jasper turns to me and grins, and the lines at the corners of his eyes bring to mind the sunrays I drew as a child. "See there, Romie? No reason at all to worry, huh."

I lean over and kiss his cheek, pleased to give him this *I told you so* moment. Jasper takes the two bottles of wine we brought from Etter Vineyards, the upstate winery where we now work, from the back floorboard, and we climb out of the Jeep. We are grabbed in turn by Jimbo, who claps Jasper on the back hard enough that the sound echoes against the woods. Then he opens his arms to me. "Looky here at the college genius. How's school treating you? Don't you be getting too smart for us, you hear me, Romie?" He lifts me off the ground and spins me around until I'm as dizzy and giggly as a toddler. And then I see Missy.

She's standing just inside the glass storm door, leaning against the doorframe with her arms crossed. She's watching us. Though we're a good hundred yards away, I see that her hair is a tousled mess, and her expression is sullen, the opposite of Jimbo's. My own appearance must change, because Jasper sees me, cocks his head to one side, then looks toward the house to where I stared a moment too long.

Jimbo rubs the back of his neck. "Yeah, she's having a tough time of it."

"Of what?" Jasper asks. I want to kick him for asking. She's closed us out, so she's none of our business anymore.

"Ahhh, she's been trying to get a monkey off her back." Jimbo's face reddens, and he drops his head, shoves his hands into his pockets. "'Bout a year ago she tried an Oxy or two, you know . . . help her sleep at night. She had insomnia, see? We're in this new house, new place away from what few kin she has left, and y'all are gone. I'm working doubles, she's feeling alone and afraid, can't sleep." His voice thickens, and he clears his throat. "I didn't know until a couple of months into it. You know how we get, Jasper—walk in the door dog-tired after pulling sixteen or eighteen hours underground, shower, and hit the hay. It's as much my fault as hers." His voice softens. "I should have seen it coming."

My throat aches, and I turn away, stare into the woods. An owl hoots, and I blink hard, scan deep into the trees until I see it, perched alone on an upper pine bough, alert despite the noon hour. Some say an owl in daytime is a portent, an omen of death. I look again toward the front door as Missy rubs her arms and steps back into darkness, disappearing. I'm the one who should have seen it coming.

That night comes back to me—my shoes making sucking noises in the muddy yard in front of Jimbo and Missy's old trailer, the ground softened by snowmelt and rain runoff, my breath making clouds in the white glow of their porch light. My fingers were nearly numb as I cradled the paper grocery bag containing stock bottles of Paw's OxyContin—and I wring my hands now, as if to fight off the chill, though the summer air is warm. What I did was wrong. *I* was wrong. Knew it then, know it again now, fresh wrong crawling over me like ants. I scratch my throat and look back at the Jeep. I wish we'd never come here; wish we could leave right now.

"Where are my manners!" says Jimbo, his voice artificially bright. "What say we go in and have us a cold beer?" He sidles up between Jasper and me, drapes an arm around each of us, and ushers us toward his house.

My legs are heavy and stiff as we climb the steps to the deck, but I blame it on the three-hour ride. Jimbo swings open the glass door and sweeps his arm to welcome us inside. "After you, Miz Grodin," he says, doffing an imaginary top hat.

I walk through the doorway, automatically sidestepping Jimbo's work boots on the plastic runner just inside the door. My feet haven't forgotten what it's like to live in a house with a coal miner, even if the rest of me has tried. I blink as my eyes adjust to the sudden darkness. Though it's August daylight outside, winter draperies still cover the windows, and they're pulled shut, blocking out late-summer's glow. The house isn't all that's brand new. There's a new couch and loveseat, new recliner, new tables and lamps. Everything even smells new.

Jasper notices, too, and he pokes a finger at Jimbo's ribs. "Look at you," he says, then waves a hand across the room. "You can't hide money."

Besides the new furnishings, something seems off to me, and I study the living room and the kitchen that sits off to the right. A worn copy of *Field & Stream* is squared with one side of the coffee table, a dog-eared edition of *Gun World* lined up with the other. There's last Christmas's sale catalog from *Cabela's* on an end table. Jutting from the kitchen garbage can are two frozen-pizza boxes and a flattened beer carton. The house is clean, but it's all wrong. And then it dawns on me; it looks like a single man lives here.

"Missy!" Jimbo calls out. "Want to come say hello to our *best friends?*"

I hear Jasper's tight swallow from where he stands beside me. "Jimbo," I say. "If she's not feeling well . . . ." He places the Etter Vineyards wine bottles on the countertop between the living room and kitchen.

"Aww, she'll be out in a minute. Probably sprucing up. You know how you girls are, always dressing up for each other." His smile is strained, and he hustles past us into the kitchen and opens the fridge. "Get you a beer?" He tosses a can to Jasper without waiting for an answer. "Romie?"

"No thank you." I glance at the door; I'm ready to leave.

"Pepsi? Water? Want to open your fancy wine?"

"Water's fine."

The three of us sit—Jasper and I side-by-side on the loveseat, while Jimbo adjusts the heating pad on his camouflage-print recliner before he sits and kicks it back. We make small talk about the weather, the drive downstate to Stump Branch, and the deer hunting Jimbo did in the fall.

"Gonna sell my tree stand," he says to Jasper, "let you have it free, you want it."

"You get a new one?" Jasper asks.

"Nah." Jimbo puts a hand to his low back. "I hunt from the ground. Can't shinny a tree like I used to. Old man's getting stiff."

Old man, I think. He's every day of twenty-four years. I study the lines on his face, the dark hollows beneath his eyes, the scabs on his knuckles. He could pass for thirty-five, easy. "You had no business picking me up and swinging me around like you did, if your back's acting up, Jimbo."

He paws at the air, shooing away my words. "You're still light a feather, Romie. Was like swinging a cat by the tail."

I laugh, and it feels good.

"You been up to see the homeplace?" Jimbo asks Jasper.

"Nah. Might ride by there, after 'while. We gonna go tend the graves. Figure we'll go up and see our old trailer. See if the folks who bought it are taking care of it."

I uncross my legs and recross them in the other direction. I like going by the Grodin homeplace, though we've got it rented out for a pittance right now. And I like going to the churchyard; like tending my parents' and in-laws' graves. Especially, I want to cup my hands around the two marble angels that sit between Momma's and Daddy's graves, the ones that mark no bodies, just the memories of my lost babies. But I've got no longing to see the trailer that was mine and Jasper's first home together. When I said goodbye, I meant it.

"You might want to rethink that," Jimbo says. "The trip up the mountain to your old trailer, I mean." He swallows a drink of beer, squints one eye. "You can't get to it no more."

"Can't get to it?" Jasper asks. "Coal trucks tear up the road or something?"

"I didn't reckon you knew. Prospect's bought up that whole mountain, every last acre of it."

Jasper's leg stiffens against mine. "Say what?"

"That couple you sold it to? Probably thought they were young marrieds, didn't you?"

"Yes," I say.

"I did, too," Jimbo says. "Turns out, the girl's one of Blackstone's nieces from down in Tampa, and the guy's his nephew. They went around acting like they needed a place real bad, struck up good bargains. Bought up eight properties like that with Blackstone's money. Soon as the ink was dry, they signed 'em over to Prospect Mining."

"You're joking," Jasper says.

"Don't I wish. What folks on that mountain weren't hoodooed by them two was pretty much forced off their land."

"Forced?" I huff. "They sold out, you mean. How you gonna force somebody off family land if they don't want to sell?"

"Cut brake lines," Jimbo says. "Bullet holes in the side of your house. Dead pets on your front porch. I even heard somebody broke poor old Widow Shrewsbury's bedroom window in the middle of the night, dumped in a box of timber rattlers and copperheads. And her blind as a bat in broad daylight." Jimbo's lips twist sideways, and he shakes his head. "They's ways of forcing you off, all right."

A shudder ripples my shoulders, and Jasper puts his arm around me. He clears his throat. "The law didn't do anything about it?"

Jimbo harsh-laughs at this, too loud and too long. "You been gone a while now, boy, forgot what it's like. Prospect *is* the law, 'round here."

My nails bite into my palms, and I release my clenched fists, flex my fingers. "I don't see how you can still work for those devils, Jimbo."

"Not everybody tucks tail and runs." I jerk my head toward Missy's voice. Don't know how long she's been standing there in the hallway, listening. She steps out of the shadow into the living room, her eyes shooting fiery sparks in my direction. Her auburn hair is now twisted into a loose bun, and she's wearing makeup, a sundress, and a lightweight sweater that's slipped off one naked shoulder. She's barefoot, and she is simply beautiful. I know I would tell her this if her words weren't so ugly.

Jasper's jaw muscle flexes like it does when he's feeling defensive, but I can't tell him her comment isn't meant for him. She said it to me, said it *for* me, just like she said that very same thing to me almost ten years ago.

We were fifteen then, and it was the first anniversary of my parents' deaths. Much like the day they died, the cold bit at my skin, though snowflakes flurried the air, instead of the sleet that caused my parents' fatal accident. The Stump Branch High School homecoming game was scheduled that night, and it seemed wrong to be celebrating on the anniversary of such an awful day. The principal canceled afternoon classes for a pep rally. Missy was a junior-varsity cheerleader, and I was captain of the pep squad, but I had no pep to give. She watched me with a clouded face as she performed the cheers from the gymnasium floor, and as soon as the varsity cheerleaders took over the court, she jogged to my side.

"Wanna get out of here?"

She didn't have to ask twice.

We stop in the girls' bathroom where Missy slips on a pair of royal-blue leggings that match her cheerleader skirt, then we slick on strawberry lip-gloss and head out into the cold. I don't recall either of us asking or saying where we were going; it is as if we are pulled along the highway by an invisible string toward the one-lane that runs up the hill, then down the dirt road to the old mountain cemetery settled in the arms of the holler.

I dust the snow off Momma's grave first, then my daddy's, tracing the letters and numbers on the headstones with a finger, their final dates the same as today's, except for the year. Without turning to look behind me, I know that Missy sits on the back steps of the Gaston

Ridge Primitive Baptist Church, the oldest and smallest church in the county. She'll sit there quietly, never rushing me, until I catch up my folks on all they've missed, confess my sins, get my cry out. Missy gives me just the right mixture of company and solitude. It's the kindest thing anyone has ever done for me.

"Tonight is the homecoming dance," I say to Daddy's stone. "But you don't have to worry none. It's juniors and seniors only, so I'm still too young to go." I pick up a snow-dusted twig that still has dark, curled leaves attached, and I fling it away from Daddy's grave, wish I'd arranged pine boughs and pinecones tied with a ribbon like we did in Home Ec class, brought it for decoration. I try to keep their graves as neat as I can, hoping the preacher won't raise the monthly fee he charges to keep them mowed and tended. Momaw pays his bill, but I try to help when I can, give her the money I make dusting the what-nots in Mrs. Maxwell's antique store in town once every month or so.

I kiss Daddy's headstone, give it a final sweep to clear it of fresh-fallen flakes, then I take a step to the right and kneel before Momma's name. "Got something for you," I say. I open the top buttons of my peacoat, reach inside and remove the apple-sized red and yellow badge from the school sweatshirt I'm wearing, pricking my thumb in the process. I suck away the freckle of blood, then hold out the badge toward Momma's marker. "I made *A* honor roll, see? Wasn't sure I was gonna make it, but Mrs. Hutchins gave me two extra days to turn in my essay, seeing as how I was out sick and all." My nose begins to run, and I pull the sleeve of my sweatshirt from under the cuff of my coat and wipe my nose. "It was a personal essay called a *memoir*. I wrote it about you and Daddy." My voice splinters, and I look at the sky and clear my throat.

I pull the stickpin at an angle from the badge's back to make a kickstand; then I brush the dusting of snowflakes from Momma's headstone and prop the badge on top. "Here, Momma. You keep it." I sniff, and the sound seems too loud in this silent space. "You earned it," I whisper. "You're an A-honor-roll mom."

I kiss her stone, and I stand. Behind me, Missy's cheerleading sneakers crunch the stiff, snowy grass as she walks toward me. The weight of her hand settles on my back, and I turn and we hug, and when she finally drops her hands, I walk around the church toward the dirt road without looking back.

The wind picks up, and the sky turns to cold steel by the time we reach the blacktop one-lane, and Missy and I link arms, walk huddled against the snow-swirling gusts. A minute later, light shines from behind us, and we quick-step off the edge of the road as a pickup tops the knoll we've just descended. I turn as it nears, see that it's new, red, and shiny, clean despite the mud, coal dirt, and salt that stains the roads in Stump Branch this time of year.

The truck slows, then stops, and the passenger window lowers. Missy's hand tightens on my arm. Two of the handsomest men I have ever seen are in the truck, and even in the gloaming, the driver's dark eyes glitter like coal when he smiles at us. The broad-shouldered, blond-haired passenger has on a letterman jacket, burgundy and white, not the blue and gold of Stump Branch High. I can't see the name or the mascot, but even if he wasn't wearing it, I would say with assurance that they aren't from around here. These boys are new-moneyed.

"It's awfully cold for a walk," the blond one says, and Missy squeezes my arm again.

"It sure is," she says, straightening her back and smiling.

I tug against her, and she turns and gives me a sharp look that says *Don't ruin this*.

The driver leans over the steering wheel to peer around the blond, and when he grins, his teeth are whiter than the snow that falls around us. "Give you a ride?"

"Yes, please, we'd *looove* that," Missy coos before I can think of what to say. Again, I am glad to be her friend, happy that she has taken a liking to me from the minute we met in seventh grade, thrilled that she is bringing me into another adventure alongside her.

We unlink arms, and I start toward the bed of the truck, as that is how we hitch a ride around here, hunkering in a truck bed against the cab, out of the winter wind. But then the strong-jawed blond swings open the truck door, steps down, and throws out his arm with a flourish.

"Offer you a leg up, milady," he says, and Missy pushes me toward him.

I seem to age two or three years when I put my hand in his, my frozen knuckles contrasting red against his warm, pink palm. He presses a big hand firmly against my waist and pushes, practically tossing me into the truck, where the driver catches me before I land on top of him.

"Whoa, there," he says, and his breath is honeyed with whiskey.

My heart beats fast when I mutter an apology, and suddenly Missy is beside me, and there's no room for the blond, whose jacket says he is a football player from Beeson, the private college the next county over.

"I would hate to ride in the truck bed in this kind of weather," the blond says, his green eyes smiling at Missy. "Would it trouble you to sit on my lap?"

Missy giggles in a way that makes me jealous of her coquetry. I mouth the word that I recently learned in class, hearing our English teacher's voice in my head. *Coquetry.*

"I'm okay with it, if you're sure I won't hurt you," Missy says. She scoots closer to me, pushing me snug against the dark-haired boy, who slides his arm around me to help me situate.

I look at him again, our faces so close I can feel his breath on my cheeks, and I see that he has high cheekbones and a ponytail. He is an Indian of some tribe, probably Blackfoot or Cherokee. Shawnee, maybe. Exotic and dangerous. There are many around here, and Momma once told me Blackfoot runs in our blood, though my hair is the brown of a squirrel in winter, and my eyes are gray-green, so I must not have soaked up enough native nectar to make me look interesting.

"What's your name?" the Indian asks me.

Native American, I remind myself. It's what they tell us to say in school. "I am Romie, and this here's my best friend, Missy."

He offers me his hand, and I sit taller, take his hand and shake it proper, though we've practically hugged already. Nestling so close to him seems odd, but pleasant, like the strange and satisfying tingle that's humming low in my belly.

"That's a pretty name," he says. "I'm Nick."

I'm a little disappointed, wishing him to have an unusual foreign name that I could brag about to the kids at school. He stretches his arm in front of me, offers his hand to Missy.

"The man beneath you is Big Mike," he says to her, and I hang onto the word *man*.

We are riding with *men*. That means we are *women*. This is true to me on the deepest level of anything I have ever known. From this moment until forever, we are no longer girls. I shiver.

"You two must be freezing," Big Mike says, boldly grasping Missy's hips and sliding her sideways on his lap, leaning her against his shoulder as if to warm her. He rubs her arm briskly to make her blood flow, and then from nowhere, he pulls out a small bottle, its bottom half wrapped in a paper bag. He puts it in Missy's hand. "Here. A sip of this'll warm you from the inside out."

She looks at me, her eyes big and round, and then she opens the cap and closes her eyes as she takes a big swallow. She gulps it down, and somehow, she doesn't make a face, though I know it must burn her throat. Big Mike passes the bottle to me. "Milady," he says, and I grin my thanks for this name he calls me.

I hesitate with the bottle halfway to my mouth, but Missy's head gives a half-nod, so I put it to my lips and pull a swig. I swallow it down, but I can't hold my face still like Missy did, and I grimace and strangle, cough down the fire that thickens to syrup in my throat.

The men laugh.

I prove I'm worth my mettle with another, bigger swallow, and Nick whistles. "Whoa there, Romie," he says, then shows me his pretty smile again.

I wipe my mouth on the back of my hand like I've seen tough guys do on TV, offer him the bottle.

He takes it, finishes the last of it, puts down the window and flings the bottle over the bank where it crashes through bare limbs and settles into winter silence. I look for a landmark, telling myself I'll come back here and retrieve the bottle, because we can't be messing up this good land.

"We good?" Nick asks us.

"Couldn't be better," Big Mike says, and Missy shifts deeper into his arms, her blue-and-gold cheerleader skirt and JV jacket contrasting as prettily with his college letterman as if the two of them belong on the cover of a coed magazine, as if they belong together.

Nick drives us slowly down the road, and we have all the time and none of the cares this world offers. When we get to the main road, he turns away from Stump Branch, toward Pinehill. This worries me, as it will soon be dark. The whiskey makes me brave enough to ask, "Where are we going?" and Nick gives me that smile again that makes my belly buzz.

"Just a little ways down the road," he says. "Thought I'd stop and get us another bottle, since that one ran dry." He reaches across me, his elbow brushing my chest, and he turns on the radio. A Van Halen drum solo I know bursts from the speakers, and my loose head bobs on my neck to the beat. Nick breaks into the song, his voice a near-image to David Lee Roth's, so mirrored I think I'm sitting next to a rockstar in the making.

When the song hits the bridge, I harmonize with Nick, and he leans close so that our heads touch, and we fill the cab with voices so pure you'd think we'd practiced together for years. The song ends, and he kisses me on the cheek.

"Wow, Romie," he says softly, "you've got a voice," and the glow that warms my face is more than just whiskey.

We round a bend and near an old clapboard beer joint that sits between the road and the swollen creek branch, its square shape sharply leaning backward, as if the winter wind might push it into the water at any moment. Nick cuts the wheel and turns into the gravel parking lot, pulls right up to the building. I shoot Missy a *What now?* look.

"Do you ladies mind waiting here for a minute?" Nick asks, and I let out a breath, glad that he doesn't expect us to go inside, because I know we cannot get in. We may be women now, but we are still too young to be let inside a beer joint. I nod, and Nick opens the door and starts to get out, then turns and slides a hand into my hair, cupping my head, and he kisses me full on the lips—short, but not too short, enough to let me know that it is *me* he really likes, really wants, though he does not even know me. It is a perfect promise.

Big Mike glides an arm under Missy's legs, lifts her into his arms, then slides out from under her. Like Nick did, he kisses Missy, but unlike me, Missy pulls his face close, kisses him deep, using her tongue. It makes me feel a little bit gross, but a whole lot curious, and again my belly grows warm. I cannot wait until Nick kisses me again, so I can try it.

The boys—the men—clap each other on the back as they walk toward the door of the beer joint, and they disappear inside. Missy and I collapse into giggles.

"Oh, my God," Missy says, taking the Lord's name in vain in a way I've never heard her say it before. "They are *so* good-looking!"

"You kissed him!" I say. "I mean you really, really kissed him."

Missy flips her hair over her shoulder, pulls down the passenger visor and opens the mirror. "Yeah? Well . . . I'm going to do it again, too." She winks at me, and I laugh. "Hand me your lip gloss. Hurry, before they come back."

We gloss and fluff and primp, and Missy unzips her coat, reaches into her bra and lifts her titties higher. Following her lead, I unbutton my pea coat and stretch my sweatshirt taut across my chest, wishing I'd worn that vee-necked sweater today, the one that Momaw says is getting too small for me. I have budded some, but Missy has full-out blossomed, and her breasts and hips curve in ways that make the grown men at church turn to stare.

"It'll be dark before long," I say, and Missy rolls her eyes.

"They will take us home. Don't worry. Besides, you're spending the night at my house, and I told Momma I might have to stay after school for cheer practice before the homecoming game tonight."

"But you aren't cheering. It's varsity squad only."

Missy grins at me. "Momma don't know that."

I squeeze Missy's arm, again grateful for her forward-thinking ways, always one step ahead of the grown-ups who worry too much about us.

Nick and Big Mike saunter out of the beer joint, each holding a brown paper bag, and when I see Nick's dark eyes, that ponytail hanging over his leather-clad back, I feel myself swell with a heady mixture of pride and desire. No one at school will ever believe my luck.

Missy grabs my thigh. "College guys, Romie. We have us a couple of *college* guys." She lets out a soft, shrill sound of joy, and I laugh.

Nick swings wide his truck door, kisses me again as he climbs inside. "Miss me?" he asks.

"Every minute," I say, and it is true. His whiskey-manly-mountain smell fills my nose, and I want to drink him down. I take the bottle he offers, drink from it, instead. I turn when Missy holds her bottle toward me, and we clink them together. "Cheers!" we chorus, and we both drink as the men laugh.

"Hell yeah!" Big Mike says, and he and Missy kiss with tongues again as he slides his hand up and down her blue-covered thigh, just a little ways beneath her cheerleader skirt.

I am glad when Nick turns his truck back toward Stump Branch, but I also don't want this evening to end, and I hope he is not going to take us home just yet. I think I shouldn't ask it, though, so I bring the bottle again to my mouth, but this time take only a tiny sip. I don't want to be greedy, so I offer it to Nick, who takes a big slug.

Just past the STUMP BRANCH, UNINCORPORATED sign, Nick turns the truck onto a snow-speckled dirt road I've never ridden on, and we drive up it a short distance, then pull onto a narrow, rutted drive that goes deeper into the holler. The truck tilts from one side to the other as it lurches across big rocks pocking the ruts, but it's only a few yards until the cabin appears. *Cabin* is probably too good of a word for the little shack, though it's made of logs, like a proper cabin ought to be.

Nick and Big Mike nod at each other, and Big Mike says, "Wait here," then the two of them get out. It's almost full dark, but since the snow has stopped and the stars are out, there's light reflecting off the white ground, making it bright enough to see a short distance without the headlights Nick doused along with the engine. They peer into the cabin windows through cupped hands, then Big Mike shoulders the door open and steps inside.

I hold my breath. They have never been here before, don't belong to this house.

Big Mike comes out, waves us to join him.

Missy flings open the door and hops out. "C'mon, Romie. What're you waiting for?"

We grab the liquor bottles, and I wrap my coat tight against the wind, hustle toward Nick's open arms. He pulls me close, leads me inside, and Big Mike pulls out a lighter and sets a lantern aflame. The cabin is somehow smaller on the inside than it looked from outside, holding only one tiny card table and two chairs, a rusted metal cooler, a rolled-up sleeping bag, and the lantern.

"Hunting cabin," Nick says.

I look around again, but there's nothing more to see. "Whose is it?"

"My uncle's," Big Mike says too quickly, but the way his eyes gleam in the lantern light, I know it is a lie.

I don't care.

Big Mike pulls Missy into his arms, and the two are kissing like star-crossed lovers. I am grateful when Nick takes my hand and pulls me toward the corner, just out of the lantern light. He takes my face in his hands and kisses me tenderly. This time I feel his tongue, and it is not gross. When it touches my own tongue, a match strikes to flame, and my insides melt. Liquid runs from my chest into my belly, then lower, down into my thighs, warming every inch of my body, though I shiver in spite of it. Soon his hands slide inside my coat and pull me even closer against him. I feel his hardness grow against me, and I swell with the power I have to move him in this way.

My control over him grows hungry and bold, and I slide my fingers up into his ponytail, loosen the elastic tie, fan out his spice-fragrant hair across my face. I am in heaven.

When I come up for a breath of air, I see Big Mike shaking out the bedroll, and he spreads the sleeping bag on the floor, then slips off Missy's jacket. He offers her his bottle again, and Missy takes it, her eyes meeting mine before she lifts it in a toast, then drinks.

Nick looks over his shoulder to where I am watching, and he laughs. It is a deep, throaty rumble I can feel in my chest. He presses me against the wall, and he rubs his groin against me, and I know that he wants me, but I know, too, that I will not give myself to him. I am puffed with authority, and I arch against him just as his cold hands slide beneath my sweatshirt and across my stomach. He is slow, a gentleman. He will not go any further.

I am proven right when he removes his hands and again takes my face in them, groans as he kisses my forehead, my nose, then hugs me tight against him. He rocks me, then again plunges his tongue into my mouth. "I need you," he says through clenched teeth, and it is this moment I first feel afraid.

I glimpse a flash of white, and I see that Big Mike is pulling Missy's leggings down, baring the skin of her thighs. Missy's hand juts out to stop him. Nick's icy hands find my belly again, but this time they go higher, slide beneath my bra, cup my breasts and squeeze. I push him away.

"It's okay, baby," he says. "I won't hurt you." He gently kisses me. "We'll take it slow."

Missy lets out a muffled yelp, and I peer around Nick's lean body to see her struggling to get Big Mike off her. He's got her sweater up around her neck, her white stomach glaring like bright sunlight, her pale knee struggling to get beneath his leg for leverage. "Stop it!" she yells, and Nick turns to look, then whips back to me, roughly presses me against the wall and pins me there.

He kisses me hard, his teeth smashing my lips until I taste blood. "Settle down, now," he says. "We can do this the easy way, or we can do it the hard way. If you behave, I'll leave the choice up to you."

My body trembles, shivers in a way that rattles my bones together.

This is womanhood.

I don't want it.

I want to be a child again. I want my mother to be alive. I want to be safe in her arms.

Missy's struggling grows louder, and maybe it is my imagination that the sound of her quick breathing amplifies, reaches my ears louder than my own. Her cries, once muffled, come louder now. "Stop it! Quit! Get off me! *Stop!*"

Nick laughs and turns to look at Big Mike, who whips off his belt with a slapping sound, and that's when I crash my knee into Nick with everything I've got. He gasps, his black, glittering eyes going blank, and then he sinks to his knees. I hurdle him and send a boot into Big

Mike's side, but it doesn't faze him. Instead, he bloats to twice his size, reaches out and grabs my other leg, sends me crashing to the cabin floor. My head hits the floor so hard that lights flash in my eyes, but I am conscious enough to pull away, scoot back against the door out of his reach.

"You little—"

Nick retches in the corner, and Big Mike raises up again. "Run, Missy!" I yell, and I bolt out the door.

I run for the truck, fling open the door, realize that Nick pocketed the keys. The cabin door swings open again, and Big Mike stands bellowing. "Get back here!" Then to Nick, he shouts, "Hold her. Don't let her out." He slams the wooden door shut, and I know he's behind me. "I will hunt you down!"

I flee into the woods, crashing into brush and tree limbs. My eyes haven't adjusted to the darkness, and I trip over a root or a rock, cracking my chin hard on the ground. I taste more blood, and it throws me into the memory of my dreams, and I wonder if I'm awake or asleep. Then I hear Big Mike's roar, "Get back here, runt!" and I get my bearings enough to run again.

"Momma," I whimper. This is my dream, my nightmare, of running, of searching, of looking for my mother in the thick woods on a frozen night.

Ejected is what the police officer told my grandmother. *Flew through the trees like a ragdoll. Landed a hundred yards down the hill. We liked to never have found her.*

"Momma!" I rush into a thicket that tangles in my arms and hair, and I fight to get free. I understand then that this is no dream. I pull loose, push forward, my heart crashing in my ears so loudly I cannot hear if Big Mike is following me. Fire has taken root in my lungs. I thrash blindly forward.

Come.

I stop. Listen. Will my heartbeat to silence so I can again hear her speak.

Come.

Ahead of me, toward the left. It is my mother's voice, and I know it cannot be of this world.

Hurry.

New strength fills my legs, and I run harder than I ever have run before, my arms and head somehow missing the branches that grasp for me, my feet flying over rocks and roots and ruts. In what seems mere seconds, I am standing on the paved road at the bottom of the hill.

It is some hour later, if time can be trusted, when I reach Missy's house, miles closer than my own. I huddle out back of their barn, praying, waiting under the eave for her to arrive. I don't wait long until I hear the rumble of Nick's truck, see the headlights round the bend toward the farm. The passenger door opens, and Big Mike pushes Missy out into the driveway, where she stumbles, falls to her knees, struggles to stand.

Nick peels out, flinging gravel and a wave of snow and dirt that motes in the faint glow from the porch light. Before he's out of sight, I am by Missy's side, helping her to stand just as her mother opens the front door.

"Girls?" she says, holding a hand to her forehead, shielding her eyes from the stark yellow glow of porch light.

We stand outside the round moon of light reflecting onto the snow, and I am glad the darkness covers us. "Yes, ma'am?" I say, blocking Missy from her view, just in case. "We're going to pet the horses before we come inside, if that's okay with you." Missy's mother never tells me no, not since I lost my own momma. It seems a hard thing for most grown-ups who know about the accident to deny me what I ask of them.

"Well," she says. Her head tilts to one side, and she stays silent for a moment. "Don't rouse them too much, then." She backs inside, closes the door behind her, and I can breathe again.

It's warm inside the barn, but my teeth won't stop chattering despite that I am not cold. I pull the chain to light the bare bulb overhead, and the horses softly whinny. Missy's leggings are ripped at the knees, and her kneecaps are bruised and bloodied. I hold her arms, help her balance while she kicks off her cheerleading sneakers, slips out of the leggings, and uses them to wipe the blood trickling down the inside of her thigh. "Oh, Missy." It is all I know to say.

She looks at me hollow-eyed, her face made of stone.

"I am so sorry. I—I thought you would run."

She almost shakes her head. "Couldn't. They trapped me."

I am sick in my heart for leaving her, for letting those animals feast upon her body.

"Besides," she says, pulling a twig from my hair, "I marked him good. Marked his face for life." She reaches inside her jacket pocket, then holds out her fist to me.

I open my hand to receive what she's offering, and she drops into it my honor-roll badge, the stickpin still thrust outward, the backside of the badge smeared with blood. A shiver ripples through me.

Her voice is flat and dry. "Not everybody tucks tail and runs, Romie."

Never have we spoken of that night since, and the closest we ever came to alluding to it was some weeks later when Missy held open her purse for me to see a tampon inside. We both breathed easier, knowing there'd be no baby to mark that awful night, but it would be something neither of us would ever, could ever, forget.

Now Jimbo twists his body awkwardly in his recliner to look at Missy. "Hey, baby! Glad you could join us. C'mon in, sit a spell." He narrows his eyes. "And play nice."

Jasper takes my hand in his and squeezes, an effort to comfort or maybe warn me to keep quiet, I don't know which.

Missy sits on the couch beneath the double windows that would overlook the back yard and the sunny day if the heavy curtains didn't cordon it from us. She smooths her dress over her knees, folds her hands in her lap, stares at the blackness of the flat-screen television. The way we're sitting, the four of us make a triangle, and I think of the pyramids, and how I once read that triangles, pyramids, and mountains draw power from the universe. I look toward some imaginary point far above the ceiling, wonder if there's energy flowing now into us, and if it'll ever be enough to make us what we once were, make us the hopeful souls we used to be.

When Jasper loosens my hand, I turn to him, but he's watching Missy, maybe waiting for her hello, maybe waiting for his own. Finally, he stands, and in one long stride, he's across the room, arms outstretched. "Hey, little sister." Jasper's always called Jimbo his brother and Missy his little sister, though she's almost three months older than he is, and they're nowhere near related.

Missy stands, and from where I sit, her hug looks wet-paper weak. She glances at me over Jasper's shoulder, and there's hurt in her eyes. I think I might cry, so I study my hands. I look up when Jasper returns to the couch, and I'm surprised to see Missy right behind him. She holds out a hand, and I take it, stand, and pull her against me. The throb in my chest is as real as any pain can get. "I've missed you," I whisper.

She stiffens against me, and her breath is hot against my ear. "You didn't have to."

Jimbo clears his throat and lowers the footrest of his recliner with a thud. "Jasper, what say we take a gander at that tree stand, let these here ladies talk hair-dos and makeup."

I wonder if he's talking cosmetics or forgiveness, but before I can even drop my arms to protest being left here alone with Missy, Jasper has risen and is following Jimbo down the hallway. A door opens somewhere toward the back of the house, shuts again, closing me inside.

Missy stands watching me for a moment, then takes my hand

and pulls me toward the couch. A memory comes to me so sharply I feel its stab beneath my ribs; a memory of my mother taking my small hand in hers, leading me toward an old floral couch, where she'd lift me onto her lap.

"Let's sit," Missy says, jarring me back to the now. Her hand is cool, and I fight the powerful urge to hold it against my burning face.

I wonder if she's waiting for my apology, and I think I owe it to her, but not because I left West Virginia. The hollowness around her eyes and the lovely frailty of her body tell me the Oxy addiction has been a harsh battle. Sorrow swells in my stomach, fills my throat, threatens to spill from my eyes. I open my mouth to offer contrition.

"I heard about you losing another baby," she says before I can speak, and my words die on my tongue. "And you six or so months along, too."

I want to nod, to speak, but I am frozen. This is the awful point where people say they are sorry for me. Where they say something stupid like the Primitive Baptist preacher did about it being God's will, about me being young enough to try again. About there being plenty of time for more babies. I steel myself for the stupid words I know will come. I am to blame for Missy's addiction, so I stifle the anger that she didn't come to comfort me, didn't even call.

"I started to call you," she says, as if reading my mind, "tell you I was sorry to hear." She turns loose of my hand, straightens her spine. "But then I realized that was a lie. Sometimes people get what's coming to them."

I suck in a breath, and before I can think, before I can stop myself, my hand lifts with its own intention to smack hard against her cheek.

Missy leans forward, juts her chin, ready to receive my blow.

I drop my hand, refuse to give her the punishment she seems to want, the pain she thinks she needs. This meanness is hers alone, and I will not be a part of it. I stand and turn toward the door, walk out on her. The sorrow that had swollen inside me shrinks, becomes tiny and hard, uncomfortable and irritating to the point of causing pain, like a pebble in a shoe on a long, uphill climb toward home.

CHAPTER SIX

JASPER

I lean against the hoe and suck on the blister that's popped at the base of my middle finger. By mid-morning, I'd tossed aside my work gloves, the smothering protectors that caused my hands to sweat and itch. I like the feel of the hoe in my hand, its hickory handle smooth against my palm, its once-varnished surface now bare and silky from use. My breath bottles in my chest when I look out over the vineyard, see how the light-orange ground glows in wide rows between the grapevines as the sun lights the soil. I like to think I'm a part of this growing, this increasing, these vines that produce swollen grapes. Times like this, I think Romie might have been right, because it feels good to give back to the land I've stolen so much from.

The hum of the electric golf cart whizzing toward me causes me to turn, and Bobby jerks a thumb over his shoulder and slows. "Snap out of it. The boss man cometh," he says, then spits tobacco juice onto the ground. "Better look alive."

I grin and wipe the sweat from my forehead onto my sleeve as Bobby accelerates and whirs past me, his cart bumping toward the big warehouse where we store empty oak and steel wine barrels. Bobby, like most of the field workers at Etter Vineyards, dislikes Willie Etter, one of two brothers who inherited the vineyards and surrounding land from their grandfather. Willie can be gruff, but he's always respected me, no doubt because both of us were once coal miners.

I glance in Willie's direction, and the ambling way he shifts his weight from one foot to the other as he navigates the reddish-orange dirt between the rows of grapevines reminds me again of Daddy's walk. I turn back to the dirt, scuff the hoe against the hardened soil to loosen a weed, bend to pull it by the roots before it takes over, leeching life from the weathered vine.

My wheelbarrow is over halfway full of weeds when Willie reaches me, and I straighten, arch my back to stretch out the kinks, and lean against the hoe handle. "Morning, sir."

"Almost noon." He pulls out a handkerchief so white it glares in the sunlight, and he mops the sheen from his forehead. "It's a hot one for this time of year," he says.

"Yessir. It is." I smile at him, but he looks beyond me toward the warehouse in the distance, nods in that direction.

"Got us a problem."

"Sir?"

He fixes me now with his gray-green eyes. "We got ourselves a thief."

"A thief?"

"Did I stutter? A thief."

I squint against the sunlight, but keep my eyes on my boss, determined not to look away, lest he think I'm unnerved by guilt. "What you got missing?"

Willie's shoulders sag, and I'm not sure if he's relaxed or defeated. "Gol-durned oak barrels. I've lost mebbe a dozen, best I can tell. Some of the French ones, too." He shakes his head and makes a sucking sound with his cheek. "Nearly a thousand a pop. Gone." He gives me a hard stare. "I hate a gol-durned thief."

"Yessir," I say. "That's a shame." I look toward the warehouse, watch Bobby's cart and the puff of ginger dirt that clouds behind it shrink in the distance. I turn back toward Willie when he speaks again.

"You wouldn't know anything about it?"

"Sir? No sir. Wish I could help you."

He eyes me a moment, but his gaze isn't suspicious of me. "Mebbe you can."

"How's that?"

A stiff breeze, far too brief, rushes past us, cooling the sweat on my neck and lifting the long hank of steel-gray hair that Willie combs over his bald spot.

"I want you to keep an eye on things. Let me know if you see anything out of the ordinary over there." He nods toward the storage warehouse. "One of 'em is making off with what don't belong to him, and I aim to catch him."

I nod, study the patch of dirt I've hoed around the base of the chambourcin vine, how the pale-orange clay looks almost blood-red when it's turned. I'm the new kid in town, new to Etter Vineyards by only four months. I imagine I must be guilty by association. I turn back to Willie. "You didn't ask me if I did it. Why is that? I'm the new guy, so it stands to reason you'd pin it on me."

The look that flits across his face is nothing if it's not pure amusement, but he quickly turns stoic. "I would know if it was you." He watches my face, studies my eyes. "We were coal miners, and miners are honest to a fault with each other. I don't believe you'd do that to me."

I swallow the knot that hangs in my throat, but I don't look away. I know plenty of miners who aren't honest, and I've yet to meet a coal-company owner who wouldn't steal life itself from man and earth for a dollar.

"Besides," he says, his eyes crinkling in the corners. "It started happening 'fore you came."

Without another word, Willie turns and heads back toward the main house, and as I watch him navigate the rows, occasionally pausing to finger a vine or taste a grape, part of me is relieved to be free of his suspicion, but another part of me toughens, angry that he finds me too honest, too meek, too incapable of doing what I've already done.

My face must have registered enough surprise that Willie thought me innocent when he mentioned that the theft had been going on for some time. In truth, I had no idea that someone else had been stealing the empty barrels. Given that two of us have been stealing, it's no wonder we've been found out.

Romie and I had been browsing antique stores, fruit stands, garden shops—most any roadside stand or business alongside the country roads leading like spokes from around the hubs of Shepherdstown and Martinsville—and of course I noticed the used, wooden wine barrels for sale. At an antique shop where Romie was inspecting Fenton, Blenko, and Depression glass, I coughed out a laugh at the $900 price tag on an empty, 60-gallon wine barrel. When the store clerk asked if he could help me, I explained that the cost of the cask seemed outrageous.

The red-headed clerk patted the barrel and ran his thumb along its spine. "Actually, this is toasted French oak, so it's quite a bargain."

"You actually move any of them at this price?" I ask.

"All the time. Tourists who come through here to visit one of the area's vineyards, folks from DC and Baltimore, wine connoisseurs . . . they make tables out of them, use them for bar stools, planters, what have you. American oak barrels are a little cheaper, say, six or seven hundred, depending on the condition, but I get top price for these toasted French barrels." He bends toward the cask and sniffs deeply. "Ahhhh. Smell it. You'll get a whiff of vanilla from the wood, a bit of the burned smell, sometimes even the scent of the wine, if it wasn't sanitized before we got it." His teeth appear yellow against his amber mustache when he smiles, and one shows the silver line of a filling near the gum. The name on his badge reads *Eric*.

I do as he said, and the smell of the barrel takes me right back to the first day I walked into the warehouse at Etter's. "Eric, where do you get your barrels?" I ask.

The man's face hardens. "Here and there. Different places." He clears his throat. "There are wineries all over these mountains, nowadays. Sometimes an oak barrel goes bad—not rotten, mind you—but I'm told if they aren't sterilized on a regular basis, they'll get moldy or rancid or something. Can't make wine in them no more, so they sell them to me."

I bent and sniffed the barrel again. "Doesn't smell rancid to me." I'd sanitized plenty of barrels my first weeks at the vineyard, mixing citric acid and potassium metabisulfite, turning the barrels every week to make sure the oak soaked up the cleaners, then washing and washing and washing again in water hot enough to scald any sin from the heart of the wood.

Eric smacks the barrel with his palm, causing a hollowed-out thump. "This here's a good one, then."

"Not a bad barrel?"

"No sir, not a bad—" His eyes narrow as he realizes I've caught him in some admission of guilt. "Where you from, boy?"

"Down the road a piece." I squat and examine the side of the barrel, looking for markings. A small area where the wood is soft and pale tells me someone has sanded it to remove the name of whatever vineyard it came from. I looked up at the man. "I work at Etter Vineyards."

The man's eyes widen beneath his bushy red eyebrows, and he links his hands behind his back. "Now look here, this barrel ain't one of yours. We pay top dollar for used barrels, and I ain't about to buy any that I know are stolen."

When his face turns a shade redder than his hair, I know he is lying, and it's then that I cut him a deal. Five hundred dollars a barrel for toasted French oak, three fifty for American. He wants them used, but clean, worn-looking enough to entice the shabby-chic crowd, no mold, and no rancid smell. I deliver my first to him a week later.

Romie don't know I steal the barrels. I've only stolen six so far, and I feel no need to tell her about it. She'd be plenty mad if she found out, but I don't see it as any worse than the drugs we sold to Jimbo. As for the money, well, I keep it stashed away in the toe of one of my old mining boots. I tell myself it might come in handy if we get in a bind, or that I'll use it to buy a surprise for Romie sometime, or if I save enough, we can put it down on a house of our own, get out of the apartment we're renting near the university. I really don't know what I'll do with the money, why I'm keeping it a secret, or why I want more of it. Sometimes a man gets tired of having important things taken away from him, so he takes something important in return. Sometimes a man just wants something he can keep all to himself.

The night I stole that first barrel was awful. The delivery went off without a hitch, but sleeping afterward was like resting on a bed of railroad spikes. I hardly slept at all, and when I did, the dreams were terrible. I dreamed once of being in the mine, only the shaft was closing in around me, getting tighter and tighter. I faced nothing but a coal seam, and I kept digging ahead, but I had to use my hands instead of a continuous miner like we used at Prospect to bore through the heart of the mountain. The worst was that I kept hearing a baby crying on the other side of that wall of solid coal, and I knew it was our baby, Romie's and mine, one of the ones that died, though I still don't know which one. My fingers were raw and bloodied from scraping against the rocks, and when I looked down at them, wine poured out instead of blood.

I woke from that one in a sweat.

After I stole the next two, I slept easier. I guess it's true that a man can get used to just about anything, like stealing, or even picking up and leaving the only home he's ever known.

When I think about Romie and me leaving West Virginia and moving to North Carolina—and I think about it nearly every day—I tell myself that I don't regret it for a minute, even the times when I do. Things changed for us in more ways than I can number, namely us losing another baby, but we were told that would have happened even if we'd stayed put in Stump Branch. We ran through a fair share of money moving down there and then back up here, then there's college tuition, but I can't say I regret any of that much. You can't miss what you've never had, and we still have a little more now than we started with. I reckon what I regret the most is how moving away from Stump Branch changed our relationships with Jimbo and Missy, and how those changes hang on our shoulders like sodden blankets.

"Jasper!" Bobby calls to me before he reaches me. He's driving the golf cart as if he's qualifying for the Daytona 500. "Let's get us some grub!" He stops the cart, and I wedge my hoe in the back and jump in just as he presses the pedal again.

"Hold up!" I say, grabbing the roof to keep him from flinging me out. "Let my butt hit the seat before you take off."

Bobby laughs and floors it, and I hold on with both hands as we bump and jump the ruts and gullies between the rows of vines.

"What'd the boss man want with you?"

I steal a glance in Bobby's direction, wonder if I should tell him about Willie's suspicions. "He asked me a serious question, something awfully important that's been bothering him."

Bobby turns toward me, and my somber expression is reflected in his blue-mirrored sunglasses. "Oh yeah? What's that?"

"He's torn up about it."

The golf cart slows to a crawl, and Bobby rests an arm on the steering wheel, giving me his full attention. "What is it?"

"He wants to know why it is that you get uglier and uglier every day, while I manage to get prettier and prettier."

Bobby's jaw drops, then he curses and shoves me so hard I nearly topple from the cart. We laugh, and he floors the pedal again, and I'm hanging on with both hands as we surf the ruts of our landscape, going airborne more than once.

Three days pass before Willie corners me in the barrel warehouse. I'm driving the forklift, rotating the barrels that have to be turned weekly, when he motions me to stop and come talk to him. I get a few sideways glances when Willie drapes an arm around my shoulders, and it's all I can do not to shrug it off.

"Got us an idea," he says.

Us. Like this is my business, too. Like we're in something together, like we're co-conspirators or partners. I like it.

He leads me to his Hummer and opens the hatch, and I know right away that we are definitely in cahoots.

"Whatcha think?" he asks.

I let out a soft whistle. Stacked boxes of high-tech surveillance equipment fill the back of his SUV.

He adjusts the bill of his *Etter Vineyards* cap and thumbs toward the boxes. "You think you can hook this up?"

"Me? Uh, no. I mean, I don't know how, sir." I pick up a box that holds a DVD player, the words *8 Night Vision Security Cameras Included* emblazed in red on the side of the box.

He jabs a thick finger at the box I'm holding. "Says here it's easy installation. You're a smart man. I think you can handle it."

"Okay." I heft the box, realize there are six or seven more just like it inside the SUV. "That's a whole lot of cameras, sir. These for the barrel warehouse?"

He nods. "There, and for the tasting room, and for the gift shop. And anywhere else I think a thief might abide." He grins and slaps the top of the box nearest him. "Got me a good deal on these."

"I see."

"Ride with me up to the main house, and let's load these in your truck."

"Sir? My truck?"

"Boy, I know I don't stutter, but you're beginning to make me wonder if I might echo."

"I'm sorry, sir. It's just—"

"We'll put these in your truck, and tonight after everyone's gone home, you can come back out here and get these installed. Start with the barrel warehouse tonight, and you can do the gift shop tomorrow night, and the tasting room the next. I want every inch of the barrel warehouse covered, so take your time. And put them so nobody'll notice. Gol-durned thief don't know I'm watching, he'll be easier to catch."

I look back toward the barrel warehouse, notice that Bobby and Lurch are watching Willie and I at the rear of his SUV, and my face gets hot. I put the box back inside and reach to close the hatch when the door closes of its own accord.

Willie chuckles. "Climb in, boy," he says, and he heads for the driver's seat.

On our ride to my truck, I try to figure a way out of this, but excuses escape me. "I'll need help," I finally say.

"Already thought of that. I'll send Carlos from the house to help you."

"Do I know a Carlos?"

"My yard man and farm hand. He's old, so he can't monkey around on the ladder, but he's fair with electrical work, and he can help you with the wiring and camera angles and such. You'll put the TV and the recorders in my office, of course. Carlos will have a key."

I nod, still a little stunned. "I could just ask Bobby. He's smart with computers and such."

Willie shoves a finger toward my face, and I catch myself before I knock it away.

"No," he says, and his lip curls. "I don't know what he ain't the one stealing."

"Bobby?" I shake my head. "I can't imagine he'd do such a thing." And then I realize that, a mere month ago, I couldn't imagine doing such a thing myself. "Sir, I just remembered that my wife has plans for me tonight." When he glares at me, I know I have to acquiesce. "B-but I can install the cameras in the warehouse for you tomorrow night. I'm sorry about that . . . but short notice and all. You can count on me to take care of it for you, you know, tomorrow night."

Willie grunts, then nods. "That'll do. It'll give me a night to explain it to Carlos. His English is a little rough, but he understands *me* okay."

I wonder if Carlos is even legal. Some of Romie's friends at the university complained that last September, instead of using local seasonal help, the Etters hauled in a truckload of immigrants they picked up in Florida to harvest the grapes. "Old Willie might as well steal tuition right out of our pockets when he does that kind of thing," Romie's pretty friend Winter said.

We pull into the employee parking lot behind the main house, and Willie opens the hatch and stands with a fist on his hip while I work. By the time I've loaded the boxes into my truck and covered it with a tarp, I've figured I can get three more wine barrels out of the warehouse tonight, before I install the surveillance equipment tomorrow. With any luck, they'll be French oak. I tell myself it's the least Willie deserves for not hiring local.

It's shy of two weeks later when Willie calls me into his office upstairs in the main house. "We got him, boy." He points to his computer, and I step around his massive desk to see a dozen square images on the screen. He taps one and it expands to full size, filling the screen. "Watch this."

I hold my breath, and my gut tightens when I see Bobby drive the forklift cradling a wine cask out the back-bay door. Time rolls forward at the bottom of the screen. Bobby returns the forklift empty, parks it, then strolls out of the bay. I open my mouth to speak, to say how I can't believe Bobby would do such a thing, to sacrifice my new friend, knowing he's done nothing I haven't done myself.

Willie jabs at the screen. "Right here. Caught him red-handed."

Lurch, the tall, flat-headed guy who trained me my first days in the warehouse, lopes into the camera's line of vision, leans to peer out the back bay. He pauses there, then throws up a hand, toward Bobby, I guess. Then he looks around before stepping up to a keg that rests at the bottom of the rack, and he rolls it forward, easily tips it upright. It's empty. Empty, even though those stacks should be full barrels. With a foot, he shoves it to the side, then disappears from the frame for a moment, only to reappear within seconds, rolling with effort a cask that's obviously heavy and full of wine.

"Bastard's been hiding empties among the fulls, then switching them out."

I let out a breath, part of me glad to know it's Lurch and not Bobby who's been stealing. Lurch's plan is brilliant, much smarter than my simple method of delivering an empty keg to the woods behind the barrel warehouse, rolling it down the weedy bank, then retrieving it after dark.

Yet I didn't get caught.

I clear my sticky-feeling throat. "What now, sir?"

"Now is when I fire him."

"Fire him? But he—he lives here." I swing my hand toward the back of the main house, toward what they call "the little house," a house that's really not so little, but smaller than the main house where everything happens. "He's the manager. He does the tastings and tours and—"

"Steals. He steals is what he does, and I can't abide a gol-durned thief."

It's hot in Willie's office, and I turn to look out the window, where the sun has nearly disappeared and evening dark sneaks across the vines.

"Go get him," Willie says. "Take a cart and drive him back up here. Sumbitch has stolen his last from me."

"Are you sure, sir? You might want to think—"

Willie's face is suddenly inches from mine. "Think about what? Letting him stick around here and steal some more from me? That man oversees the gift-shop till, the tasting-floor till, and the warehouse. If he'll steal barrels from me, who knows what else he's thieving? Probably stuffing his pockets with cash from the registers, too." He shakes his head and rolls up his sleeves, as if ready for a fight. "Been living right here under my roof, free of charge, getting a salary, and stealing from me." He opens his desk drawer, pulls out a bottle of pastel antacids, shakes out a handful. "And him my nephew. Don't that beat all." Willie tosses back the tablets and chews, the crunching sound filling the room.

"Lurch is your *nephew?*"

Willie's nostrils flare, and he swallows loudly. "You don't think *Lurch* is his real name, do you?"

"No, sir, I—"

"Carson Clayton; he's my brother Charles's son. Wife remarried after they divorced. Charles let her husband adopt Carson when he was a baby, so he'd have the same last name as his mother. Probably what messed him up, made him feel like taking what he missed out on by birthright." Willie's lip curls. "Hell, I always treated him like family, gave him a good job, place to live. What more could he want?" He slams a fist on his desk. "He's as selfish as his real daddy. Go get him. I want him outta here."

"Yes, sir." I rub the back of my neck, wonder if there's any way out of this, wonder if I should confess, if it might save Lurch's job. But he's on tape. No question he's guilty. And so am I.

"Sir, tomorrow is Saturday, and we have a full schedule of tours and tastings. Maybe you want to wait until—"

"I want him *gone*. You and your purty wife can do the tours, and Bobby can do the tastings. I'll help Mother—Mabel—with the gift shop this weekend. We'll figure out the rest as soon as I clear that gol-durned thief out of here. The sooner, the better. Now go get him and bring him to me."

Sometimes it seems like a long drive to reach the barrel warehouse at the far end of the vineyards, but tonight the distance closes too soon. The golf cart's headlights bounce across the dirt path in front of me, and a rabbit scurries from the vines on one side of the path to the other. I think of the kits I snuffed out in Greensboro, and I wonder if I'll ever see another rabbit without thinking of death. The rabbit seems like a sign, and when I taste the tang of blood, I realize I'm chewing my lip raw, dreading what's going to happen.

Part of me wants to cry, and I tell myself to stop it, and I pound the steering wheel with the heel of my hand until I have to stop for fear of breaking the steering wheel. Yes, I stole some barrels, but I had a good reason. It was easy money, money I need to buy a house for Romie and me I let go of the only home we had—got cheated out of it by that bunch of Blackstones—then we rented out the Grodin homeplace for a pittance, the place where I was born and raised. That's my fault, I know, but it was the only choice we had at the time, so I chose it. Romie and I've got no one else, no one to save us except each other. We are orphans, and it's my job to take care of her, to provide a place for us, to make a real home for us. And if that means stealing, well.

And Lurch . . . he's got two daddies, now, don't he? Probably has two mommas, too. And he's got an uncle who gave him a nice house to live in, free and clear. Willie don't have no kids, so Lurch is probably heir to the whole winery. And yet he goes and steals? There's no good reason for that. No reason at all.

I'm driving like Bobby does by the time I reach the barrel warehouse, despite it being too dark for such speed, and when I slam on the brakes, the cart whines to a stop on the concrete loading pad in front of the big metal building. I bury my face in my hands and take a deep breath, trying to get control of myself before I go in there.

I find Lurch toward the back of the warehouse, clipboard in hand, tallying the daily barrel count. He looks in my direction, clearly surprised to see me after quitting hours. "What are you still doing here, Coal Miner?" He stuck me with the nickname after he found out I'd worked underground at Prospect. "I didn't authorize overtime."

Any other time, I'd have probably laughed, but his comment

causes my shoulders to tense, and when I speak, my voice has a deep, rough edge to it. "Willie sent me to get you. Cart's out front." I turn and walk away, not giving him time to ask why, not believing he deserves an answer.

I sit in the golf cart, waiting for Lurch to join me, and I think of how different we are, us two thieves, and a memory comes to me of Momma holding *The Children's Illustrated Bible* on her lap. She has it open to the story of the crucifixion of Christ. Jesus is on the cross, and thieves are hanging on shorter crosses, one on each side of him. One thief confessed to stealing, Momma said, and because he asked for forgiveness, he went to Paradise. The other one didn't, and he died hell-bound.

I rub my face and look around me, and in the aura of floodlights around the barrel warehouse, the trees are showing the first frosting of fall color. The twilit sky scatters a few eager stars against its deep blue backdrop. This here is my Paradise, the only one I expect I'll ever know. I think about Jesus hanging on the cross between those two thieves. It takes me only a second to know I won't tell Willie what I did, because if I confess, my West Virginia Paradise will disappear.

I look toward the brightest star, promising that from this point on, I will never steal another thing from anyone else, ever in my life, no matter the reason. I pray God will have mercy on my soul.

CHAPTER SEVEN

ROMIE

I place another pair of Jasper's boots into the wieldy cardboard box, tape it up, and stack it on top of the growing pile that's replaced what used to be our decent-sized living room. It seems only days ago when we moved into this apartment in the Shenandoah Valley, and here we are leaving it behind less than a year after we moved in. I tell myself it's a fresh start—it is, in so many ways—and I have become good at fresh starts. They give me a chance to be a brand-new me, and each new me is smarter than the old one.

This new me will have a new job, since part of Jasper's and my agreement with Willie Etter is that I'll work part-time at the winery. I'll mostly help his mother Mabel—they call her "the Widow Etter"—at the gift shop, but I'll also tend the vines or help with bottling or do whatever they need as the seasons change. Jasper's a supervisor now, and our labor, plus a decent wage for Jasper, is in exchange for rent on what they call *the little house*—though it's nearly twice the size of this apartment. The little house sits to the far side of the vineyard, surrounded on three sides by acres of grapevines. It is a quiet little dream home, and I cannot believe our luck.

The apartment door swings open, and Winter strides in without knocking, as if she's the one who lives here. "Are you ready?"

Winter and I take turns driving to class, and the rider has to pay for coffees, so I check to make sure I have enough cash to cover our habit. "Ready." I grab my psych and anatomy textbooks, and we head out the door and climb into her car.

"Are you taking a load of boxes over this afternoon?" she asks. "If you do, I want to go. I need to see if this so-called little house is worth letting you leave The Taj Mathal."

I laugh at the nickname she's given The Wiesenthal, our apartment complex that's filled mostly with university students. "Sure, but if you come, you're carrying boxes."

"Duly noted," she says, and she examines her wine-red lipstick in the rearview mirror.

Winter's name somehow fits her, though she hates it. She came here from Jamaica as a child, making her exotic as well as beautiful. Her skin is as dark as midnight, and her hair is coal black. Her cheekbones are sharp enough to slice tomatoes, and the slight tilt of her eyes calls to mind a svelte black panther. She even moves like a sinuous cat. When we walk side by side, I seem to disappear, as all eyes watch her, which disproves what she always tells me, that I am beautiful.

When we reach student parking, we climb out of Winter's Mazda, and we lift our paper coffee cups in toast to good luck. We part and head toward our separate classes, knowing we'll meet up in an hour and a half for the psychology class we're taking together. Winter has changed her major from nursing to psychology—I'm certain she did it because she has a crush on Dr. Hart, though I've seen Dr. Hart's husband and know she's arrow-straight—so now Winter practices analyzing everyone. She thinks she can make the world a better place, and I don't have the heart to tell her that the best any of us can do is to make it through another day alive, and that sometimes, maybe that's not even the best option.

Winter likes our new house, though I keep telling myself not to call it *our house*, because, like everything else this world pretends to offer, it's tenuous and temporary.

"I'd like to burn some sage the next time I visit," she says. "You know, to clear the house of any bad energy, since the previous tenant left against his will."

It sounds dumb to me, but I figure no harm can come of it, other than the house smelling like a pizza. "That'll be okay."

She smiles and laughs in that odd way she laughs, from deep

within her throat, without opening her mouth. "Okay, yes; it'll be okay. It'll be a very good thing. Trust me." She walks down the hallway from the primary bedroom, back through the center of the house, and I follow her to the two bedrooms on the other end. She leans against the doorway of the first, looking at the pile of boxes we've stashed there. "What a great house for starting a family. Plenty of room for kids."

Sharp pain twinges at the back of my throat, and I curl my toes inside my shoes. I can't respond.

Winter smiles at me, her catlike eyes shining, and she turns and moves to the next bedroom. "That room for a girl, and this one for a boy," she says, waving her hand through the air like she's making a regal decree. She steps into the room, peers out the window overlooking three huge maple trees and acres of vineyards. "You can hang a tire swing from that tree for her, build a tree house for him." She waves a hand over her shoulder toward me, without turning from the window. "Or vice versa. You'll want to wait until you've finished your degree, of course. A lot of women juggle kids and work and school, but there's no need making it harder on yourself." She runs her hand along the windowsill, inspecting or appraising, I'm not sure which. "You'll make a great mother."

I can't take anymore. Her words cause my body to ache, and I need to sit down. My ears roar, and I lean against the wall to steady myself.

"What do you think? Romie!" Winter rushes to me. "Are you okay? What's wrong?" She takes my face in her hands, and they feel cool against my burning skin. "You're clammy," she says. "Are you getting sick?" Winter slides her arm around my waist and tries to guide me down the short hallway, but I push against her.

"I'm okay. Really. Let go." I feel claustrophobic, trapped, and part of me wants to run down the hallway and out the door, wants to leave this space that feels too small and too big for me. I peer into the empty bedroom, know it will never hold a boy, my son. I hug myself and rub my arms. Out of nowhere, I feel exhausted, needing rest, needing sleep.

"Let's get some water," Winter says. I watch her take a few steps down the hallway, and I wish she'd keep going, but she pauses and turns to make sure I follow.

I step to the bedroom doorway and peer in, wonder who closed their eyes here, who slept here before, who dreamed. They've left nothing behind, nothing to mark their existence, no trace of life. It will be the same for me, the same for Jasper. We will leave nothing and no one behind, and when we die, it will be as though we have never lived.

"Romie?"

I push away from the doorway and follow Winter into the empty kitchen.

"Do you have any glassware unpacked?"

I shrug.

Winter begins opening and closing cabinet doors, and she finally pulls out a left-behind wineglass with *Etter Vineyards* stamped in blue on the side. She holds it up and smiles. "Imagine. A wine glass at a winery." She fills the glass with tap water and offers it to me, but her forehead is creased, and she's biting her lower lip. She studies me for a moment, and when she speaks, her voice is soft. "Want to tell me what that was about?"

I cross my arms against my chest, still holding the wine glass. It takes me a moment to realize I'm thirsty, and I take a sip before I answer her. "We don't—I can't . . .."

How do I tell her, this woman who I want—*need*—to be my friend? How do I admit that I am *less than*, that I am unable to carry a child? How do I put into words what has happened, what I have lost, what I can never have, or do, ever—*ever!*—again?

She gently touches my empty hand, slides one finger into my palm, and my fingers close around it, gripping it as if I am an infant holding onto her mother's finger. "It's okay," she whispers.

I break into a sob, and Winter holds me, rocks me against her, and she strokes my hair. Out of nowhere, I begin to giggle, and she takes my face in her hands and looks into my eyes, all concerned, but soon she is giggling, too.

"We must be crazy." She wipes her eyes, still laughing.

"One of us is," I say, "but I'll never admit that it's me."

"You can talk to me, you know. I can help."

Winter and her psychology, and her hocus-pocus paganism. How can she help me, when I can never tell her, or anyone, all the wrong that I've done? Images flit through my mind: Missy's pale thighs against Big Mike's dark jeans, her skinned and bloodied knees. The paper grocery bag full of OxyContin bottles I placed in Jimbo's hands. The blood—so much blood—on the floor of the emergency room, and the doctor's footprint right in the middle of it when he told me my baby was gone. How can I tell her about the dreams, the nightmares?

Last night I had the one about the crows and babies again. A *murder* of crows, they call it. How appropriate. Flocking and flooding the air around me, and then they're no longer birds, but babies. Babies and toddlers dressed in black bonnets, black short pants, black christening gowns. I woke up whimpering, Jasper's arms curling around me, closing me in, when all I wanted was for him to let me go, so I could join those babies and fly away.

Winter unloads the last of my boxes from her car, sees to it that I'll be okay waiting alone for Jasper to get off work, and then she leaves. After she's gone, I stand on the back deck of the house, overlooking the acres and acres of grapevines, and I feel small, as if I've shrunk. I wonder if it's true, if I've become smaller each time I have moved, if I've left behind broken-off pieces of myself, like a trail of breadcrumbs, so I can someday find my way back to whatever place might once have been home.

Our first winter in the little house turned out to be better than I thought it might, and to keep Christmas from seeming so lonely again, Jasper and

I drove up to DC to see the giant Christmas tree harvested from West Virginia, glowing on The White House lawn. We kept busy, and the lonesome season passed almost before we knew it had arrived.

Our studies helped. Turns out that Mabel Etter is a big fan—*proponent* she calls it—of education, as she retired from teaching English comp at the university in the eighties, shortly after her husband, Willie's daddy, died. She told her son Willie that school was more important than working in the gift shop and vineyards, so instead of punching a clock, I just help out as I'm needed. I make sure it adds up to at least twenty hours a week, to be fair, but now I have flexible hours.

Mrs. Etter also coaxed Willie into sending Jasper to the university, which Willie said he'd planned to do all along. He's got Jasper taking some horticulture class about winemaking. Willie said he wants his supervisors and managers to "know the business from the vine to the fine wine," and now Jasper repeats that phrase all the time, singing it like a song. Jasper loves being a university student, but I have to wonder whose idea it was to give college credits for tasting wine. Winter and I think it's funny and brilliant, so we plan to take the same course next semester, though it has nothing to do with our majors. She says it'll make us well-rounded and more cultured, and that we all can use a little more culture.

I open the oven door now, and visible waves of heat wash over me as I peer at the grape pie nestled inside its butter-crusted cocoon. It's still a good ten minutes away from bubbling, but the house is already fragranced with grapes and cinnamon. Of course, even without a pie in the oven, the little house often smells like grapes, or wine, or sour-wine vinegar. It's comforting to me, the routine that has become our new life since moving here. I spend early mornings making Jasper's breakfast, helping the widow Etter open the storefront of the winery, and then I head into town to the university for late-morning classes, or to the hospital for the lab credit that one day will land me a nursing job.

I perch on the barstool in the breakfast nook overlooking the kitchen, and I refocus on my study of the circulatory system. *The heartbeat is the universal sound of life*, I read. No kidding. I've learned firsthand that the absence of that rhythmic pulsing is the universal sound of death.

Winter tells me I need to talk about how I've had more than my fair share of death and dying, so that I can recover. What Winter doesn't understand is that grief isn't an illness, so there's no such thing as recovery. If I could, I'd tell her that, instead of illness, it's more like ever-present waves that wash over me. Sometimes they're calm, lapping at the edges of my mind, but other times, they crash into me, pull me under, nearly drown me. I stay quiet, because when I open my mouth to explain this to her, I never know which kind of wave will come out.

I push away these thoughts—best *not* to think about it—and continue reading, making notes as I go. I'm just getting the hang of the directional flow of blood—from the body into the right atrium, to the right ventricle, and then to the lungs to pick up oxygen, on into the left atrium of the heart, then to the left ventricle, where it then pumps that freshly oxygenated blood to the whole body, before returning depleted to the right atrium to start over again—when with perfect timing, my cell phone produces the sound of the human heartbeat. I grin. That's Jasper's ringtone.

"Hey, doll baby," he says over the speakerphone, and I can hear the smile in his voice. He seems happier now than I've known him to be since we were teenagers, though sometimes the sense that something is missing hollows out a space between us. We both know that the emptiness is our missing babies, but we don't talk about that anymore, because I couldn't bear it if we did.

"I got a surprise for you," he says. "Jimbo just called, and he and Missy are on their way up here. Can you set a few more plates for dinner?"

Jimbo and Missy. My jaw tightens, but I try to sound more pleased than I feel. Jimbo means the world to Jasper. Missy . . . well, she's my oldest friend, but I could take her or leave her these days, and most times, I'd rather leave her. "Sure. You know what time they're coming?"

The three-hour drive from Stump Branch isn't something you'd typically make without planning ahead, but then again, Jimbo and Missy aren't plan-ahead kind of people.

"Should be here around four."

The clock on the microwave reads 3:02 PM. "Not much notice." I chasten myself for the sharp edge to my voice, and I speak with more energy. "No problem, though. I'll make macaroni salad and cut up some fruit to fluff up supper." I'd put a roast in the Crock Pot after Jasper left this morning, so there should be plenty to go around. And then I think to ask, "What's the occasion?"

"I'm not sure. Jimbo says he's got good news." He chuckles. "Must have won the lottery, he's driving all this way to tell it."

"That'd be like him, wouldn't it? Throw money away on a long drive just to talk about having it. He'd be broke and borrowing again in a week." I envision Jimbo throwing hundred-dollar bills in the air, his face black with coal dust, and I grin.

Jasper and I laugh, say our goodbyes, and I mark the page in my textbook, head toward the pantry and pull out a box of elbow noodles. "Right atrium, right ventricle, lungs, left ventricle, left atrium, body," I mutter. Or is it left atrium, left ventricle?

I head to the bedroom, change into a university sweatshirt, so Missy can see how I've grown and changed, become more educated and cultured, while she's stayed the same. Back to the kitchen, I put on pasta to boil, then hustle around the house, dusting, straightening, fluffing pillows on the guest bed, in case they plan to stay over. Not that it should matter. Missy's never been much of a housekeeper. But that's all the more reason to make things look nice for Jimbo. Right atrium, left atrium . . . no! Right atrium, right ventricle. I return to the kitchen to stir the pasta, think maybe I can get in another few minutes of study time, when just as I lay the wooden spoon across the top of the pot to keep it from boiling over, there's a knock at the door. It swings wide open. Out of some weird tribute to Paw, I just can't bring myself to lock the front door.

"Whassup!" Jimbo's voice fills the house, and the smile on my face feels genuine when I head to the living room and stand on my tiptoes to drape my arms around his shoulders. Jimbo's hug lifts me off the ground, then he sets my feet gently on the floor. "Still light as a feather," he says, and I know he means it as a compliment.

"Brought you something," Missy drawls, and she offers a brown paper bag filled with apples. She slides the bag into the crook of my arm, and I hug her with the other. "We stopped at the orchard just down the road a piece. Got some apple butter out in the truck, too. We can put it on biscuits in the morning."

So they're staying overnight. Or for a few days, or a few weeks. No way of telling. "Thank you, Missy," I remember to say.

The two of them follow me to the kitchen, where I push aside my textbooks to make room for the bag of apples.

"Sure smells good in here," says Jimbo.

"Got a grape pie in the oven," I say.

Missy wrinkles her nose. "Grape pie? I never heard of such."

"Where's Jasper," Jimbo says, looking around as if he expects my man to materialize out of thin air.

"Working the vines," I say, and I pick up my phone to text Jasper. "I'll let him know you're here." Before I can press *send*, the back door off the kitchen opens.

Jasper's big grin makes my heart soar. "I tell you what, Romie," he says, "you'll let just about anyone or anything in here." He strides across the floor, and he and Jimbo wrap each other in a backslapping bear hug, growling like a couple of frolicking cubs.

Missy and I laugh, finding common ground in the knowledge that our husbands are overgrown boys, though I recognize the tiny prick I feel as jealousy stabbing me at the place in my heart where a close friend belongs. Since the gully formed between Missy and me, I don't really have a best friend. I hold out hope for Winter if she'll lay off the psychoanalysis of my every word. Maybe us not having a history together is a good thing.

Jasper and I once talked about his friendship with Jimbo, and he thinks the two of them are so tight because they had so many near-death experiences in the mines. "Builds brotherhood," Jasper said, "those life-and-death situations. He's saved my life a time or two, and I've saved his at least that many."

I've been in a few life-and-death situations myself—losing both parents when I was a young girl, my momma-in-law's sudden death, watching my daddy-in-law waste away, losing two babies before they were born—but I have never had a friend save me from any of those things, so I think a close woman-friend is something I may never have.

I remember to check the oven, and Jasper, Jimbo, and Missy follow me to the kitchen. The pie is done. Missy peers over my shoulder to examine the jammy juice bubbling at the crust's slits, anxious to escape its confines.

"Well," she says, and turns away.

I close my eyes and let out a breath, already ready for her to leave.

"I'm up for a big ol' slice," Jasper says. "What about you, Jimbo?"

I put on a smile and turn to face the boys—*men*, I suppose I should think of them. "It needs to rest a bit before I slice it. Let's save it for dessert, okay?"

Jimbo whistles and rubs his stomach, and I notice the beginnings of a potbelly. It makes me happier.

"Shoo-weee!" he says. "I wasn't the least bit hungry until I walked in this here door, but now I could eat a cow—hooves, hide, and all."

Jasper claps his long-time buddy on the back. "What say we head out back for a bit, get out of the kitchen before the ladies put us to work?" He shoots me a sneaky look and ushers Jimbo toward the kitchen door, which opens onto a deck overlooking the St. Vincent vines this side of the vineyard.

"What can I do to help you?"

Missy's offer surprises me, but I take advantage and point toward a cabinet door. "Plates are in there. You can set the table if you please. Silverware is the drawer below." She steps across the small kitchen, her high-heeled mules making a snapping sound against her heels. It's too chilly out for open toes, but it isn't my feet getting cold.

We make small talk as we putter around each other, and a time or two I have to remind myself to be amicable and kind. We boo-hooed and hugged and patched things up after our argument at her house in Stump Branch, but I've yet to figure out what it is that makes me feel bitter toward Missy, besides the fact that she's beautiful even when she's rumpled, which is always, and that she strikes me as lazy and careless. It aggravates me, too, that she always takes the easy way out of everything like a teenager will do, even though we're grown now.

"Romie," Missy says, "why haven't you offered me some of that fine wine you and Jasper are always making? Did you forget your manners?"

I don't point out that it's lack of manners that causes her to say such a thing, and I pull down four wine glasses from the rack that Jasper built and hung above the island countertop, where I'd sat studying in peace minutes earlier. I take a bottle of white wine from the refrigerator and offer it to Missy, along with a corkscrew. "Let's start with white Manseng, and then you can open a cab to let it breathe for dinner." I think of Winter and hope I sound cultured.

"Sounds good," she says, and I am encouraged.

"After dinner, we can open the port we helped Mrs. Etter bottle a while back. It tastes like chocolate and blackberries, and it'll go great with the pie. So yummy!"

"Listen at you," Missy says, waving her hand in the air. "Sounding all hoity-toity and high-society since you've been living at the winery, getting college educated and all."

Despite her grin, my face burns. I'd meant to sound pretentious, to rub her nose in how much better we're doing now, how leaving Stump Branch has been good for us, but she can't let me have even one small triumph. And how can she call me *hoity-toity*? I glance down at the wear-faded knees of my jeans, stained from kneeling under the vines to shove props beneath them when they grew heavy with ripening grapes. I turn my back on her, pretend the macaroni salad needs my attention. "More pepper." I take out my frustration on the grinder.

My shoulders tense when the cork softly pops behind me. I turn and accept the glass Missy offers. "Thank you," I manage, before taking a sip of the cool wine. Missy downs hers in one motion, then pours another as Jasper and Jimbo come in from the back porch, laughing. This time, she only pours a small splash in her glass, but fills the other two for the guys, emptying the bottle.

Jimbo's laugh strangles in his throat when he sees Missy with the wine glasses, and a look flashes across his face that I can't quite name—anger, concern, and frustration braided together, but it's gone in an instant. His eyes dart to me, then to Missy, and I know that whatever good news they came to tell us really isn't good news at all. I wonder if she's back on the Oxy.

Missy offers wineglasses to the guys. "A toast to celebrate our good news," she says.

Jimbo accepts the glass but clears his throat. "I thought we were gonna tell them at dinner."

So, they popped up here with only minutes notice, but planned ahead as to when to break their news?

Missy shrugs. "Okay by me." She makes a shooing motion with her hand. "You boys wash up and head to the table. We're about ready."

We are about ready?

Stop it. I'm trying to be a better person—an important goal for every human, according to Winter. Missy's got some good traits, after all, or at least she *had* some good traits. Some must stick with her, or else Jimbo still wouldn't be so smitten with her.

Minutes later, we're sitting at the table, and as Jasper slices the roast, I notice the bottle of cabernet sauvignon is nearly half empty, though everyone at the table still has a bit of white left in their glasses, including Missy's, whose glass still has a splash of wine, just as she poured it earlier. She must have caught me studying the bottle, because when I look at her, she glances away, picks up her water glass and takes a dainty sip. She has drunk straight from the bottle!

I'm so caught up in my astonishment that I don't realize the conversation has turned, until Missy speaks across from me.

"It's actually as much of a request as it is an announcement," she says. "A *big* request."

"To go with a big announcement," Jimbo says, and when I look at him, it appears he will explode with whatever is bottled inside of him.

Missy's giggle sounds fake and forced. "Go ahead, Jimbo. You tell it."

Jimbo stretches forward and grabs both mine and Jasper's hands in his, and Missy follows suit, her hand small, cool, and dry, compared with Jimbo's big, warm grasp. Our stretching arms form a cross in the center of the table, intersecting the roast, and I think of the heart's four chambers: right atrium, right ventricle, left atrium, left ventricle. I wonder which one I am. I look up, and everyone is smiling but me, so I pantomime.

When Jimbo's eyes lock with Missy's, I notice he is near to tears, and it hits me then what their news is.

"We're going to have a baby," Jimbo says.

Jasper gasps. He looks at me and, without speaking, he reflects my pain, but his expression tells me to be happy for them.

He coughs out a laugh. "That's wonderful! Congratulations!" We release hands, and he lifts his wine glass, each of us following suit, and our glasses chime in celebration.

Without meaning to, I gulp down every last drop in my glass.

Missy takes a long drink from hers, too, and I notice the gentle touch of Jimbo's fingers on her arm, a subtle reminder—maybe a request—not to drink any more.

"It's—that's—that's wonderful news!" I'm pleased that my voice sounds right, that it doesn't carry the acid that fills my throat and mouth. I reach for the cabernet and, ignoring Mrs. Etter's rules for wine service, I fill my glass first, far beyond the portion that will allow the wine to breathe. The bottle's nearly empty.

"There's more," Jimbo says as I reach to fill his glass.

"The request," Missy says. "We have something very serious and important to ask you two." She rushes her words, or maybe they just come together quickly in my head. "You don't have to answer right away. You can take some time to think about it. You should, I mean. You should think about it, first." Her brown eyes, usually doe-like, widen even more to convey her seriousness. She turns toward Jimbo, and he nods solemnly, the weight of his question lowering his head a bit when he looks at Jasper.

"Jasper," he says, then glances at me, "Romie." He again looks at Jasper, and another wave of heat washes over me from nowhere, as if I'm still standing at the oven door. "We'd be honored if you two would be the godparents of our firstborn baby."

Missy's face shines, and she bounces up and down on the dining chair like a small child. "Say yes," she pleads. "Oh please, say yes!"

Jasper lets out a huff or a sigh—I can't tell which—and he manages a surprised smile. "Well, of course. The honor is ours . . . right, Romie?"

Jimbo leaps from his chair, sending it backward a few feet, and he stoops to grab my face in both of his big hands and plants a kiss on my lips. He rounds the table to hug Jasper, half-lifting him off his seat in the process. Jimbo's happiness makes it easier to smile. This really is a joyful moment for the two of them, and I wish I could be happy for them. Intoxication might help, so I take another long drink of wine, but my throat closes around the red liquid, choking me until I'm sure I am drowning.

CHAPTER EIGHT

JASPER

It's become my habit to spend my morning break in Willie's office. If you'd told me when I first started working for him that I'd soon spend time sipping hot coffee while lounging in a comfortable leather chair across from his desk, I'd have said you were crazy. Shooting the breeze with Willie is now one of the things I like best about working at Etter Vineyards. I've even got my own coffee mug that's washed and waiting for me on his credenza, says *I wish this were wine*. He's got a bunch of 'em with sayings like that, some from the gift shop, some that folks have given him, and while I have no idea how that one found its way into my hands, I've claimed ownership of it. Just like I've claimed ownership of that leather chair. I still miss Stump Branch every day, but for now, it feels good to belong here.

My morning started with a flat tire on the way to Three Pines Restaurant with a load of wine, and then I dropped a case on the ground, breaking four bottles and ruining a good pair of jeans. Next, the mustard leaked from my sausage biscuit onto my shirt, so I had to run back by the house to change before heading back to work. At least I'm confident in knowing nothing worse can happen, and I head upstairs to Willie's office for that much-needed coffee break. I can already picture Willie laughing when I tell him what my train wreck of a morning has been like.

Willie's gray-haired secretary Marlene is on the phone when I reach the top of the stairs. She's got a face as round as a Moon Pie, and I always chat her up for a minute, because she tells me these half-dirty jokes, and when I laugh, she acts appalled and tells me I have a filthy mind, that she didn't mean it that way at all. I wave at her and head toward Willie's office, but she holds up a hand and gives me a funny look. I pause, and she covers the mouthpiece of the phone with her hand. "He's fit to be tied," she says in a loud whisper. "Take a deep breath before you go in there." Then she returns to her call, picks up a pen, and takes down an order.

My hand's on the doorknob to Willie's office when my phone buzzes in my pocket, and I check it, seeing Jimbo's home number scroll across the screen. I wonder why he's not calling from his cell, but I let it go to voice mail, so I can check on the boss man. Willie is even-keeled, so if he's upset, he's got good reason, and I'm anxious to commiserate as I give two quick raps and open his office door.

Eric, the red-headed clerk who I sold stolen barrels to at the antique store sits across from Willie's desk. Sits in *my* chair. A smug look crosses his face when I walk in, and I feel sick. The S.O.B. has been calling me a couple of times a month, demanding I bring him more wine casks, or else he's gonna turn me in to Willie. I told him he's guilty of selling stolen property and of blackmailing me into stealing it, and that's a worse crime. Told him he wasn't fool enough to do anything so stupid as tell Willie, anyhow. Looks like he's a bigger fool than I thought.

A big ugly vein throbs its crooked way across Willie's forehead, and when he looks at me, his face turns from red to purple, and I worry for him. He's not a young man. He could have a stroke or heart attack right here. "Willie?" I say, as softly and gently as I can. "You okay?" I step toward him, meaning to go around the desk, meaning to put a hand on his shoulder, meaning to calm him, when he blows up on me.

"Gol-durn you! Gol-durn you, Jasper Grodin! Sit your ass down here. Sit down right now. Explain to me why it is that you took up where that gol-durned thief Lurch took off. Explain to me why you been stealing out from under my nose."

He doesn't even ask if I did it, and I wonder what my face must have shown when I first saw Eric sitting here—in *my* chair. I've never been good enough at lying.

Willie falls quiet as I sit in the other chair—the *not my chair*—and I get the sense of Romie's teakettle steaming and boiling over a raging flame, its whistle ready to go off at any moment, ready to pierce the air with an ear-shattering screech. I have the urge to cover my ears.

He's waiting on me to speak.

I know I'm caught. I think of that thief on the cross, and I decide to come clean. "I'm so sorry, Willie. It was last year—"

"Gol-durn you! You *know* I hate a gol-durned thief!"

Eric clears his throat, covers his mouth with a cupped hand a second too late to hide his snide smile. "Ett," he says, rising to his feet, this nickname for Willie new to my ears, foreign, proof that Eric has known the man longer than I have, better than I do. "I'll excuse myself now, let you handle this unfortunate situation." He drawls out *sit-chew-ay-shun* as he darts his yellowed eyes toward mine.

I grip the armrests of the chair I sit in, tying myself down to keep myself from standing and knocking him clean through the picture window overlooking the south vineyard. Willie's face is still purple, and I speak with a calm that's a lot more measured than I feel. "Why don't you stay, Eric? Let Willie hear both sides of the story, like how you been calling me every couple of weeks, threatening me with this very meeting if I don't steal some more barrels for you."

Eric's smile falls from his face, and he pales, his freckles standing out like rust spots. "I never! I had no idea the barrels were Ett's, until I got one stamped with the logo."

I slide my cell phone out of my pocket, hold it up. "Got every voice message you've left me right here. You like me to play 'em for you? Refresh your memory?"

Eric steps forward, as if to reach for my phone, and I draw it back, my hand fisting around it. He rushes for the door, flings it open, and his feet thump the stairs as he runs from his guilt. I turn to follow, intending to pound his sorry ass into a puddle of pulp.

"Stop right there!" Willie bellows so loudly it hurts my ears, and my hands rise to cover them.

I turn towards him, and shame lights fire to my face. My head is so heavy it's hard to lift it. "I'm sorry, Willie. Eric had me over a . . . ." I can't say the word *barrel.* "I never meant to—"

"No," he says, quieter now. "I'll deal with Eric later. His lying kind don't surprise me none. But you . . . ." His voice falters, and he glances toward the window, then turns and glares at me. "Get. Out." He speaks through clenched teeth, and spittle flies onto his desk.

"If you'll just look at my phone, you'll see—"

"I said *get out!* Get out of my office, get out of my house, get out of my vineyards. You're fired. I want you off my property, and don't you dare step foot back here once you're gone."

"Sir, please. Romie and I—"

"Tell your wife I'm sorry for her." His voice drops a decibel, but it holds no tone of forgiveness. "Mother loves her, and she'll be sad to see her go. But we can't abide a thief, Mother and I. You've made us fools." He looks away, then turns back to me, and hurt and anger shimmer in his eyes.

I have no argument, no reason, no clear explanation. Other than easy money, I haven't even been able to explain to myself why I did what I've done. "I have the money. I'll pay back every cent. I never spent a dime. I—"

"You got three days to clear out the house. That's more time than you deserve." His lower lip trembles. "In the meantime, don't let me set eyes on you."

I stand and step toward the door. I turn back, and the cup Eric had been holding sits facing me. *I wish this were wine.* I meet Willie's eyes, and the fury there makes me catch my breath. There's nothing I can say to fix this; nothing can change what I've done. "Yes, sir," I say. "I truly am sorry."

I'm at the bottom of the steps before I know it, and it seems the whole conversation has been a bad dream. My phone buzzes again. I pull it from my pocket to silence it and see it's Romie who's calling me this time.

Romie.

How will I tell her what I've done? How will I explain the why of it, when I don't know why, myself?

A phone call is no way to say such things, to tell her I've lied, I've stolen, and I've caused our eviction. I silence the call and let it go to voice mail, wonder absently why she's calling me between classes, anyway. She had a final exam today, so she's probably calling to tell me how well she's done. She wants me to be proud of her, and I am truly puffed up by all that she has accomplished. I wish she could be proud of me too, but when I think of what I have done to us, any sorrow I have seems like arrogance.

I walk on past the golf cart, needing to stretch the distance to the little house—no longer *our* house—needing to clear my head, needing to silence the voices yammering there. My own voice asks, How will I break this news to my wife? How will I tell her she's married to a thief? *A gol-durned thief*, Willie's voice says. Then Romie's voice repeats her words from the hospital bed when she last miscarried. *I want to go home. Back home to West Virginia*, and *I don't want to go back to Stump Branch*. How will I tell her this place is no longer home and that, without our jobs, Stump Branch is all that's left for us?

There's tightness in my chest, and I think I might suffocate beneath this burden. We'd rented out the homeplace in Stump Branch, but the lease will be up in a few days. We've already planned to go back and paint the place, tidy it up before renting it out again. The timing is good, as far as timing goes, and I wonder if this is one of those things we'll later look back on and say that it was God's good will that we were evicted just when the homeplace was due to be empty. Or maybe we'll look back on it and say that this is when the cyclone sent us spinning, sucked us down into the darkness that ruined us.

I round the corner in sight of the little house, and Romie's Jeep is parked in the driveway. I pull out my phone to check the time. It's hours before she should be home. I don't know whether to hurry in to see if something is wrong, or to slow down, put off this awful thing that I have to tell her.

The house is quiet inside, and I step softly through the kitchen and living room, unsure of where Romie may be. I find her in the bedroom, and I stop breathing when I see her. She has her back to me, pawing through the top drawer of our dresser. Our suitcase is splayed open on the bed, and a neat stack of her clothing is nestled into one corner.

She is running away again. This time, she is leaving *me*.

I was a fool not to have taken her call, not to have cried into the phone, not to have begged her forgiveness. I should have known that Willie or the Widow Etter would call her, deliver the hateful news, seal my fate.

I should have reached her first.

Romie turns, and her face is damp with tears. "Jasper," she says, her voice cracking, and she places a stack of t-shirts in the suitcase. She steps around the bed toward me, and I stiffen, awaiting the slap I deserve. She raises both arms, and I lift mine to block her blows, but she doesn't swing. She slides her arms around my neck and pulls me close.

I can't speak. I can't process her reaction to what I have done, to the job I have lost, to this home I have lost. She squeezes me and rubs my back, and over her shoulder, I see the suitcase, see pieces of her life and mine stacked inside it. Hers—and *mine*. Those are *my* t-shirts she placed in the suitcase. She isn't packing to leave me. She's taking me with her.

I rub her back, still staring at the clothes in the suitcase—no cardboard boxes—realize this is not how she would pack to move.

I unwind her arms and take her by the shoulders. "What are you doing?"

She blinks rapidly and opens her mouth, but nothing comes out.

"Romie . . . the suitcase?"

"I—I thought you knew. Missy said she would call you."

I can't make sense of what's happening, of why Missy has anything to do with this. I look again toward the suitcase, and Romie follows my gaze.

"We have to go." She takes my hand. "Jasper . . ." She's trying not to cry. "Jimbo's been hurt. He's real bad. Roof fall." Her voice catches, and she sniffles, then she turns away and yanks down some blouses from our closet. "They're air-lifting him to Charleston." A sob strangles her next words. "Jasper, it's so bad."

A roof fall.

Jimbo and I worked shoulder-to-shoulder, bolting up the roof over our heads, building cribs, cross beams, and setting posts. So we all remained safe. Sometimes a big slab of slate would shear off, or a thick wedge of coal would break loose and fall, threaten to take us out. We'd always been careful, inspected the roof four, five, ten times if necessary. We always had each other's backs.

I don't know who's partnered with him since I left, never wanted to know who took my place. Whichever sonofabitch it was didn't protect Jimbo like I would have. I never would have let this happen to him.

"Get your toothbrush and shaving kit." Romie stacks jeans in the suitcase, then throws in several pairs of socks. "Then you need to call Willie. Tell him this trip can't wait. He'll have to call in help for the weekend. We've got to go now. Missy's due in nine or ten weeks, and she'll need us, too. Shock and stress could put her into premature labor."

My legs are wooden posts, but somehow they manage to bend, to propel me toward the bathroom where I gather my things. When I catch my expression in the mirror, my face is slack, and I look old and haggard. This bad dream has turned into a full-on nightmare.

A heavy thump brings me back, and I grab my shaving kit and meet Romie in the hallway as she's dragging our suitcase out of the bedroom. "Here, baby," I say, reaching for the handle. "I've got this." She turns to head toward the kitchen, but I grab her arm, pull her back to me. "How bad is bad?"

Her lower lip trembles. "Crushed his legs. They're gonna try to save one, and maybe the other one, too, if they can find it."

If they can find it. My chest hitches when I try to breathe, and I steel myself against the heaviness that tries to crush me, too, as if I were deep in the mine with Jimbo when the earth crashed onto him.

I pull our suitcase toward the front door, pause to look behind me at this house we've called home. Whatever happens to Romie and me, wherever we next call home, I need to believe—have to believe— that she will never leave me. She doesn't even know it, but she's the only thing keeping this world from burying me alive.

As I'm putting the suitcase in the back of the Jeep, Romie calls to me. "Got everything you need? I'm ready to close up." She's got her purse on her shoulder, and she dangles her keys for emphasis.

I rub my forehead and think for a second or try to. Do I have everything I need? I need it all, *we* need it all. We only have a few days to get everything all out. How can we do that if we leave now? I look at my wife, but I can't speak. So much has happened in the past hour, I can't seem to form an answer. Thankfully, I don't have to. Romie closes the front door of the little house, and she locks it. Romie never locks that door. It seems to me such a significant motion, this closing and locking of the door on this house that's no longer our home, and I think I might sink into the ground.

Romie is already in the Jeep before I climb in. I'm fumbling with the car key when she grips my knee. "Want me to drive?" she asks. She searches my face, and I realize I must look like I feel—half crazed.

"No." I shove the key into the ignition, shift into gear, and drive down the long, graveled drive. I've turned onto the highway and driven half a dozen miles, when Romie again touches my knee. "Jasper, we've got to hurry."

I glance at her and check my speed. I'm doing almost forty in a fifty-five. I accelerate to sixty and tell myself to focus.

Romie clears her throat. "Did you call Willie?"

"Huh? Um, no."

She's pressing numbers on her phone. "I'll call him, put him on speaker, so you can talk to him. Just keep driving."

I reach out to stay her hand. "Romie, wait."

This time I really get the, *he's losing it* look from her.

"There's time for that. Let's just concentrate on getting to Jimbo." I can tell she's not buying my hesitancy, so I offer the most truthful explanation I can give her right now. "Willie's had a bad morning. Nasty meeting with some asshole the next county over. He about popped a vessel this morning." I give her what I hope is a sorrowful, caring look, and I speak quietly. "He's got a mess to clean up, so believe me when I tell you he's not missing me right now. I'll call him later this afternoon, after we get to Charleston."

She shrugs, and I'm glad it's over. *For now.* I try to think of how to tell her, how to explain, how to break it to her that where we live is no longer where we live. I can't think of anything to say, no words at all to make clear what has happened and will happen to us.

We turn onto the four-lane, and I'm navigating traffic when I notice she's again punching numbers into her phone. "What are you doing? Stop that!" I reach toward her phone, and she jerks it away, out of reach.

"What in God's name?" Her doe eyes grow even rounder. "I'm not calling Willie." She sniffs, and I let out a long breath. I nod, and she resumes punching numbers.

"So who you calling?"

Again with the sniff as she lifts the phone to her ear. "The Widow Etter. I want her to check the house while we're gone and tell her I can't work—"

"We don't live there anymore!" Before I can think of what I'm doing, before I can stop myself, I knock the phone from her hand, striking her face in the process. The phone slams against the dashboard, where it bounces and smacks hard against the passenger-side window. Romie shrinks away from me, her hand pressed against the cheek I've hit. Tears spring to her eyes, and my stomach lurches.

Though I never intended it—I never imagined I could do such a thing!—I have hit her. I have hit her, and she is crying. She is crying as she huddles against the door, her lip trembling, her face full of fear and confusion.

And then she changes. It's as if a cloud crosses her face, or maybe a dark shadow. Whatever it is, the change occurs in an instant, in the space of a thought or a memory. Anger— *rage*—rage like I've never seen from this wisp of a woman comes over her, comes through her and out of her.

"STOP! Stop the car! Stop right now!"

I glance between her, this woman who has become someone I've never seen before, and the road, then I change lanes, slowing the Jeep.

"I said *stop!*" She is growing, swelling, filling the seat next to me in a way that's impossible, and yet it's happening. I am definitely losing my mind.

"Now! Pull over *now!*"

Romie grabs my arm, her bony little fingers sinking like talons into my forearm, and she yanks, causing me to jerk the steering wheel hard to the right. A horn blares as I struggle to gain control of the Jeep, and its tires squeal and loose gravel flies as I brake, and we skid onto the shoulder. I jerk my arm away from her, my elbow coming dangerously close to her chin, and she is all over me, striking, slapping, punching. She is a wild animal, a wildcat, scratching and clawing and screeching.

"Don't you *ever* hit me! How dare you! How dare you do this right now!"

I manage to grab her wrists, fold her arms together, pull her tight against me, pin her close. "Shhhh. Shhhh. Romie. Stop. Settle." I soften my strangling voice, hoping to calm her. "Hush now. I'm sorry. I didn't mean—"

Sobs break from her chest, and we are both crying. I rock her as if she were a child, a little baby, blowing shushing sounds into her hair. She crumbles apart in my arms, and it is as if all the pain in the world pours out of her, and I want to soak it up, but it is too much. I don't know what is happening to her, to me, to us.

She pushes away from me, and I am almost grateful to have the small, cool space between us. There's a red mark rising on her cheek, and her chin quivers when she hiccups out a question. "Who—who is—is she?"

I stare at her, wondering now if my wife is the one losing her mind.

She struggles to slow her jagged breathing. "What's her name?"

"What?" I squint, as if it will help me see more clearly what is happening, as if it might help me understand her. "Her who? Who are you talking about?"

"The w-woman, the bitch you're l-leaving me for. Who is she?"

I shake my head, and it takes me a moment to grasp what she's said. "Romie. There's no one. I'm not leaving you!" I reach for her, and when she stiffens and winces, I suck in a breath. "Baby, please don't." I hold up my hands, then slowly guide a hand toward her arm, touch her softly with my fingertips. "I would never hurt you; you have to believe me. I overreacted. I only meant to keep you from calling Mrs. Etter."

A tractor trailer barrels past us, and the Jeep shudders in its wake. I should have told her right away. I should have said that I lost my job, and I lost our house.

"Then what's the money for?"

Why can't I make sense of my wife's words? Why does it seem we're talking in different languages? I search her face for clues. "What money, Romie?"

"The money in your boot. A whole sock full of bills. Thousands. Yes, I found it weeks ago, and I've been watching to see what you were gonna do with it. You've been hiding it from me. You talk about that woman all the time, tell me her dirty jokes. Is it her? Willie's secretary?" Her voice catches. "You said we don't have the house anymore. I thought you planned to leave—"

"No! Oh, God, no. Baby . . . I thought *you* were leaving *me*." I bury my face in my calloused hands, scrub until my cheeks feel raw.

"*What?* Jasper, you're not making sense. What are you talking about?"

Sitting on the side of I-64, as traffic grows heavier and rain begins to fall, I hold out my hands to her. "That woman is Marlene, and she's a nice old lady, older than Willie. And I stole the money. I mean, not the money. I stole wine barrels. That day we went antiquing, that guy at the shop, I knew those barrels he was selling were stolen. Logos were sanded off the side. I thought I was being smart, like a businessman, cut myself a deal with him. Seemed real smart at the time, easy money. Thought I had him where I wanted him. I didn't know Willie then like I do now. Once I started liking him so much, I quit. I stopped cold. That guy at the shop, he threatened to tell Willie if I didn't keep stealing, so I called his bluff." I shrug, realize words have been tumbling out of my mouth almost faster than I can say them. "Except he called mine. He was in Willie's office when I walked in today, and Willie fired me."

"Why didn't you tell Willie what you'd done when you decided you weren't gonna steal anymore?"

And there it is, the question I have worried around my head so many nights in bed. "I thought he'd fire me." I pick at a hangnail on my thumb, and it starts to bleed. "Reckon I was right."

A soft huff comes from Romie. "Even if he had, you'd have felt better than him finding out this way. Sometimes a man has to admit he's done wrong."

My throat shuts tight at these last words because they aren't

Romie's, they're my daddy's, and I can hear him say them in my head. I stare at my hands until they blur, wishing Daddy and Momma were still alive, because then they wouldn't know what I've done. They wouldn't be looking down on me right now, seeing this mess I have made, seeing this awful man I have become. The cry busts out of me, and it's not a man's cry at all, but a boy's cry, and I am ashamed that I cry like I haven't cried since my daddy died. I break and fold in half, lay my head in Romie's lap, and she strokes my hair, and now it's her shushing me.

Get up, son. That's enough. Again, there's my daddy's voice in my head, stern but kind, and I know he means it. I sit up, clear my throat, wipe my face on my sleeve. "I'm so sorry, baby. I'll find a way to make this right. You have my word."

Romie turns away from me and stares out the window into the browning weeds that follow the curve of the hillside up toward the woods. Her silence is worse than her screams.

"Baby, please say something."

She wipes her eyes, then she turns to me. "We need to go. Jimbo needs us. He needs you."

The slow, heavy way she shakes her head is the most sorrowful thing I have seen since . . . since we lost our last baby. How could I have done this to her? She has lost so much, and now I have taken this place from her, too.

She lets out a long, weighty breath, and she deflates in front of me. "We will talk more about it when this is over. I can't just deal with it right now. We need to get to Charleston." Her eyes are bloodshot when she looks at me. "Are you good to drive?"

I nod, check the traffic, and pull onto the interstate. Long minutes—painfully long minutes pass, and the only sound is the damning rhythm of the windshield wipers. *Goldurn you   goldurn you—goldurn you.*

Their chanting is silenced when Romie places her small hand

on my thigh. "Secrets aren't good for anybody, Jasper. Don't ever keep anything from me again, you hear me?"

I want to thank her, to apologize yet again, but my throat is too swollen to speak. I nod and blink hard to keep from crying. It's some mile or so later before I can talk. "You have my word, Romie. My word and my love. I will tell you everything there is to tell about anything, right up until the day we die. No secrets between us. No more. Not ever."

When I turn toward her so she can see my sincerity, she looks away, hiding whatever is in her eyes. I can only pray, as we drive toward whatever comes next, that she believes me.

CHAPTER NINE

ROMIE

Jasper offers his hand as we exit the parking garage through the automatic doors that open into the hospital lobby, and I accept it, not for his comfort, but for my own. Who else is here to hold me to this black piece of earth, when all of me wants to fly away?

His hand briefly squeezes, then loosens, like the flicker of a dying flame, and I know this to be his nerves. Even though he earned his EMT cert, Jasper hates hospitals for the same reasons I love them: the antiseptic smell, the endless corridors and wings, long hallways offering navigation by colored tiles or paint stripes on walls, clinicians striding purposefully among people who are confused, or sick, or both. I look down at my jeans, and oddly, I'm glad I'm not wearing scrubs. I've always liked the respect I get when I'm in uniform, how people believe I can help them, save them, make them whole again. Now I realize it's an illusion. No matter what I wear, there's no way I can make Jimbo whole again.

Jasper's grip on my hand grows tighter when we walk down the hallway ramp into the surgical unit's waiting area, and I realize we haven't spoken since we entered the hospital. I search the twenty or so faces in the large waiting room for one I recognize, but I don't see Missy anywhere. One of the three flat-screen televisions hanging on the far wall has a list of colored numbers that I know are patient numbers, and beside each is a time and an alpha code. I nudge Jasper and whisper, "When we learn his patient number, we can tell when he comes out of surgery into recovery, and then when he's assigned to a room."

He stares at the screen and then looks at me. "Good to know." He tries to smile but can't do it. "I know some of the medical part, but not the hospital part. I'm glad you know the hospital stuff. It'll help." We stand, both of us awkward and hesitant, unsure of what to do next.

I tug his hand. "We should check in at the nurse's station."

As we turn to leave, Missy walks in, and there's a coal miner I don't recognize at her elbow. I'm stunned to see how round her belly has grown, how the purple sweater she wears hugs it like a warm blanket. There is need in her eyes, and any bitterness I have felt for her washes out of me. Tears blur her image as I reach for her, and she slides into my arms, her unborn child snugged between us. We hold each other until our sniveling subsides.

"Preacher," Jasper says to the coal miner.

I look up to see the two men in their own brief embrace, their handshake between them, and when they step apart, I wonder why the man's face is still coal smudged, but his hands are starkly clean, and why he's still wearing his oil-stained, navy coveralls. I notice the familiar Prospect Mining patch, take odd comfort in the gold-and-white reflective stripes across the chest, down the arms, and around the hem of his overalls, how this measure of safety catches the light as he moves.

"How is he?" Jasper asks the man. Missy dabs at her eyes with a wadded tissue, looks at me, then turns toward the man and nods.

"Ahhh, Jasper, he ain't good."

The man extends his hand toward me. "Sorry for my manners," he says. "Pastor Robert Beggs. I worked with your husband."

He clasps my hand in both of his, pumps it up and down as he leans forward, peers earnestly into my eyes. He's a preacher, all right. *Bobby Beggs.* What a perfect name.

Preacher Beggs cuts his eyes toward Jasper as we shake hands. "We miss your husband every day. Sure would like to have him back at Prospect."

I wonder if it's a sin not to like a preacher.

He drops my hand, and we all look at one another for a minute, so I break the silence, ask what no one is saying. "Can they save his legs?"

Preacher Beggs pales a shade, looks at Missy.

Her lower lip trembles when she starts to speak, and I am

ashamed of my callous question.

"They're gonna try to reattach the one what was cut clean through, said it was a good cut,—" she makes a coughing sound, "—whatever that means. The other one, the one what stayed attached, I think it's pretty mangled. Doctor said loss of blood is the first priority. Jimbo was unconscious when they got him out of there."

Preacher nods. "That's a blessing." He steeples his fingers together. "He couldn't feel pain if he was unconscious."

I look down, and it's then that I realize the stains on the legs of Preacher's overalls aren't oil, but dried blood. "You were there?" I ask softly.

He looks from me to Jasper, his lips in a firm line. "I was behind the continuous miner, saw the slab come down. Me and Nicewander got it off him. Had to use a jack. We pulled him out. Got him on the ambulance that took him to the chopper, then we went and got Missy. We came straight up." He stares at the floor a moment, then meets Jasper's eyes again. "Redd Truby found his leg, gave it to the EVAC medic, helped him put it on ice hisself." He nods toward the double glass doors. "He just left. Said he couldn't be here. But you know Redd," he says to Jasper, "he'll be back come morning. He won't rest a lick until he sets his eyes on Jimbo again."

I recall something Paw once said about how coal miners behave after an accident, how some will stay by the hurt man for days, visit his family, see him through to total healing. Others, they can't get far enough away, as if accidents are contagious, as if being near a hurt man will bring hurt on themselves. I wonder which kind of man Jasper will be.

Jasper clears his throat. "Who's Nicewander?" he asks, an edge to his voice.

"Guy who took your place. Stinson brought him down from Prospect's Kentucky Number Ten."

Jasper's face darkens, and his hands curl into fists just before he shoves them into his pockets.

"What time did this happen? Why was Jimbo on the dayshift?" he asks.

It's Missy who answers. "He switched a few months ago. Traded shifts with Hippie, so he can be home nights to help me with the baby." Her hand rests on the mound of her stomach, and something low in my own belly tightens.

Preacher nods. "Just so happened Cuddy's got the flu, so I stayed on until they could find somebody from one of the other sites to relieve me." He shakes his head. "It's a blessing I was there when I was. The Good Lord always knows, don't He. Praise Him."

Praise Him? Praise Him for what? For letting the roof fall on Jimbo? For making Jasper and me homeless? For letting my babies die? How can anyone praise God in a time like this?

Jasper makes a humming sound, and I wonder if it's in agreement or disbelief.

Preacher puts a hand on Jasper's shoulder, one on Missy's, and looks right at me. "Let's have a word of prayer, shall we?"

I glance around the room, embarrassed that we're going to do this here, now, in front of everyone, but it is as if we're invisible, unseen by these people who have their own problems, their own loved ones under the knife. I bow my head, grateful to shut my eyes against all that's around me. Whatever words the man says wash right over me. I think of the little house, and all the packing I'll need to do, and I wonder where Jasper will find work, where we'll live, and where we'll go. I imagine my husband stealing wine casks, see them lined up like round tombstones in the dark of night. I'm thinking of all that money he'll hand back to Willie, wishing we could keep it, when Preacher's "Amen" reaches my ears. I feel guilty for thinking of Jasper and of myself, instead of Jimbo, who's as close as the only brother I'll ever have. I swallow hard.

I touch Missy's arm. "When will you know something?"

She looks toward the flat-screen monitor that hangs across from us, lifts her hand toward its colored numbers and letters. I'm appalled when I see her fingernails, usually painted and pretty, now chewed to small crescents in beds of red skin.

"His number is the one that ends in sevens," she says. "Lucky number seven. It's his favorite number." She smiles at me, or tries to, but there's yearning behind it. "Letter *D* means he's having surgery."

"How long?" I ask, and when she gives me a blank stare, I clarify. "How long has he been in there?"

"It switched from C to D over an hour ago. The nurse said it could take until the early morning. Said they will have at least four surgeons working on him . . . maybe more."

Four surgeons. I try to think of what kinds of surgeons he would need. Orthopedic, vascular, neurosurgeon, maybe? What else? A replantation specialist? An image of the bone saw I held during a lab assignment comes into my mind, and I remember its heft, and how sharp the saw-toothed blade felt against my fingertip, and I feel sick. Blood and bodily fluids never bother me, but this is Jimbo's body, Jimbo's life.

". . . coffee? Something else?" It's Preacher talking at my elbow, and he's looking from Missy to me. Missy nods, but I shake my head.

Missy's gaze darts around the room, and she puts her hand on Preacher's arm. "I'll go with you. I need to . . . I need to get out of here for a minute." She turns away from me, and Preacher puts a hand on her back and steers her gently toward the automatic glass doors.

I'm left standing alone, and I turn, searching for Jasper, find him in a corner with three other coal miners wearing Prospect garb who've trickled in; ones who, as Paw said, will stay by a hurt man for days. One claps Jasper on the back, and they all laugh, and it seems a betrayal to laugh while Jimbo is fighting to live.

He looks at me as if I've reprimanded him aloud, and his face colors. He says something to the men, then comes to where I stand. "Where'd Missy go?"

I shrug. "With Bobby *Beggs*." I think of the Primitive Baptist preacher on Gaston Ridge, of his pink, moist palm held out to me, of how I'd put Momaw's check into it, or the cash I'd made dusting Mrs. Maxwell's antique shop, just so he'd keep Momma's and Daddy's graves mowed or swept. In my young girl's mind, I imagined he'd dig them up if I didn't pay him, that he'd fling their rotting corpses over the bank into the briary woods. It was money we didn't have to give that paid for his new Cadillac every year. And Jasper wonders why I don't like preachers.

Now Jasper's lips press into a line, and he motions to two chairs distanced from others by a large end table. We sit. He reaches for my hand, and though I let him take it, it lies motionless in his, like a cold fish. He has stolen, and he has lied to me, and he can't even tell me why.

He stares at our hands, and when he finally raises his gaze to me, his head remains downcast. "I am so sorry, Romie." His thumb strokes the back of my hand. "I will make this up to you. You have my word."

"For what that's worth." I pull my hand from his, and I stand, refuse to look at him. "I'm going to find Missy."

Outside the glass doors, I turn away from the hallway leading toward the elevators just as four men in heavy coats with *MSHA* patches step out—Mining Safety & Health Administration inspectors— heading toward the waiting room, no doubt to interview the miners about the roof fall. I head in the opposite direction, ride the elevator up, step off and turn left, then right, until I have no real idea where I am. I stop before a large picture window looking out across a parking lot, and beyond that, another bland hospital wing. I stare, searching for something to rest my eyes on, but I find no answers here, no comfort, only a view of nothing at all.

Missy settles in the chair beside me, returning from another of her frequent bathroom breaks. Jimbo now has been in surgery for five hours. We're about thirty minutes past-due an update.

She is quiet, elbow on the chair's armrest, her chin in her hand.

Her eyelids are heavy. "Want this?" I ask, offering her one of the folded, beige blankets that a unit volunteer passed around to the few of us still in the waiting area. A stack of bed pillows rests on a nearby coffee table. They offer us what small comforts they can.

She opens her eyes wider, searches my face as if trying to focus on who I am. Her pupils are pinpoints.

"Missy!" I hiss, leaning close to her. "Are you—what did you take?"

She blinks sleepily. "Nothing." She waves her hand slowly, as if moving it through mud instead of air.

I lean against the chair arms between us, grip her wrist, lean even closer. When she again searches my face as if seeing me for the first time, I smack the back of her hand. "Missy!" I glance around, thankful no one is watching. "What are you on?" She rolls her eyes, and I jump to my feet. "I'm getting a doctor."

She reaches for me, grasps my arm, but her grip is weak. "Sssit down! It's nothing. Just sssomething. Something the nurse gave me to . . . to help my nerves. My husband could die, you know!" Her eyes are large now, and it seems she is rallying to return to the here and now.

I sit again in the seat beside her, noting that Jasper, who slumps on a chair across the room, is half-asleep, half-focused on the news channel broadcasting from a ceiling-mounted flat screen in the corner. "What—did—you—take? Missy, you can't take drugs when you're pregnant!" I whisper fiercely.

She sits straighter, places a hand to the small of her back. "You don't know everything. You're not even a nurse yet, so don't go playing doctor." Her eyelids again threaten to stay closed when she blinks.

I pull her up and make her stand, and she half-swats at me. "What're you doing?" Her voice is thick-tongued, and her frown is sluggish to appear.

"We're going for a walk. Come!" I pull on her, looking over her shoulder toward where Jasper sits, his eyes now closed. When we reach the doorway, I call to him. "Jasper, we're going for air."

He jerks awake, turns toward me and his eyebrows lift, but I wave him off, knowing he'll nap again.

I turn left in the hallway, hoping to find another empty corridor with a big window overlooking the parking lot, a quiet place where we can sit and talk. We needn't walk that far, as the hospital is surprisingly quiet, and the lights are dimmed in this corridor, the padded benches empty. I guide her to a bench and sit beside her, my hand on her arm. "Missy. What did you take?"

She pulls her arm away from me. "I told you. Something for my nerves."

"What was it? Where did you get it? And don't lie to me. There's no nurse on this planet who would give you something that would knock you out like this while you're pregnant. You're not even a patient here."

She shrugs. "Brought it with me." A drunken grin slides across her face. "Ain't you ever heard of 'mother's little helpers?' I'm gonna be a mother, so I'm practicing the helper part now." She laughs too loudly.

I want to slap her. I recall her slugging back wine early in her pregnancy, realize that if she brought drugs from home, she's probably been taking them the whole time. "What was it? Missy, you know better. Whatever goes into your mouth goes into the baby, too."

She covers her face with her hands and stifles a scream. "Look, I'm scared, okay? I keep thinking . . . Romie, you don't know . . .." She rubs her face. Her eyes are damp, and I can smell the sweet-sour sweat of her.

"What? What are you afraid of? What don't I know?" When she doesn't answer, I huff. "I'll tell you what I don't know," I say, "I don't know how you can do this, how you can take pills when you have an innocent little baby inside you. Why did you even start?" My face aches from tightness, and I work my jaw to ease the tension there.

"I saw him." Missy's voice is shrill, and I glance around to make sure no one can hear us, feel relief to see we are alone.

I shake my head. "Saw who?"

"*Him!* Jimbo and I were near Huntington. Jimbo went into a convenience store, and then *he* came out. He was wearing . . . ssscrubs. He got in an SUV." She squints as if trying to see the man again. "There was a woman and two little kids in his car." She wipes her forehead and leans back, closing her eyes.

I gently shake her shoulders, trying to keep her awake and present. Missy's daddy skipped out when she was two, and I can't imagine how she'd recognize him now. "How did you know it was him?"

Her eyes open wide again, and she gapes until she can focus on my face. "Can't miss him," she says. She traces a lazy finger down her cheek. "I told you; I marked him good."

My breath catches, and I release her shoulder. She's not talking about her father; she's talking about her rapist. *Big Mike.* A hand flies to my mouth as I take in everything this could mean.

"When?" I finally manage. I again rustle Missy, and she sits up straighter this time.

She offers a shrug. "Two years ago. Y'all were in Carolina."

"Have you seen him since?"

She shakes her head in wide, slow arcs. "Nooooo." Then she nods. "But I keep looking. I look everywhere I go."

I am breathless for a moment, and my skin tingles. Two years ago. Two years ago, I was pregnant with my own baby. Missy started using Oxy then, right after she saw him. Big Mike is the reason she started using drugs.

I stroke her hair, smoothing the rumpled auburn waves, and she tilts her cheek into my palm. "We'll go to the police," I say. "There's no statute of limitation on rape. It's a felony."

She pulls her head away. "No!" Her voice echoes off the wall and down the long hallway.

"Shhh." I rub her arm, trying to calm her. "Does Jimbo know?"

Missy presses her fists against the sides of her head. "No! No! No! And you're not going to tell him! No one can know!" She wraps her arms around herself and begins to rock softly, her swollen belly complicating her movement. "Besidesss," she says, her voice quieter, "it's too late to prove anything. His word against mine."

"And mine," I say.

"And Nick's."

Nick. Maybe she's right. Two against two. But Big Mike has a scar.

I think about what it would mean to tell our story, to go to court, to face the two men who took advantage of Missy and me when we were still girls, when they were still college boys. I imagine Big Mike married with two kids. I look at Missy and see what this is still doing to her all these years later.

"Romie," Missy drawls out, and her eyes are half-closed again. "Promise you won't say anything. Promise. We've kept it secret all these years. No sense telling now."

I shake my head. "And look what it's doing to you." I think it's worth it to go to the cops, but when I watch Missy struggling to keep her eyes open, I wonder if she's too far gone to handle facing Big Mike again.

"I am *coping!*" Her voice is again too loud. "I never shoulda told you! I don't want to go through that again, tell people what happened, people looking at me, feeling sorry for me."

I again imagine Big Mike now, what he might look like. Big Mike wearing scrubs. He could be a doctor now, helping people. Repenting for his sins. Every time he looks in the mirror, he sees the scar, sees again what he has done to my friend. He could be a much better man. Or he could be raping someone else.

Missy lurches forward, the effort lifting her feet off the ground. She puts her face close to mine. "Don't you tell a ssssoul."

"Look what this secret is doing to you. It's tearing you up inside."

"It's my sssecret. And I ain't about to tell it." She rubs her nose with the back of her hand. "Besides, it ain't got nothing to do with the pills, anyway." She leans back and holds her round stomach. "Me and the baby just need a little break." When she turns to me, there is hurt behind her heavy lids. "Jimbo ain't never gonna be the same again, Romie. What's this baby gonna do with a crippled daddy? If it even *has* a daddy. What am I gonna do if Jimbo dies? He's all I got that loves me."

Her words jab my heart. I've been unfair to her. "*I* love you." I'm pricked deeper as I realize how much I mean those words. "Missy, *I* love you. And Jasper loves you, too."

A sob heaves her swollen breasts, and she falls against me, and I hold her while she weeps.

It's another hour later, and the D on the patient monitor has yet to change to the E that'll indicate Jimbo is in recovery. Missy is curled on her side on a loveseat in the waiting room, sleeping. I cover her with a blanket, and my throat tightens when I adjust it over her pregnant belly. I wonder if the baby within her is all right, or if it is already an addict, like its mother. For the first time in many years, I find myself in silent prayer, asking God's grace on this baby and its addicted mother, its damaged father—and before I can stop myself, I ask for God's grace on Jasper and me.

My face grows hot when Jasper appears at my elbow. "I'm glad she's resting," he whispers. "She's got to need it more than the rest of us."

I nod, tilt my head toward the door. "Let's step out for a bit."

He looks over his shoulder to the far corner, where two of the three coal miners are playing rummy on a table that they've dragged between them. The third is sleeping with his cheek resting on a wadded Prospect jacket.

In the hallway, he turns toward the left where he's seen me go a few times, but I shake my head. "Outside. I want to go outside."

When we step out into the parking garage, the night's chill reaches my bones, and I point to where our Jeep is parked. "Let's get my jacket." As we walk between the cars, the odor of the parking garage seems weightier than it did when we arrived, gasoline and exhaust fumes hanging heavy in the night air. "Can we go outside of here? Where we can breathe?"

Jasper nods, holds my jacket for me while I slip my arms inside, and he slides his arm around me as we walk toward the exit. Even through my hurt, or maybe because of it, I am grateful for his embrace.

Out in the open, a thick, damp mist has settled in the downtown streets lying between the mountains, a wet rug slung over the city's shoulders. It makes a yellowed aura around the streetlights leading away from the hospital, and I want to follow wherever the lights lead, wherever is away from here.

"She's doing drugs again, Jasper." My words come out in a frosty cloud that adds to the misty air. "She's stoned right now. God knows what it's doing to that baby."

"Are you sure?"

I don't answer, don't need to. We both know his question is one of wishful thinking.

His exhale seems to come from a deep place of hopelessness, and it makes me even sadder. "That's the last thing Jimbo needs." He touches the side of his finger to his eye, and it's then I realize he's tearful.

I lean against him, and he wraps his other arm around me, holding me there on the sidewalk. It is some minutes before we turn loose of one another, and when we do, he wipes his face with both hands.

"Listen," he says, and he sniffs deeply. "I know this may sound crazy, but maybe we lost the little house for a reason. Maybe it's a sign that we need to move back to Stump Branch."

My legs feel weak, and I start to shake my head. He holds my shoulders to steady me.

"The lease is up on the homeplace in just shy of a week. Willie will surely let us stay in the little house that long, I think. We can move into the homeplace, help Jimbo get through this—you know he's gonna need a lot of help when they send him home." He pauses, then speaks more softly. "And you can keep an eye on Missy. Maybe having you back there will keep her from feeling so lonely. Remember, Jimbo said lonesomeness is what caused her to start popping the Oxy, anyhow."

I now know lonesomeness was never the cause, and Jasper and I were never to blame. But I can't tell him this, though it feels like a burden too heavy to carry. I am so very tired, and I look around me for a place to sit down, but there isn't one. I gaze toward where the streetlights lead, out to the highway toward the busy interstate where people are driving, heading to a place that's not the place they left behind. I want more than anything to go with them.

I look at my husband, at the hurt and hopefulness etching lines into his face even as we stand here. I wonder if those lines are a map that will always lead me back to him.

It's as if my whole life already has been decided for me and I haven't been allowed to make any of the choices. "Stump Branch," I say on a breath, and around me, I feel the mountains exhale. "I reckon it's as good a place to live and die as any."

CHAPTER TEN

JASPER

"Hold it tight," I tell Romie, more out of habit than of need. She knows what she's doing. Her knuckles are red as she grips the two-by-six, holds it steady against the sawhorse as the SkilSaw sprays us with a light coat of sawdust. This is our third day working in Jimbo's front yard, building the switchback wheelchair ramp that'll let him enter his own home. We'd have finished it in one day, two at the most, if Jimbo and I had been building it, and it pains me to think we've probably built our last of anything together.

Romie and I work good enough together. We've stayed busy these last three weeks since we moved back into the homeplace; painting, tearing up stained carpets, painting, patching up what Shirley Gunter's grandkids tore up, and painting some more. Shirley let the grandkids she was keeping for the summer pick the colors of their bedroom walls, so we walked in to find my old bedroom Barney-purple, and the guest bedroom pitch black with glow-in-the-dark stars and psychedelic posters glued all over the walls and ceiling. Momma's sewing room had been turned into a playroom with one wall covered in chalkboard paint and enough chalk dust to choke us. Momma's and Daddy's bedroom, where Shirley slept, was painted strawberry pink. "Pubic pink," Romie called it, and I laughed until I choked over that one. It was the first time she'd smiled in a long while.

We worked hard, filling the space with talk like, "Hand me the scraper," and, "We're gonna need a third coat of primer to cover that black."

We never mention why we ended up here, and I find myself grateful, for a change, for the part of Romie that pushes down the hard stuff and pretends it never existed.

Now Romie glows yellow with a fine coat of sweet-smelling sawdust. She sneezes, and it puffs around her like the dirt clouding off Charlie Brown's buddy, Pigpen. I laugh, and she scowls.

"It ain't funny, Jasper. I'll never get this stuff out of my hair."

"Missy'll get it out for you."

As if I've conjured her, Missy's belly, followed by her head, pokes out of the opening screen door. "Want some iced tea?" She's holding a glass in each hand, the door held open by her hip.

I put down the saw, and Romie hoists herself onto the deck to get the tea. The three of us turn toward the sound of a muscle car coming up the seldom-traveled road. "You have a customer today?" I ask. "I thought you were beautifying the old ladies at the nursing home this afternoon."

One day a month, Missy volunteers at the skilled nursing facility at the edge of town, cutting and curling old-lady hairstyles with lots of teasing and hairspray. Sometimes Romie goes with her and gives manicures to the ladies, and when they get back, we giggle at their unbelievable repeated stories of times we've never lived. Missy is still doing hair out of the beauty shop that Jimbo built for her in the back bedroom of their house. He gave the salon its own driveway and entrance, put in a sink with a neck-rest, a salon chair, and mirrors all around—his idea to keep her from being so lonely during his long shifts in the mine. She named her beauty shop "Sheer Perfection," but Jimbo teases her by calling it "Curl Up and Dye."

The dusty Camaro slows and pulls into the gravel drive, follows it not to the garage, but to the back of the house, toward the salon entrance. I recognize the car and the asshole driving it. "Weasel's your customer?" I say. As soon as I speak, I know that she is *his* customer, not the other way around. We all went to school with Weasel, a picked-on runt when we were little. Weasel's daddy came into some big money when a relative died, built a huge brick house on the side of the hill that overlooks the four-lane, and Weasel became an instant asshole. Now he's *the* local drug dealer, and his name is now earned as much for his sneaky ways as his pointy chin, skinny nose, and slitted eyes.

Missy shrugs. "He has to get his hair cut, same as everybody else, I reckon." She lets the door slam shut behind her.

"Give her a minute," I say to Romie, "then go in and check to make sure he's in the chair. I don't believe for one second that the rat bastard is here to get a haircut." I smack the sawdust from my hands and look around me for a bat-sized piece of lumber that'll fit my hand and Weasel's head.

"Jasper," Romie says, holding out her gloved hand, palm-down. "Don't."

It's scary how that woman can read my mind sometimes.

She puts down her tea glass and heads into the house, careful to let the door close quietly behind her. I don't think she's had time to get down the hallway to Missy's beauty-shop room, when the dirty blue Camaro rumbles to life and backs out of the driveway.

"What's *wrong* with you, Missy." I grab the three-foot piece of two-by-four from the ground, spit sawdust from my tongue, and head toward Weasel's car. When he turns and sees me, I wave the board in the air. "Stay away from this property, you hear me, Weasel!"

His slitty eyes grow big behind the dusty window, but then he grins that shifty grin of his, and I fling the two-by-four at his car as he peels out of the driveway onto the road, slinging gravel and dust into the air. The board misses and bounces end-over-end on the blacktop. I despise that sonofabitch.

"Missy!" I yell, and I hurdle-jump onto the stairless deck to reach the front door. I fling it open too hard, and it smacks against the side of the house, but I don't care. "Missy!"

Missy pads into the living room in her sock feet, a look of shock on her face. "What!" She turns to glance at Romie, who's followed her up the hall. She props her hands on her belly. "What is *with* you two! Weasel just stopped in to check on Jimbo. Y'all are making a big deal out of nothing."

"It ain't nothing." I realize I'm pointing my finger at her, and I drop my hand. "That piece of trash don't care about Jimbo, and he never did. He and Jimbo *ain't* friends." My finger flies up again, and I shove it in Missy's face. "And he ain't *your* friend, either. Don't you think for a minute that I don't know why he was here."

Missy rolls her eyes, but then she smiles in that lazy way of hers and, unbeckoned, my gaze falls upon the heave and heft of her pregnant breasts as she breathes, then lower, to her ripe, swollen stomach. My tongue goes dry, and I look to Romie for salvation.

"Jasper Grodin!" Missy's voice calls my attention back to her, and I think my face must betray my sin. "If I didn't know better, I'd think you was jealous that me and Jimbo have friends other than you and Romie." Her voice rises and sweetens. "You've been gone a long time, you know. What'd you think? That we was gonna sit here and pine over you two while you were gone?" She huffs a mean laugh. "Weasel *is* our friend."

Romie speaks from behind her. "Then why didn't he come in and visit awhile? Why did he stay in his car, and why did he leave the minute I stepped out the salon door? And what did you give him?"

"What are you talking about?" Missy runs a hand through her hair.

"I saw you hand him something. Was it money? Did you buy drugs from him?"

Missy's lips press together, but they don't stay that way. "How dare you! Why are you always accusing me of using drugs? You know I'm doing better. You know I'm trying. I'd like a little bit of support, here."

"I know it's hard." The softness of Romie's voice, the compassion there . . . it surprises me. "It's called *addiction* for a reason. But you have to fight this, Missy." She places a sawdust-speckled hand on Missy's belly. "You need to fight . . . for this little baby. *Your* baby."

The shimmer in my wife's eyes cuts into me, causes my throat to close up, scrapes me in a raw place I didn't know was still there.

Missy's nod is slow, and when she turns toward Romie, Romie's arms open, and she holds Missy and rubs her back, the unborn baby between them.

Romie and Missy don't come with me when I go to pick up Jimbo from the hospital's rehab center in Charleston. To her credit, Missy spent many a night and day in the hospital with Jimbo, but now the drive is tougher on her, and she has to stop to pee so often that it makes hauling her up there a chore.

Romie talked Missy into cooking a big welcome-home dinner for Jimbo, and the two of them are making Swiss deer steaks with homemade rolls and all the fixin's for our return. I'm glad this'll give me some road time with Jimbo, and besides, I figure a big part of him won't want his wife to see me pick him up like a child and set him in the Jeep.

I'm surprised when there are crutches leaning against the wheelchair when I pull up to the hospital entrance to get him. The nurse has a cart beside her, and I load up clear plastic bags holding rubber straps and plastic bins and all sorts of hospital paraphernalia. Then I see his temporary prosthesis, the one he wears a few hours a day until his new one will be fitted for him. The partially severed leg they reattached is doing fine; it's the one that was mangled that he lost. Seems crazy to me that part of him is gone forever. I put his prosthesis on the back seat with the bags, then pick up some odd-looking thing and study it a minute.

"Not that one," Jimbo says, pointing to the padded thing I hold. It looks like two short, tube-shaped pillows with a stretch of cloth between them, and I hold it up to him, like a question. "That's my stump rest," he says. "Keeps it straight. Lay it on the console, and I'll fix it when I get in."

My face is hot, the word *stump* now meaning something other than the name of a creek branch, something other than the place I think of as *home*.

Jimbo turns to the nurse, and the two share a look I can't name.

"You've got this," she says, and he tries to smile.

He takes both crutches, holds them together in front of him, puts all his weight on them as he shifts to the front of the wheelchair. Then he separates the crutches enough to get the reattached leg in between, and he hoists himself to standing, the white-capped stump hanging, a forgotten flag of surrender on a flagpole. His smile is both pride and pain. "Whatcha think, old man?" he says to me. "Didn't think I'd stand again, did you?"

The nurse is careful to keep the chair a scant few inches behind Jimbo, in case he falls back, but he manages the two careful hop-steps to the Jeep, and he turns his back toward the seat. He's bashful when he speaks again and pushes the crutches toward me. "Gonna need your help a minute, buddy."

I lean his crutches against the side of the Jeep, follow his instructions, let him use my shoulder to push on. I start to hoist him by the hips into the seat. He seems a little shorter than he used to be and lighter than I'd imagined, and I feel bad for wondering how much a man's leg weighs. With both hands, he eases his good leg—his only leg, only good because it's all that's left, left full of rods and pins and who-knows-what—into the floorboard. "Lord, that hurts," he says through clenched teeth.

Over my shoulder, the nurse says, "Breathe through it, like we practiced. It'll get easier as the muscles get stronger. You're doing fine."

He nods toward her, then he slides the cloth of the strange, double-tubed pillow beneath the stump, putting one tube between his good leg and the stump. The other tube sits between the stump and the console. "See?" he says to me. "Keeps it straight and protected."

The nurse's smile is proud, like she's taught a child to tie his shoelaces, and I'm dumbfounded by all that Jimbo is having to learn anew.

"Did you confirm that your wheelchair was delivered? Your walker?" the nurse asks, and Jimbo nods.

"Wife said they came yesterday."

"Perfect," the nurse says.

I step aside but leave the door open, thinking she'll want to give her prize pupil a hug to send him off into this harsh, new world, but she's already turned away, pushing the vacant wheelchair back toward the entrance, dragging the empty cart behind her, like he's nothing at all to her.

We are mostly quiet on the ride back to Stump Branch. During his weeks at the hospital and rehab, we talked about the accident, about me not being there—Jimbo told me to stop apologizing for that—about Missy slipping a pill here and there, and about that slimy Weasel she's been buying them from. Jimbo seems comfortable with the quiet between us now, and usually it's the same for me, but not so much today. There's this thing between us now, this raw-pink stump like a white-bandaged ham that's propped on the seat beside me. I try hard not to look at it, but it's always there, brightly glaring at the side of my vision, somehow never quite out of my sight, even when I'm turned away.

After we leave the interstate and head through town, Jimbo begins to talk, only a little at first, then his words are like water flooding into the Jeep. He flits from talking about the lawsuit money his attorney promised him, to pointing out the new fast-food joints that have opened since we moved away, to how he's gonna teach his baby to deer hunt, and I realize he's nervous about going home.

"You found a job yet?" he asks, the first thing he's said that needs a reply.

"Been working part-time at Walker's Garage. The hourly pay is good, but it's only part-time. I need something full-time."

"I reckon Prospect's hiring," he says.

There's a thrill in my chest when he says this, as I've been thinking about coal mining again since I first set eyes on those Prospect uniforms in the hospital waiting room, but I figured he'd think me a backstabber if I even considered it.

"Heard they're a man down, need a new roof bolter." He grins at me, but I can't manage to grin back.

"Jimbo, I should have been there. I should have—"

"I *don't* want to have to tell you *again* to stop that," he says. "Even if you'd been there, there's no sign that you could have stopped it. Roof was soft is all. It happens. Hell, it happened to us a time or three, but we were lucky."

"*I* was lucky," I say. "You . . . not so much."

He smacks my arm with the back of his hand. "Yeah, not so much." He grins, and we are high-school boys again, though my cheeks still sting.

"Gotta stop for gas," I say, and I pull into the new 7-Eleven—new in that it wasn't here when Romie and I moved to North Carolina, built a few years ago at the base of a hillside stabbed with knife-thin, low-income apartment buildings. I park beside the pump, hop out, realize Jimbo can't follow me. Again, I feel hot and flushed, and I wonder when I'll do these things right, when I'll get used to him being so different. I clear my throat, open the door again. "You need anything?"

He nods, stares straight ahead. "Water would be good."

I pump gas into the Jeep, watching the fumes curl around the nozzle into the air. I don't even think to look at the price when I replace the pump handle, and I thread my way through the overfull parking lot, then head inside. I grab a couple bottles of water, think of how our fridge at the homeplace now always holds a dozen plastic bottles just like these, something it never held before. Romie refuses to drink well water in Stump Branch, won't even cook with water from the faucet until it's been boiled.

I'm paying at the register when I see the blue Camaro pull into the parking lot. I drop a twenty on the counter and head for the door, as the clerk calls out to me.

"Hey, buddy, don't forget your change!"

"Keep it for damages," I say, and I break into a run as I see Jimbo fling open the passenger door, hear him yelling threats at Weasel. "Stop it!" I shout so loudly my throat clenches. I shouldn't have told Jimbo about Weasel coming to his house, but at the time, it seemed a good idea. I thought he ought to know.

Weasel is out of his car now, that sneer of his begging for a fist. "What you gonna do, cripple?" he shouts, and people turn to look. He holds out his wiry arms, welcoming a fight. "You gonna crawl over here and do something? You a big man, now you ain't got no legs?"

The roar that comes from Jimbo is nothing I've heard before, and every stare is turned toward him. "I'll kill you, you sonofabitch! I don't need legs to put a gutshot through you." He turns, reaches behind the seat for his crutches, but when the crutches catch light, folks must think he's grabbed a gun. A woman screeches and shoves her little boy into her car, hops in, and guns it out of the parking lot. Weasel backsteps and then runs toward his Camaro, and I try to intercept, but he's in it and squealing tires out of the parking lot before I get there.

"You okay, buddy?" I ask when I reach the Jeep's passenger side.

Jimbo's lips are still curled back, and anger is rolling off him in hot waves. "I swear, I'll kill him." He shouts, his voice loud enough to be heard the next county over. "I will hunt him down and I will kill him!"

The meanness in his voice is new to me, and as much as I can't stand Weasel, I find myself praying their paths will never cross again, because the chill that shudders me says Jimbo means what he is saying. I put a hand on his shoulder, an effort to calm him, and the stone-cold hardness in his stare is such a shock that I yank my hand away, burned. Slowly I step back, and I close the door, taking my time to reach the driver's side. I'm in no hurry to climb in beside the hate I just saw in him.

We don't speak again until we reach Jimbo's driveway, when he lets out a whistle. "Won't you look at that," he says softly. "You built me a racetrack."

I laugh, as much out of relief as anything else, and I jerk a thumb toward the crutches. "I might have been premature, huh. Looks like you'll be climbing stairs again in no time flat."

He shrugs, and the grin I know him for returns. "It'll be a while. I can only walk a few steps at a time, but I'll get there. Once they fit me for a prosthesis, I'll have to learn to walk yet another time, so there's gonna be time to practice making that turn right there at high speeds in my wheelie-chair."

"Did you say *wheelie*-chair?"

"Oh yeah." He's serious now, his face back-lit. "I watched one of the young vets in rehab popping wheelies in his chair. Could do it one-handed, too. Spin around like a top. Won't be long, I'll have me some *new* skills."

I laugh. "Don't throw out them crutches, then. Sounds like you'll need 'em again one day soon, you act a fool like that."

He points to the front door, where Romie's face peers from behind the glass, and she waves. "Looky here," he says, when Missy appears beside her. "I got me a welcoming party."

"That you do," I say, "and I have it on good word that there's a table full of Swiss deer steak at that party, too."

"Stop wasting my time then, son, and go get my wheelie-chair. Jimbo has finally come home."

After dark, while I lie beside my sleeping wife, a sickle of moon knifes the blue-black sky outside our bedroom window, and I think about my best friend's words. *Jimbo has finally come home.* I study the same ceiling that hung over me as a child lying in my parent's bed, and I wonder if I can say it and mean it: *Jasper has finally come home.* This place has been home to me since my earliest memories, but too often—times like right now—I wonder what will be the next thing that makes Romie say we have to up and leave it.

Our days are settling into a new normal, though I'm on the edge of it, still too uncertain to dive right in. Mornings, I get up first, start the coffee, wake Romie before I climb into the shower. She makes breakfast for us, we eat, then it's her turn in the shower. Later, I follow her off the mountain, and she's in the Jeep, while I'm in the beater truck that Hippie sold me for eight-hundred dollars. When we get to town, we blare horns, then Romie blows me a kiss in her rearview, and I flash my headlights, and she turns onto the four-lane towards the medical park, while I hang a left down Main, heading to Walker's Garage.

After my five-hour shift (six on a good day), I head for home and do a chore or two while I wait on the crunch of the Jeep's tires. There's that awful span of minutes between when it's time for Romie to come home and the time when she actually gets here when it's hard to breathe, when I'm strung so tight I think I might rip down the middle, when I think maybe today's the day she won't come back to me, the day when she just keeps driving to someplace else.

Today she pulls into the driveway, and I walk out to meet her, help her carry in the groceries, ask her about her day. She tells me about the two patients who got into an argument in the waiting room about presidential candidates.

"They're about to come to blows," she says, "and Carla's got the phone in her hand, ready to call 9-1-1, when the older man says something about, 'Idiot Republicans.' The younger one looks at him all blank-eyed, says, 'Hell yeah! That's what I'm talking about!' They see they're on the same team, start slapping one another's backs like old buddies." She shakes her head. "Stupidest thing I've ever seen. I hate politics."

I laugh, thinking of how quickly she fell back into the anti-MTR meetings held at the garage twice a month. "Yet you got plenty to say your own self."

She deadpans me. "When it comes to hurting us or this land we live on, you know straight up I got plenty to say."

I don't want to venture down this road with her, get her smoked and steaming before we're even in the front door. "Got a surprise for you," I say. "Couple of surprises, really."

Her frown fades, but her face says she's suspicious. "Oh yeah?"

"Winter called a bit ago. She's coming to see us tomorrow. Said she'll be down before noon. I asked her to stay the weekend, but she said she can't, so it's just for the day."

"That's awesome!" Romie's whole face is a smile. "What's next?"

"Sorry?"

"You said you had a *couple* surprises. Can't imagine there's a better one than that, though."

"Come inside and see."

I switch the plastic grocery bags to one hand so I can open the door for her, and I offer a little bow as she enters. I follow her through the living room toward the little nook off the kitchen that we call our dining room, and I watch her face when she sees what I have done. On the table are two lit candles, and in the middle stands a bottle of wine from the grapes we grew and helped bottle at Etter Vineyards. I've grilled steaks and baked potatoes, but I know it's the wine that'll get her attention.

"Where did you . . ." She turns to me, and there's a glistening to her eyes.

"Guy at the liquor store got it for me. Been waiting on it for a few weeks. He called me yesterday. I made us a special dinner to go with it."

She walks to the table, picks up the bottle, studies it. "Did you ever?" Her smile is the prettiest in the world.

I'm the warmest I've felt all day, and I have to stop myself from running to her side, picking her up, and carrying her to the bedroom. *This* Romie, this one right here in front of me, she's the one I fell in love with when we were just teenagers running these ridges barefoot in summertime. "I'm glad you like it," I manage, thinking my own grin might bust my jaws.

"Here." Remembering my manners, I pull out her chair and seat her, then lift the bottle from her hand. I quickly round the corner to the kitchen and snag a dishtowel from countertop, sling it across my forearm, and perch the bottle just so in front of it as I re-enter the dining nook. "Milady, may I interest you in our finest cabernet?"

A look I can't decipher flits across her face—alarm, fright, shock?—then settles into an unsettled smile. She composes and her eyes brighten again, and there's her giggle. "You're so silly, Jasper."

"What was *that?*" I ask, then wish I hadn't.

Her eyelids spasm like hazard blinkers. "What?"

"That look on your face." Even as I speak, I realize I've reminded her of our life at the winery, of those precious days in the little house, of how I took it away from her. "Never mind." This was a stupid idea. "See if I cooked your steak okay." I turn away to open the wine bottle, do it with my back to her. My jaw clenches. She needs to get over this. I can't take back the past, what I've done. I've said all the *I'm sorries* I care to say about that. Isn't a woman supposed to forgive her man when he does a foolish thing out of love, or grief, or whatever it was that caused me to steal those barrels? How much more can I be asked to pay for what I've done?

"Honey," Romie says from behind me, "this steak is perfect. So juicy! Did you grill it with butter?"

I nod, realize I've been nodding for a minute, then make myself smile before I turn around. "Indeedy I did. Nothing but the best for my bride."

Her eyes roll back in her head, and she moans in pleasure as she chews, making whatever irritation I feel turn to dust.

CHAPTER ELEVEN

ROMIE

Milady. Jasper said the word that shoved me back in time, shoved me against the wall in that dark and frigid cabin the night that Missy and I hitched a ride. *Milady.*

Jasper saw it in me. My face never has been able to cover what my mind is thinking. And I lied to him. Again.

I stack our dinner plates in the sink, add a squirt of Palmolive, and run hot water over them. Bubbles foam and pop, and I breathe in the clean fragrance of soapsuds, think that maybe it's time I come clean myself, time I tell Jasper what happened when Missy and I were younger. My chest hitches a little at the thought.

"Here, baby. Let me do that." Jasper stands close at my back, so closely his breath moves my hair against my cheek.

"You cooked," I say. "Let me clean." If I keep my hands busy, it'll be easier to talk about this awful thing, to finally say what I've kept from him far too long.

Before he can argue about helping with the dishes, as I know he will, before he reaches in front of me to take over this little chore, the new doorbell he installed chimes three pleasant notes.

I turn to him and shrug, part of me relieved for the reprieve of telling my story. "You sure Winter said she'd be here tomorrow and not tonight?"

"I'm sure. And I ain't expecting company," he says. He leaves my side and goes to the door, while I hurry to the table to straighten the placemats and retrieve the wine glasses. I'm back at the sink as Jasper opens the door, part of me wishing he'd turn away the visitor, tell them it's dinnertime—*our* time—but we don't do that around here. Jasper grilled only two steaks, which we devoured, so I think of what I have to offer a guest, knowing the house must smell like food. I remember there's half the chocolate pie that I'd made over the weekend still in the fridge. I can make coffee to go with it.

"Well, if it ain't Redd Truby!" Jasper says. "Come on in! Hey, Romie, Redd's here," he calls.

I quickly peer around the corner to see the men exchange handshakes and shoulder slaps, then dry my hands and greet the man I haven't seen since we stood shoulder-to-shoulder at Jimbo's hospital bedside in Charleston. Something seems odd about him, then I realize it's because he's dressed in jeans, a flannel shirt, black cowboy boots that look like they've been spit-shined, and a blue and gold WVU cap, instead of the Prospect Mining uniform I've always seen him wearing.

"Have a seat." Jasper waves toward the sofa, and I offer Redd coffee and a piece of pie.

He pats his belly. "I'm full up, Romie, thank you. But a glass of water would be mighty fine." Redd motions toward the nook and our small dining table. "Mind if we sit there? Got some business to discuss, and I've always thought it best to discuss business at a table."

Jasper tugs at his ear. "Sure, okay." He pulls out a chair for Redd, cocks an eyebrow as he looks toward me to let me know he hasn't a clue, then takes his usual place at the head of the table.

I fill two glasses with ice and bottled water and deliver them to the men as they speak in generalities, realizing Redd is waiting for me to leave the room before he talks whatever business it is he needs to discuss with Jasper. I don't like it.

I return to the kitchen, plunge my hands into the hot water and wash the dishes quietly, keeping an ear turned toward the dining nook.

"How you been spending your days, Jasper?" Redd asks.

"Sir?"

"You still part-timing at Walker's?"

There's a pause, and I imagine Jasper nodding, hope he's smiling. When he speaks, his voice doesn't sound like it's coming from a smile.

"Ah, you know. I'm getting a few more hours now. Making ends meet. You know how we do." The room is quiet for a moment, then Jasper adds, "Been a good thing, really. Gives me time to do a little maintenance on the house, and I help Jimbo out. Been driving him to therapy a few times a week, helping out around his house when I can." He clears his throat. "Romie helps 'em quite a bit, too. Missy's getting close to her time now. Only got about five or six weeks to go."

"Yeah?" Redd says. "I reckon she is ripe to pop soon. I stopped in to check on Jimbo a few weeks ago. He's looking good, ain't he. Coming right along. Hard to keep a good man down."

"How're things at Prospect?" Jasper asks, and my jaw clenches.

"Wouldn't know. Wednesday a week ago was my last day."

"No kidding! What will they do without you, Redd Truby?"

"Oh, I imagine they've already replaced me." He coughs that deep, chesty, coal-miner's cough that's so common around here, and I say a quick prayer that it's not black lung. I been praying more since Jimbo's accident, since Missy's drug use came to light, since . . . well, *since*.

"Shoot, the day after Jimbo's accident," he continues, "there were thirty-two applications turned in. Men standing in line to get into Stinson's office while the MSHA folks were still swarming around like ants on a sugar hill." He grunts. "You know what they say, 'Men are dying to get into the mines . . .'"

"'. . . And dying is how they get out,'" Jasper finishes for him.

I despise that saying.

Jasper clears his throat. "Say you got some business to discuss?"

It aggravates me that he dropped his voice a decibel when he spoke, like he don't want me to hear.

Chair legs chuff across the floor, and I think it's Redd who has turned his seat to face Jasper head on.

"Yeah, I do. I want to offer you a job, Jasper."

That does it. I drop the wine glass I'm washing into the dish drainer where it clashes and rings against a plate, grab the dish towel from my shoulder and round the corner toward the men.

"How dare you, Redd Truby! Don't you do it," I snap at the man. "Jimbo lost his leg—nearly lost his life! And you come in here trying to get Jasper to replace you, try to get him back in that mine where the same God-awful thing could happen to him?"

Redd Truby chuckles, and I think my head might pop right off my shoulders. He holds out a hand, palm down, and motions for me to calm down, or have a seat, I'm not sure which. But I'm not about to do either one.

"I ain't talking about Prospect, Romie. This here's something altogether different."

His eyes twinkle when he tries not to grin, and I feel both foolish and angrier. I open my mouth to speak, but Jasper fixes me with a look telling me that I've said enough, and he turns back to face Redd.

"I reckon you best tell us what it is, Redd." Jasper's voice deepens. "Tell *me* what it is."

Redd pulls a long sip from his glass of water, while I stand here fuming, not speaking, but not about to leave the room, either.

He puts down the glass, takes his time wiping his lips with the back of his hand. He glances at me before he clasps his hands atop the table and leans toward Jasper. "I inherited a patch of land up in Tucker County when Aunt Lil passed." He looks at me again. "You two been up to Tucker County in a while?"

I don't answer. His question might be some kind of trick. I feel my blood pressure ratchet up another notch.

"It's been a while," Jasper says, and if he's impatient with Redd's tale, his voice doesn't betray him.

"You've seen the big windmills up thataway?" Redd says.

"Windmills?" Jasper asks. "Turbines, you mean?"

Redd grins. "Turbines, yes indeedy."

Jasper nods. "Yeah, we did drive through there, top of that

mountain where it levels off." He turns my way. "You remember, Romie? Right before we moved to Greensboro."

"Yes." I rub my still-damp palms on my pants, not sure where this conversation is heading, or why it's bothering me so much.

Redd nods. "I'm gonna put a whole field of those mechanical daisies in the ground up there on Aunt Lil's place. Need me a couple of strong, young backs to help me get 'em planted."

Jasper stares at Redd for a minute, then he looks away, but not toward me. It's as if he's hiding what he thinks, doesn't want me to see it on his face. He's learned that trick from me.

The room is quiet for so long it feels stiff and uncomfortable, and finally I can't take it.

"Those turbines don't come cheap, Redd. I'll bet they're more than a new truck, maybe two," I say.

At this Redd laughs. He doesn't chuckle, but he laughs a real, loud, belly laugh that at first makes me feel foolish, but when I see the tears in his eyes, I can't help but start to laugh with him.

"Shoo!" Redd says, wiping his eyes. He chuckles again, but he finally composes himself enough to talk. "Romie, I *wish* they cost as much as two trucks. Hell, I wish they cost as much as three or four. One of them commercial windmills costs over two million dollars."

I gape and rest my palms on the table, then look down, surprised that I'm sitting. I don't recall when I sat down.

Jasper whistles long and low. "*Two million,* you say? And you're gonna plant a whole field of 'em?" He cocks an eyebrow. "I know you said your Aunt Lil left you the land—and not to dig deep into your business, Redd—but was she a Rockefeller? I mean . . . did she leave you enough millions to do all that?"

Redd's grin turns into a workaday smile, genuine but tired. I get the feeling he's answered that same question more than a few times.

"No. No, she didn't. She did leave me a fair penny more'n I

deserve, but not enough to do all that needs doing. The good thing is that the D.O.E.," he nods toward me, "D.O.E. is the U.S. Department of Energy, Romie—the D.O.E. kicked in some grant money, and I've already secured the loans I need, some using the land as collateral until the wind farm is up and running. It sounds awfully complicated, but it was easier than you think, 'cause the income was calculated based on the megawatts each turbine produces, and thanks to the wind farm that's already up and running across the county lines of Tucker and Putnam, the wind evaluations are already in place, so that saved me a small fortune."

He places his fingertip against a droplet of sweat sliding down the outside of his water glass, and it strikes me that he may be sweating as much as the water glass. He wipes his wet finger on his jeans. "That's a whole lot of jargon to say that a little over two dozen windmills and twenty million dollars have me ready to plant." He takes a deep, satisfied breath, and his smile grows brighter. "I reckon you can tell I been working on this a while." He nods, agreeing with himself, I suppose. "About six, maybe seven years."

He leans forward and splays his hands on the dinner table. "See, the energy that the windmills produce is sold to the power company, plus a couple other businesses I've already got contracts lined up with. I secured the loans back when I did my business plan, so the capital is in place to purchase the turbines. I just have to provide the land, which I have in spades, and some more transmission lines. Then I've got to build a road and supply the labor to get the windmills planted and keep them running." He softens his voice. "And security, of course."

"Security?" The way he quietly tacks on this last requirement doesn't sit well with me, and I shift on my seat. "Why would you need security?"

He fixes me with his stare. "Romie, you of all people ought to know the answer to that. You and your people in that MTR group know good and well how anyone fares when they go up against the mining companies."

My face burns, and I look to Jasper, whose eyebrows lift and drop. I wonder how many people know I'm involved in those meetings. I wonder who else at Prospect Mining knows, and if they knew before we left. I wonder if I'm safe, if Jasper and I are safe.

My mouth is dry when I speak. "So . . . so you're saying the coal companies cause trouble for the wind farms?"

He nods. "Oh yeah. It's money outta their pockets. Out of the dirty politicians' pockets, too. And of course, there's the environmentalists who are on the wrong side of the debate, who say dumb things like, 'Turbines kill birds. Turbines kill bats,' and other such nonsense."

Jasper looks at me, then at Redd. "Well, don't they?"

"Yeah, sometimes." When he shrugs, his shoulders appear tired. "Mostly not. Most birds are smart enough to steer clear and change their paths, though we did have to submit to a study during migration season to show that Aunt Lil's land—*my* land now—doesn't sit in a migration path. Can you believe that? A migration study." He grunts. "That cost me a pretty penny, let me tell you.

"Truth is, cats kill hundreds of millions more birds every year than turbines do."

I don't know what my face shows because Redd waves his hand toward me. "Don't look at me like that, Romie. It's true. Stanford University did a study on it. I looked all this up and reported it on my business plan. I had to have my ducks in a row, see." A grin slips across his lips. "The ones that cats don't kill, that is." He chuckles at his joke. "Seriously y'all, airplanes kill more birds, and power lines and cell towers electrocute more birds, even nuclear power plants kill more birds than wind farms ever do. And them there's facts. You can look it up yourself." He leans back and crosses his arms, as if he's won some major debate and there's nothing left to argue.

Jasper clears his throat. "Sounds like you've got it all figured out,

Redd Truby. When do you plan on getting started with all this?"

I feel my jaw drop open, and I close it. I stare at my husband, want him to look at me, but he won't do it.

Redd grins. "Oh, I *started* years ago. I'm just ready for the boots-on-the-ground part, now. That's where you come in."

Hopefulness lights fire on Jasper's face, and there's pure *joy* in his smile that seizes the breath in my chest. I haven't seen him like this since . . . since we first lived at the vineyards. I turn my head and squeeze shut my eyes to stop the well that tries to spring up. As much as I want him to be happy, there's no way I want him to do this dangerous thing. I open my mouth to protest, but Jasper speaks first.

"What do you have in mind?" he asks Redd Truby, and his voice is so full of optimism that it makes my throat tighten.

Redd leans back in the chair again, and his chest grows broader. "Oh, there's plenty to be done." He raises an eyebrow. "Back-breaking labor, some of it. The top of the mountain has a long, bare patch where I'm gonna install the first line of windmills, but we got more land to clear, and we got to cut in a road." He pauses and sucks at his lower lip. "I heard you learned to clear land down in Carolina when you was working for Billings Construction."

Jasper's head bobs like an eager puppy. "Yeah. Yeah, I know how to do that." His face clouds for a moment, and I'm not sure why. He drops his head, but when he raises it again, that funny look is gone. "How'd you know what I did?"

"You know that Mack Billings and his sister over in Fairmont are old family friends? No, don't reckon you would, huh. We don't talk often, but it's a small world. Keep that in mind." He looks toward me as he says this last, and it feels like some kind of warning, like he knows something that I don't.

Redd picks up his water glass, downs every last drop in one long drink. He holds the glass toward me. "Can I bother you for a refill, Romie? All this yammering makes me thirsty."

I know his request for what it is—a reason for me to leave the table, to let the men talk without me there. Begrudgingly, I take his glass and shoot him a look that says, *watch yourself*. It doesn't faze him.

In the kitchen, I pull another bottle of water from the fridge and refill Redd's glass. Their voices are low mumbles, and it irritates me. I toss the empty bottle in the recycle bin under the sink, and I stand still, picturing again the optimistic happiness in Jasper's face a moment ago. He deserves to be happy like that, doesn't he? To do something that makes him proud? There's probably good money in this venture that we can surely use, and maybe insurance and other benefits, too. I think of what Jimbo told me about how Prospect treated poor old Widow Shrewsbury. I think of the other horror stories I've heard about Prospect since moving back to Stump Branch. Wouldn't taking away some of their mining business be worth the risk? Could it possibly put some of those devils out of business? It'd be better for the environment, no doubt.

I wonder what Winter would say about all this, and I hear her voice in my head telling me not to make this decision about me. It's Jasper's opportunity, and the choice should be his. How I react to it is up to me. She'd say this job's a good thing, that Jasper needs to feel like he's an equal partner in this marriage, and I find myself agreeing with what she's saying, even though she hasn't said a word.

I decide to slow my return to the table, to let the men talk privately, so I wipe down the countertop again, clean the stove, and put away the garlic salt that Jasper left out after seasoning our steaks. I give my husband time, let him make this decision—and I already know he's going to say *yes*—even if it worries me. It seems the least I can do for the man I love.

I wasn't wrong. Redd Truby made Jasper a fine offer, and Jasper gripped the man's handshake like it was a life preserver while he was lost on a stormy sea. He's still chattering on about it even now, though we've been here in bed a good twenty minutes, and I need to be up early in the morning. "Baby," I finally say, "I'm happy that you're happy, and you know I love you to the heavens and back, but would you *please* shut up?" I grin as I say it, then I can't help but chuckle when I see the whites of his eyes grow wide in the moonlight that's fingering through the slats of the window shade.

He raises up in bed, flings back the covers, and pounces on top of me. "How dare you, woman! You must pay for your insolence!" He raises his fists in the air like a warrior, stretching his arms wide.

"*In*-so-lence?" I say, making my voice as slow and sexy as I know how. "You know I love it when you use big words."

We can't hold our giggles inside any longer, and Jasper collapses atop me, our laughter metamorphosing into the hums and moans of late-night lovemaking.

I'm dreaming about the slow-falling babies again; babies and toddlers in white christening dresses and black short pants and now there are babies in yellow rompers. I'm telling myself it's a dream, telling myself it'll be over soon, like Winter taught me to do, even hearing her now in my sleep telling me these things. It helps, but I can't shake out of it. I keep seeing those faceless cherubs drifting, falling, chubby arms spread like wings. I reach out my hands to catch one when music that doesn't belong in my dream jars me, pulls me out of it, and as much as want this disturbing dream to end, I don't want to leave the babies behind.

It's Jasper's cell phone playing a John Mellencamp ringtone.

He assigned "Get a Leg Up" to Jimbo's number as a musical caller-ID after Jimbo started singing it every time he climbs in our Jeep.

I roll toward him. "Answer that, please," I mumble. "Make it stop."

Jasper's hand smacks the bedside table a few times as he tries to locate the offensive noise. "What time is it?"

"Evidently, it's time to wake the dead." I roll over and flick on the lamp, squinting in the violent light. I open my own phone case and read

4:08 AM. "This can't be good," I mutter against Jasper's drowsy, "Hullo." He props himself on an elbow, his back toward me.

I hear Jimbo's excited voice on the phone, though I can't make out his words. Jasper turns to me in the bed, and his eyebrows shoot upward. "We'll be right there," he says. "Be ready to go when I pull in."

"What is it?" I say, though my drowsy mind is already connecting the dots before Jasper puts down his phone.

"It's Missy. She's in labor." A sleepy grin breaks across his cheeks. "We're about to have us a baby!"

I climb from the bed, rush to our closet and pull down jeans and a blouse, then think better of my choice, grab instead a pretty tank top and a comfortable sweater to layer, knowing we will be at the hospital for a while. Part of my mind is in nurse mode—it's too early for her to be in labor, and Jasper didn't ask how far apart Missy's contractions are, or if her water had broken—while another part of me is thinking about my husband's words. *We're about to have us a baby.*

But *we* are not. It's not *our* baby.

I drop the shoe I'm holding into my lap and close my eyes, try to dredge up those babies I dreamt about only moments ago, but they're gone, alluding me. Why can't we have a baby? Why does Missy get to have a child when Jasper and I can't? *God,* I pray, *give me a baby! Just give me a baby already. You* know *I'll be the best mother I can be. Please, God. Please!* I'm not sure if I'm asking or demanding, but I wonder if it matters, either way. I wonder why He'd hear me this time, when it seems He has never heard me before, never answered even one of my many prayers for the lives of those who've died and left me.

"Are you ready, babe?" Jasper calls from somewhere else in the house, his voice muffled by walls.

I wipe my face on my sweater sleeve and bend to tie my shoes. "I'm as ready as I'll ever be."

We're nearly to Missy and Jimbo's place before I realize I haven't said a word, haven't had to, as Jasper is again talking about Redd's plan, about how he'll even have a job for Jimbo, too, as soon as Jimbo's a little more mobile, how our buddy can drive a forklift like that one-legged man at the lumber yard. I recognize his chatter for nervousness, excitement, a way not to think about what's really ahead of us these next few hours.

I again chastise myself for thinking ugly thoughts, for thinking Missy and Jimbo don't deserve this baby. Lord knows, they've been through enough and have earned this soon-to-arrive bundle of happiness in their lives. As much as Missy can sometimes grate on my nerves, she's still my oldest friend, still someone I think of as a *best* friend, even when she's not. And oftentimes, anymore, she's not.

I reach for Jasper's hand in the light of the dashboard, squeeze it, and mirror his smile. I remind myself that this is a happy moment, and I take a deep breath as we pull into the driveway and through the yard, right up to the end of Jimbo's wheelchair ramp. Pale blue morning light is creeping over the ridgeline, pushing difficult dreams and darkness into the past. I'm thankful it'll soon be full daylight.

Indoors, I find Missy sitting on the edge of a wooden kitchen chair, her knees spread far apart, one hand on her back and the other rubbing her beach ball of a belly. Her face is red and damp in the glow from the light hanging over her kitchen table. She shakes her head as I hurry to her side.

"I'm not ready for this." She blows out a long breath through pursed lips. "I mean, I'm ready for it—I want this baby outta me. I'm just not ready for it to hurt."

"You got this, little momma," I say, pushing a damp curl from her cheek. "We're gonna get you into the Jeep, head to the hospital, and in no time they'll give you an epidural to help you through those contractions." I smile at her, and maybe I imagine it, but she appears more hopeful. "Can you walk?" I ask.

She reaches out both hands. "Easier than I can get up from this chair."

I grasp her hands and lean back, offering leverage as she heaves herself from the chair.

Jimbo provides clipped details as he switches from crutches to his wheelchair. "Five minutes apart. Started at twenty-three minutes apart yesterday morning. Stopped for a few hours. Started again after dinner at nineteen apart. Been steady since. Now five apart. It's go time!" His crutches bang against the doorframe as he rolls out the door and down the ramp, Jasper behind him.

Jasper's already helping Jimbo into the Jeep, and when I glance out the door, I'm pleased to see Jimbo's hoisting himself onto the front passenger seat. I want to ride in the back with Missy. "You got your bag packed?"

Missy nods as if her head is heavy. "Jasper took it when he followed Jimbo down the ramp."

We start toward the door, then Missy stops short.

"You okay? Another contraction?" I ask.

She shakes her head, stares at the floor.

"Leaking water?"

Again, she shakes her head but doesn't take another step.

"Missy? What is it?"

Her doe eyes roll toward mine. "I—I took something."

"You . . . *what?*"

"I thought you should know. Just, you know, just in case."

"Missy! What did you take?"

She offers a slight shrug. "Just a . . . an Oxy. I'm scared, okay? I need something to get me over the hump, take care of the pain."

Now it's me shaking my head. "Why, Missy? Why on Earth?"

"You don't know! It's gonna hurt like hell!"

I grip her arm a little firmer than I should, pushing her again toward the door. "You ain't the first woman to give birth. It ain't rocket science. They would've given you an epidural if you needed one, once you get there. You know that."

She stops again right at the door. "Would have? *Would have?*"

I press her again to keep moving. "Well, I don't know. Maybe they can't give you one, now you're on Oxycontin. I don't know. We'll have to ask."

She jerks to another stop, and Jimbo lowers the passenger window. "You okay?" he yells. "Let's get a move on, unless you want to birth our baby right here!"

Missy's hand reaches out and grabs my arm. "You can't tell them." Her whisper grows fierce. "I mean it, Romie. Not one word."

I'm not sure if she means Jasper and Jimbo, or if she means the obstetrics team, but I am certain her doctor needs to know this. "Let's get in the Jeep, before Jimbo has a stroke. We can argue later."

"Nothing to argue about. You're keeping your mouth shut," she mutters.

Once we're settled in, with Missy's back wedged partway between the back seat and the door, she plants one foot on the floor and braces the other against the base of the console. She dips her head toward mine. "Promise me," she whispers.

I ignore her and grab my cell phone, Google *Oxycontin during childbirth*. I scroll and read and scroll some more. I find a medical journal entry that says Oxycontin is sometimes used during labor for pain control, and it doesn't harm the baby in those small doses. I turn my phone toward Missy, so she can read.

A grin breaks across her face and her head bobs. "See," she whispers. "It's gonna be okay."

"The doctor still needs to know," I say, and she presses her lips into a line and frowns.

"Absolutely not."

"How we doing back there?" Jasper says to my reflection in the rearview mirror.

"Good," Missy says. "I'm good."

"Oooo weee!" Jimbo says, turning partway around in the seat. "We're about to meet Jimbo Junior!"

My mouth drops open. "Please, God, no. Not Jimbo Junior."

Jimbo grins that silly grin of his, and I see the crinkles at the corners of Jasper's eyes in the mirror. "Could be Missy Junior, I reckon," Jasper says.

I turn to Missy and smile, glad for this moment of lightness. "I know you want to keep the names you've chosen secret until the baby's born, but please tell me you've picked something better than that."

"We'll ss-see," she says slowly.

Her slight slur tells me her tongue has grown thicker, and my jaw tightens. Oxy shouldn't cause her to slur, and I recall she took Xanax when Jimbo was in the trauma center. I turn back to my phone, reading more of the articles I pulled up, checking the ones about long-term opioids during pregnancy. Words and phrases jump out at me: *maternal death, birth defects, stillborn.* I put my phone away and rub my sweaty palms on my jeans.

"Missy," I whisper, leaning close to her, "have you been taking Oxy all along? You said you'd stop after Jimbo's accident."

She mumbles, then presses back hard against the seat. "Had to take it sometimes to stop the diarrhea. It's the only thing that'll—" Her words are cut short on a sharp intake of air.

"Breathe," I say. "Just like we practiced." I puff out my cheeks and blow along with her, while Jimbo turns and does the same from the front seat. Jasper stares at us in the rearview until I stop puffing to scold him. "Hey! Eyes on the road, mister!"

He's driving faster than usual, but he's the best driver I know, and I feel safe knowing it's him at the wheel instead of Jimbo, who has a reputation for being a wild man on the road.

"Just so you know," he says, "the three of y'all huffing and puffing together sound like a freight train climbing a mountain."

After a moment, Missy's breathing slows, and she releases the death grip she had on my thigh. I check my watch, and Jimbo speaks in unison with me. "Five minutes."

I rub my stinging thigh and shift in the seat. "We've got plenty of time."

"Sssaysss you." Missy slides lower in the seat, and her head falls back, her eyes now closed.

Jimbo hears and sees this, and he looks at me, wide-eyed. "No." He reaches back his hand, clasps Missy's outstretched leg. "Missy. Missy!"

She lifts her head, but it takes her a moment to focus on her husband's face. "What?"

"Missy, you didn't!"

"Aww, now." She again rests her head against the seatback.

Jasper glances between Jimbo, the road, and my reflection in the rearview. I shake my head at him.

"How many?" Jimbo moves his wife's leg, shaking it as best as he can from his awkward position. "Missy. Missy, how many did you take?"

My mouth opens, closes, then opens again before I can speak. "You know? Jimbo, you *know* she's taking Oxy?"

He shakes his head and frowns. "No. I mean, yeah, I knew she took them quite a while back. Said she had to take it to stop her from— from getting sick . . . you know, withdrawal sickness. She had been taking Xanax, but she told me you busted her when I was in Charleston." He shakes his head, looks at Missy, but then talks to me like she's not even here. "I thought it was, you know, because of me. Because I might die." In the light of dawn seeping through the trees into the car's interior, his face seems to pale. He rustles Missy's leg again. "Baby, you told me you stopped."

She rouses and stares out the window.

"You promised," he says, and his voice sounds both weak and defeated. He hitches out a half-sob and releases her leg, turns back around to face the road ahead.

I slide closer to Missy, take her hand, and rub it, trying to rouse her again. She looks at me, but it takes a moment for her eyes to focus. "You took Xanax with the Oxy, I say?"

A slow smile spreads across her face. "Didn't I tell you that part? Musta forgot." She snorts a laugh through her nose.

"Dear God," I say. "Jimbo, she took Oxy and Xanax." Then I shake her again. "Missy, how many?"

She pulls her hand free of mine, holds it out, and cups it. "About this many." She grins again, leans her head, back, then her eyes open wide. "Nnnnnnn!" She grunts and pushes against the seatback. She lifts her foot from the console and places it on the edge of the seat between us, shifting her back against the car door.

"No. No. No!" I say. "Stop! Stop pushing. You can't push yet. Breathe!" I make the puffing sounds we've practiced, and Jimbo and Jasper join me. Missy's face reddens, and she puffs once, then again makes a grunting sound as she bears down. "No! Stop pushing! Breathe through it, Missy!"

Jimbo's wedging himself between the two front seats across the console now, puffing his cheeks out as he demonstrates for Missy how to blow. She focuses on his face and begins to mirror his breathing until finally the contraction passes. "This ain't good, is it," he says to me.

I shake my head. "Missy, you can't push. I know you want to, but you can't push yet. You'll hurt yourself and the baby." Then to Jimbo, I say, "It's the pills. She's buzzed out, and she's doing what feels best to her, even though it's too soon to push."

Jimbo checks his watch. "Four minutes now. They're closer."

"So are we, buddy," Jasper says, and I'm so thankful for his soft voice of reason. He turns the Jeep onto the main road, and soon we're speeding toward the hospital. He catches my eye in the rearview again. "We can do this. It's gonna be okay. She's gonna be okay. The baby's gonna be okay, too."

He focuses again on the road as we come out of the shade of the mountain into the early morning light, and in the mirror, I see tears glimmering in his eyes. I imagine he's thinking of his drive to the hospital when I lost our little girl, praying this isn't a tragic repeat. All this time, I've been thinking about myself, about losing my baby and what Missy's pregnancy means to me, not realizing that Jasper has pinned his own hopes on the outcome of this delivery.

"Yes," I say, and I slide an arm around Missy's shoulder, rest her head against my shoulder, and kiss her forehead. "We're all gonna be okay."

In the small waiting area outside the labor and delivery suites, I touch Jasper's hand, gently pull it away from his mouth. I examine the fingernail he's chewed, and it's ragged and red down to the quick.

He pulls his hand from mine and wipes it on his jeans. "I know, I know." He stands now and walks the length of the room. "Shouldn't we be hearing something?"

We've been here for what seems like hours, though it's just barely one. A nurse quickly took Missy back and allowed Jimbo to follow. "It hasn't been that long. I'm sure they're getting her prepped . . . you know, taking a urine specimen, getting her into a gown, probably doing some bloodwork, given her . . . her . . . ."

"High," Jasper finishes for me. "She is flat-out stoned." His full lips form a thin line.

We turn toward the squeak of Jimbo's wheelchair wheels on the polished floor of the hospital's women's center. His smile is tired as he drifts the last several feet toward us. "She's doing good," he says. They're working with her now. That room is a little claustrophobic with all of us in there." His grimace is fleeting. "Thought I'd take the chance to bring y'all up to speed."

"The baby's okay?" I ask.

He nods. "Seems to be." He traces a fingertip on the top of his head. "They put in a little screwy thing on the top of the baby's head up inside Missy—said it wouldn't hurt at all, just barely hooks on the scalp—so they can monitor the baby's heart rate better. She's dilated about three centimeters, so things are moving right along." He lets out an exhausted sigh.

"You need anything?" Jasper asks. "Coffee? Pepsi? You look tired."

Jimbo sighs again. "Yeah, I reckon I am. Haven't slept since the night before."

"Did you or Missy call her momma?" I ask. "I'll call her if you haven't."

"No. Nada. Not happening." He slices a hand across the air. "Missy gave that a 'Hell, no.'"

"Why?"

He scrunches his face. "She didn't tell you?"

"She told me her momma moved away a while back. I know that much."

He shakes his head. "Yeah, *ran away* is more like it. She shut out Missy when she found out about the—about her—you know, the drugs. Said it shamed her." He huffs. "As if her running off with that missionary wasn't shameful enough."

"Mission—*what?*" Jasper says.

"Yeah," Jimbo says. "Some missionary did a revival at the Pentecostal church some months ago—when y'all was up in Shepherdstown—and when he left town, Missy's momma took off with him. Told folks at the church, 'God called me to go.'" His lip curls. "Guess he called her in the middle of the night, 'cause no one saw her leave in daylight. Missy found out a week later when she called her momma's cell and learned she was in Illinois with the preacher. She called Missy a junkie and told her never to call her again. So don't," he finishes.

I don't know what to say, so I stay quiet.

"Reckon we're all a bunch of orphans now, ain't we," Jimbo says.

I don't remind him that his own father may be alive somewhere. The man left when Jimbo was three, so I reckon Jimbo, technically, *is* orphaned.

Jasper makes a humming sound, then waves a hand toward Jimbo's chair. "How's your leg holding up, buddy?"

"Ain't bad, considering. I ain't got the energy to navigate the crutches just now, but this chair is taking up too much space in that little room, what with all the stuff they've dragged in there."

"If there're any other chairs or a table or anything in the room that are in your way, you can ask them to move them out, give you some more room," I say, glad for this change in subject.

"Yeaaaah," he drawls and rubs the back of his neck. "Truth be told, I had a few words with the doctor and decided to excuse myself before things got any uglier."

Jasper and I exchange glances.

"What happened?" Jasper asks.

"Aw, she started spouting off a bunch of stuff like, 'prenatal intoxication,' and 'neonatal abstinence syndrome.' Pissed me off is what it did. I could tell she was judging me. Judging us, I mean. I told her not to be pointing no fingers at us. Told her that, from the looks of her, she probably come from people who had plenty of experience with that sorta thing, herself."

"Jimbo!" I hop to my feet, stand over him for the lecture I'm no doubt about to give him. "You said those things to Doctor Gloria? She ain't come from no kind of people other than the very best! You know her daddy has a building named after him at Beeson College, right? That's—"

"Stereotyping," Jimbo says. "I know, I know." He stares at his hands in his lap, picks at a hangnail. "Wasn't my finest moment."

Jasper lets out a soft whistle. "Buddy, you know she's here to help you, right? To help Missy and your baby. You might want to treat her like the savior she is."

Jasper's softspoken and calm, and I'm impressed with him and a little bit ashamed of myself. His quiet way with words always accomplishes so much more than my knee-jerk soapbox sermons. I don't know how he does it.

I look toward the clicking sound of high heels coming down the hallway, where Dr. Gloria Samuel's gaze falls on Jimbo's wheelchair, and the rhythmic pattern of her steps falters a moment before she turns and heads into the waiting room where we three sit.

"Mister Kinzer," she says to Jimbo, "I'm going to change into scrubs. Your wife has dilated to six centimeters, so it won't be long. You may want to head back to the room now." She pauses and wipes the light sheen from her smooth, brown forehead, pushes back a few wiry curls.

"Doctor Gloria," he says, "I owe you an apology."

She links her fingers together, lets her hands fall into the folds of the pretty dress she wears beneath her crisp lab coat, and she pulls her shoulders back. *Regal* is the word that comes into my mind, and I think of how one day I'd like to present myself like this to my own patients—confident, expectant, but no doubt in charge of any situation.

"Yes," she says. "You do."

He turns and meets her eyes. "I'm sorry. What I said . . . it was uncalled for. I reckon I felt like—*feel* like—you are judging us. You know," he waves his hand across his legs, "that you think we're white trash or something. A bunch of drug addicts."

"Mister Kinzer—"

"Please, call me Jimbo."

A faint smile twitches her lips, then disappears. "Jimbo, I accept your apology, but let's be clear that I am not excusing your words. Indeed, what you said was uncalled for. While you were worrying about me judging you, you were also busy judging me. You don't personally know me, and I don't personally know you or your wife. I only know what you tell me. It's unfortunate that what she has told me, and what you two have represented to me, is not the whole truth." She unlinks her fingers and smooths her skirt. "I base critical medical decisions on what science shows me through test results, coupled with what my patients tell me." Her forehead creases and her lips press together for a moment before she speaks again. "When my patients aren't truthful—and withholding information is not truthful, Mister—*Jimbo*—I cannot give the best care. My decision-making may be skewed, and that could cause harm to your wife and your unborn child."

She looks at Jasper, then at me, and her eyes widen, as if she's recognizing our presence for the first time. "Are you two family?" she says, and there's hesitancy in her voice, as if she realizes she may have spoken inappropriately in front of us.

"They're the only family we've got," Jimbo says. "Closer'n blood."

Her eyes narrow for a moment, then she nods. "May I speak freely?"

"Yes ma'am, you may," Jimbo says.

"Melissa—*Missy*—has used drugs throughout her entire pregnancy. The fact that this information has been kept from me has jeopardized her, as well as your baby. We won't know how badly until she gives birth, and then we can examine the infant, run some tests."

Jimbo's face crumbles and he hitches a soft sob. "I am so sorry. I knew, but I didn't . . . I didn't know all of it, I mean, how much." His voice is thick, and I wipe at my own wet cheeks. He purses his lips and blows out a long, slow breath. "When this happened," he again waves at his legs, "they sent me home with a bottle of pain pills." His face is pleading when he looks at Dr. Gloria. "I flushed them right away. I didn't take nary a one, and I made sure they weren't in the house for Missy to get ahold of. She—she had a problem once before, but she'd been doing good. She'd been doing *real* good." He rubs his hands on his jeans. "I found out when I went for my checkup that she'd called in all the refills on the prescription. I didn't even realize the bottle had refills. I reckon she'd been taking them all along."

"What was it?" Dr. Gloria asked.

Jimbo snorts. "What else? The Appalachian prescription of choice. Oxycontin. What every doctor around here pushes and shoves at anybody what's got a lick of pain."

She frowns but doesn't argue. "And the Xanax? She said she'd taken Xanax. Was that also yours?" She glances at Jasper, then at me, as if we're also culpable.

I shake my head vehemently. "No, ma'am. She didn't get anything from us." I motion toward Japser. "We don't take any medicine of any kind."

Jimbo's face reddens and he shoots me a look so filled with anger that my breath catches.

"Jimbo," I say, "I wasn't—I didn't mean . . .."

He sniffs. "I don't know exactly where she got them." He glances at Jasper, then back to the doctor. "I have my suspicions, though. And if I ever get my hands around that man's neck . . .." His hands form into claws, and he mimes choking the life out of someone—someone Jasper and I both know to be Weasel.

Dr. Gloria steps forward and puts a hand on Jimbo's shoulder. "Now's not the time. Let's just focus on what's ahead of us, shall we?" She again looks at me, stares hard at me, really, and she cocks her head. "Do I know you? Do you work here?"

I sit a bit taller. "I work for Dr. Ed Green, and I'm in nursing school. I've just started doing my clinical hours here in the hospital." I feel my face beaming, and I realize I'm doing exactly what I was meant to do. It's a great feeling.

She offers a small and tight smile. "Good for you. We can use all the nurses we can get around here." Her face again grows serious. "You understand, then, how important it is for me—for any doctor, or *nurse*—to know what's really going on." She looks at Jasper, then fixes her stare on Jimbo. "No more secrets."

"No more secrets," Jimbo says. "No ma'am. Nary a one."

CHAPTER TWELVE

JASPER

I reach out my hands, greedy, but nervous, to hold little Paisley Grace in my arms the first time. She's so tiny, not quite six pounds yet, and while part of me worries I might break her, all of me knows I'd give anything to keep harm from coming to this fragile little girl who looks at me with such innocence it splits my heart in two. I lean to kiss her forehead, still covered in a soft, downy fuzz, and when my lips touch her, it's like a flash of recognition jolts through me, squeezes the breath from my chest. For an instant, I think she is Romie's and my baby come back to us, reincarnated, and she's finally in her daddy's arms. I break down—really break down—into a big, blubbering mess.

She is two weeks old today, and she is going home. But not to our home. This is Jimbo and Missy's baby, not ours. I cough out another sob.

"Here, Jasper," Romie says, and I can tell she's embarrassed by my display. "It's my turn to hold her now," she says, then lowers her voice to a whisper, "while you go get yourself together." She lifts the baby from my arms and holds the tiny bundle against her chest, and when I look at her, I can't tell if she's hurting for me, or for herself, but I do recognize her pain, and I know I have to get out of this room before I bawl like a little schoolgirl.

Stop it, I tell myself as I step into the hallway and head toward the men's room. *MEN,* reads the sign on the door. I'm a man, all right, *now act like one.*

Inside, I blow my nose and splash cool water on my face, but I avoid the mirror. I suppose people who are smarter than I am would tell me this is my turning point, the place where I come to terms with the loss of my own daughter, where I finally face my grief so I can start to heal.

I pull rough paper towels from the dispenser and dry my face. *You've been watching too many daytime talk shows.* I decide right now to keep the television off when I'm not working at the garage. This job with Redd will go a long way toward putting my mind right again, so I don't turn all sissified and weak. I head out the door and back down the hallway to where my wife, Jimbo, Missy, and their new baby girl are waiting for me to drive everyone home.

Jimbo rolls his way up the wheelchair ramp and into his house, with Paisley Grace in her baby carrier balanced on his lap. Once we're inside, he plays with her yellowish cheeks, cooing a bunch of nonsense sounds like a blithering idiot, and I can't help but grin at him. "That's the most intelligent thing you've said all day," I say, "maybe all year!"

"Uh-huh. I'm surprised you have the intellect to understand such brilliance." He feigns a punch at my shoulder, and Romie turns and rolls her eyes at Missy.

"Are you two sure you don't want to stay at the house with us a few days?" Romie offers again. "That'll give you some time to rest, Missy. Jasper and I can help with the baby and whatever else needs doing while Jimbo's down at the clinic doing his PT."

Romie and I have already talked about this, hoping we can convince the two, not so much to help with the baby, but so we can keep an eye on Missy, make sure she's staying clean.

Missy shakes her head. "I just want to be here at home." She leans over and kisses Paisley Grace, lifts her from the carrier so Jimbo can get out of his chair and push it away. He says he's now "off the chair" when he's at home.

"Besides," Missy says, "we need to adjust to being a new little family together for a few days. You know, get into a routine and all."

I glance at Romie in time to see her expression darken before she turns to look out the window. I recall Jimbo's words in the waiting room two weeks ago, when he told Dr. Gloria that we are "closer than family." I reckon Missy didn't get the memo.

I take Romie's hand. She squeezes mine, but she doesn't turn her gaze away from whatever's outside the window, from whatever is far from here, and I know she wants nothing more than to be away from the here and now of this house. My Runaway Romie.

"Jasper," Jimbo says leaning against a crutch and holding out his hand. "Thank you for driving us." I accept his handshake, and he clears his throat, so I know there's more to come. "I'd hoped to be able to make this drive home myself. I dreamed of it from the time I first learned this beautiful lady here was pregnant with my child." He grows quiet a moment. "Things don't always turn out the way we plan, but they tend to work out anyways, don't they."

He leans over and kisses Missy's cheek. "Another week or two and I'll be behind the wheel again. You just watch me. That ol' tough-ass physical therapist thinks she's pushing me hard, but you keep your eyes peeled. I'm gonna show her what hard is. She said I'd be driving again in a month, but I'm gonna cut that in half." He fiddles with Paisley Grace's chin. "Yessir, little girl. Daddy's gonna take you for a ride real soon!"

Romie's grip on my hand tightens, and I know this is hurting her, probably even more than it's hurting me, but I also know it's hurt that we've got to get over.

"Speaking of driving," I say, "have you seen Redd Truby lately?"

"It's been a while . . . a month or two, I reckon. What's he got to do with anything?"

"I guess it's okay to tell you. You heard about what all he's got going, up in Tucker County?"

"Can't say I have."

"He's starting him a wind farm up there. Turbines. Got the property all lined out, business plan and loans approved, got him some vendors he's working with, all his permits in hand. It's a go." I can't help but smile. "I'm going to start working for him in a few weeks. Already turned in my notice down at Walker's."

"Hot damn!" he says.

Missy shushes him. "We agreed not to start out cussing around the baby," Missy says. "I know she don't know what you're saying just yet, but now's as good a time as any to break the habit."

"Yes, ma'am!" he says, giving her a crooked salute.

I laugh and grin at Romie, and it pleases me that she manages to smile.

"Redd says he's got a place for you, too." I motion toward his crutch. "Once you're driving again. He'll need somebody to man the forklift."

Missy's mouth drops open. "He can't do that." She turns to Jimbo. "You can't do that. You'll lose your disability!"

Now my own mouth drops open. Did she really say that?

"Aw, no, sweetie" Jimbo says, and he rubs his wife's shoulder to soothe her. "They's still partial disability. And the lawyer says we gonna get so much outta Prospect that I won't need no stupid disability check, anyways. Besides," he says, "I need something to pass my time, entertain me." He looks at me and makes his eyebrows bounce. "Reckon with all the money we'll have, I can put me some shiny mag wheels on that forklift of Redd's, paint some racing stripes on it." He claps me on the arm. "We can drag race around them windmills, whatcha think?"

I laugh, thinking of Bobby and the wild way he drove the golf carts at Etter Vineyards. It's lucky for all of us that he and Jimbo have never met.

Paisley Grace lets out a surprisingly loud and high-pitched wail for a baby so tiny, and Missy bounces her gently. Missy wrinkles her nose and waves a hand in front of her face. "Shew. I think she needs to be changed," she says and heads toward the hallway.

"I'll come with you," Romie says, "help you settle her in."

"Sit," Jimbo says to me. "Stay awhile." He takes a seat in his camo recliner, rests his single crutch against the chair arm.

As soon as the women are out of earshot, I lean toward Jimbo. "There's something I want to ask you." I pause so he'll know this is serious stuff. "You could say this is none of my business, but I feel like it is. I feel like we've been through a lot together, and I want to know the truth."

Jimbo shakes his head and holds up his hands. "So say it."

"Did you throw out the Oxy they prescribed you, or did you sell it?"

His nostrils flare. "What do you think? Tell me, Mister Officer Grodin, what do you think I did?"

It's my turn to hold up my hands. "Look, I just want to know if you sold them to Weasel."

"Have you lost your mind? You think I'm gonna sell pills to the man who sold pills to my wife? The man who helped her get addicted?"

I fix him in the hardest stare I can muster. "You haven't answered my question."

He shoves a finger toward me. "You got no right to ask me such a thing. You—you and your wife who was the first to bring drugs into this here house."

I wince at his words, knowing he's right, but I don't back down. "Answer the question."

"No," he says.

"No, you won't answer, or No, you didn't sell them."

He rubs his forehead, then pinches his bottom lip. Neither of us speaks for a moment.

"Okay," he looks around the room as if searching for what to say. "I sold them. I figured it'll be a while before we get any money coming in here . . . disability, lawsuit, whatever. These things take time." His face reddens and his Adam's apple bobs. He finally meets my stare. "But I never sold them to Weasel. I can't believe you'd think I did such a thing."

I lean toward him and prop my elbows on my knees, lace my fingers together. "Who'd you sell them to?"

RHONDA BROWNING WHITE

"Darius. He stopped by here to check on me, told me if I had any pain pills to get rid of, he wanted 'em."

This is bad. Real bad. "D is on the Oxy? And him working *underground?*"

Jimbo shakes his head. "No. No, I don't think so. H wouldn't do that. See, he cut out the coke a while back, too. His old lady got onto him, said it was either her and the baby, or it was the drugs. Said one of them had to go." He nods. "D chose the right answer."

"So why was he wanting pills?"

"Why does anybody who ain't eating Oxy want it? For the money." He rocks back in his chair and crosses his arms like this conversation is over.

A high-pitched wail—almost a screech—comes from the nursery, and I resist the urge to cover my ears. "Who does D sell them to?"

Jimbo winces and his hands drop from the armrests into his lap. "Aw, Jasper. Can't say for sure, but he probably sold them where everybody sells when they have a lot to move and don't want to parse them out to a bunch of addicts. To Weasel."

A silent moment passes between us, then Jimbo lurches forward, swats at the emptiness below his stump where his calf and ankle and foot belong, his fingers clawing at the air.

I reach a hand toward him. "You okay, bud?"

"Aw, no. I'm not. Sometimes my foot itches so bad I could dig it right off, if it weren't already gone." His lips curl into a grimace. "Phantom pains, they call it."

The baby shrieks again, and I can't help but squeeze shut my eyes, as if this could block out the sound.

"Yeah," Jimbo says, nodding toward the hallway. "That's gonna be rough. They told us that she'll have that high-pitched cry for a long time. It's that neonatal abstinence syndrome Dr. Gloria talked about. Paisley Grace has got it." He stares at his fingers, picks at a nail. "Can you believe they had her on methadone in the hospital? Had to wean her off the Oxy. She was addicted before she was even born." His voice catches, and he swipes at his eyes. "And here I sold more Oxy, thinking it was a smart way to get rid of it and make us some money to live on 'til insurance comes through."

It's like he's apologizing, and I think of what Dr. Gloria said, about accepting an apology, but not excusing it. I realize my hands are fisted, so I flex my fingers and change the subject. "How long will it last?"

"Huh?"

"The neonatal abstinence syndrome. When will it go away?" In EMT school, they never talked to us about the syndrome, but then maybe it's not a thing in North Carolina like it is here. My mind flits to the millions of things Romie is having to learn to be a nurse, and once again I am proud of how smart she is.

"Could be years," Jimbo says, bringing me back to the here and now. His lower lip trembles. "The damage could last a lifetime. No way of knowing just yet. She might have developmental delays . . . you know, not walking soon enough, not talking soon enough, stuff like that."

"But she *will* walk and talk, right?"

Jimbo looks more hopeful. "Yeah, she should. It'll just be—just be a little harder for her than for most." He lets out a shuddering sigh. "I swear, Weasel is gonna pay for this one day. Mark my words."

I think of how Romie and I are the ones who first brought the Oxycontin to Jimbo. It was the pills Paw gave us that Missy took the first time. I reckon Jimbo must figure my train of thought when he speaks.

"Don't go there. It wasn't you and Romie. I sold everything y'all gave me that very same week." He shakes his head. "And yeah, I sold it to Weasel." He grips the arms of his recliner. "It was him who turned around and put them pills right back into Missy's pretty little hands. And not just Oxy—though Oxy was the one what hooked her. He sold her sleeping pills, Xannies, Percs, Vicodin . . . he's a walking pharmacy.

I heard tell he's even moving heroin now. Cheaper than Oxys for them who can't pay. Missy was doing real good, *real good*, I swear it. I thought she was off everything." His voice is tight, and his face is so red I think his head might pop like a blister. "I figure it was after my accident when she got on the pills again." He fiddles with the seam on the chair arm. "When we were in the detox shrink's office at the hospital, she told him she started taking a few Xannies here and there right when she found out she was pregnant. 'Eased her nerves,' she said."

"Jimbo," I say, leaning forward again. "It's an *addiction*. She's gonna need a lot of help fighting this. She might always need help, her whole life through."

He nods. "She's getting it. She's on the methadone now. Every morning. She has to sign in at the Wellness Clinic every single day. And she needs it. Like, she *needs*-it-needs-it. Hates it though. Says she's traded one addiction for another." His smile is strained. "We're a mess, ain't we? A cripple and his junkie family."

"Don't say that. Don't you dare talk like that. You're getting around better than some men with two legs, and your wife and your baby are both alive and here with you." My throat clenches, but I swallow it loose again. "You will get through this. And me and Romie, we're here to help you."

Romie walks into the room as if I summoned her, followed by Missy. "Yes, you know we'll help with whatever it is you two need," Romie says, though I know she has no idea of the gravity of the conversation that Jimbo and I have just had. "Whatever you *three* need," she says and smiles. I want to jump up and hug her.

"Where's Paisley Grace," Jimbo asks, and I realize we are all calling her by both names, and I think this will be how she will always be known.

Missy wipes her hands down her face. "She's sleeping, for however long that lasts." She looks at me. "She doesn't sleep long. It's wearing me out already." She sinks onto the couch.

Romie perches beside her and touches her arm. "Why don't you sleep. Go on to bed, and I'll stay here a while. If she wakes, I'll tend to her so you can rest."

A look passes between Missy and Jimbo, but I don't know what it means. "Ah, we got this," he says. "We gotta get us some practice on this new-parent thing." He grins at Romie, his face brighter. "See, Ro, we're in basic training now." Again he gives that crooked salute. "Ooo-rah!"

After working eight straight at Redd's—Blue Gold Wind Energy—I navigate the switchbacks of Dry Fork Road. I pat the dashboard of Ol' Nellie—that's the nickname I've given my old beater truck—after she handles a devilish, uphill hairpin with little more than a grunt in low gear. "Atta girl." Talking to myself is a habit on this long drive, a way of filling up the lonesome, as the radio was busted when Hippie sold me the truck. I never bothered replacing it because, until I took the job with Redd, I only drove it around Stump Branch. I'll need a whole new truck before winter sets in anyway, because I ain't going to risk breaking down in harsh weather on these two-lane blind curves through the middle of nowhere. For now, I pass the drive time thinking, and there's plenty thinking to be done these days.

I pass the neighboring wind farm and suck in a deep breath, astonished all over again by the grandeur of it all. Though I've driven past these impressive turbines dotting Backbone Mountain dozens of times now, they never cease to awe me with their remarkable stature and the lazy way they turn in the breeze. I'm not too many miles past them when I top out on a knoll and look out on devastation and destruction, what the coal companies call "area mine." (It strikes me how I'm thinking now, how I think *what the coal companies call it*, not what *we* call it—and how it no longer bothers me that I'm not a part of Prospect anymore, not a coal miner, and how a growing part of me is downright proud of that.) The huge dark plateaus of the area mine, what's left after the company has finished plundering the land, are zigzagged with gray mining roads, and the twelve-mile scab where a massive mountain once stood now looks dead, even though it's post-reclamation. Part of the government's bargain in the interest of environmental rehab is that the coal companies have to reclaim the land with foliage. They plant the area mines with patchy-looking lespedeza, a weed that grows so fast they can't even exterminate elsewhere, but it won't hardly grow at all here in this now-toxic soil.

My mouth dries out each time I drive through here, and I down the last of the water in the plastic jug beside me. I won't look away from the wasteland, though. The ghost of the mountain that once stood there, the ruins of her, speaks to me and tells me to look at her, to see what's left of her. Sometimes I think her voice sounds like Romie's, but I decide it's Romie's voice that echoes the mountain's, because the mountain was here first, made by God's own hand.

I try to imagine what the mountain looked like before she was cut down; her bottle-green in the spring, her fiery oranges and reds in the fall, her snow-covered brilliance sparkling in the winter sun. Sometimes she tells me that the work we're doing on Redd's property is important, that it'll save the lives of other mountains like her. She tells me that I am finally doing the right thing, and it's time is long overdue. When I apologize for what's happened to her, she gives absolution, even as she tells me she will never let us forget what has been done to her. When the rivers flood with every hard rain because the spine of her ridges was pushed into valleys as overfill, we will remember her. When the tornadoes rage through, tear manmade things apart because she's no longer here to buffer and block their winds, we will remember her. When our rivers turn orange with mine-acid runoff, and the missing trees that once purified her streams can no longer clean our waters, we will remember her and, she tells me, we will be sorry.

I think about the loss of her every day when I drive past, both coming and going. Stump Branch isn't looking much better, though the mountain Prospect tore up wasn't nearly as large as this one. It's no kind of relief to think devastation of a lesser area is lesser devastation.

I wonder how it will look in a few decades, in a few hundred years. I think about time, about how slowly it drags sometimes, like when we're hurting or ashamed, but how right now it seems to be barreling ahead like a freight train through the good days. The happy times always disappear too quickly, and before we know it, we're eyeball-to-eyeball with another heartache or hardship. The last three weeks have been really good ones, though, and they have passed in a blur.

Romie's nose is in a book every spare moment, since final exams are drawing near. She pops in to check on Missy and Paisley Grace almost every day. Romie told me last night that Missy is still driving herself to the methadone clinic every single day, not missing a dose. Jimbo is doing driver re-education, already far ahead of where he should be with his therapy. Redd offered him a job, but Jimbo hasn't decided if he'll take it, or if he'll stay on the draw until his lawsuit comes due. I hate that kind of thinking. Still, his dedication to walking and driving and getting back to normal is admirable. But then, he has a now-six-pound reason to do that.

Romie and I babysat little Paisley Grace last Saturday to give our friends a date night, and the baby is doing well, considering. She still squalls and screeches like a banshee, and as much as I love to see her sweet little face, those screams make my scalp crawl. I don't know how Jimbo and Missy can stand it day in and day out.

My phone dings, and I see the text from Romie saying she's home. I realize I'm making better time than I thought, so I should get home in time to help her with her homework tonight. I sometimes quiz her on her subjects, making sure I'm keeping my mind as sharp as hers, like Mack suggested years ago. I've decided to take a couple more classes myself next semester now that money is coming in steady again. Redd tells me he'll allow time off to study before exams, and me and Romie—

Romie and I—can do homework together again like we used to in the little house. I like this new normal. It feels a little like . . . well, redemption. I like the feeling so much that I belt out singing Kid Rock's "Born Free," doing my best impersonation of him the rest of the drive home.

When the weekend arrives, I'm up just as early as if I'd been going to work, though it's been in me these last few weeks to sleep in a few hours on Saturday mornings. Romie and I are heading to Summersville and Richwood this morning, where we're meeting up with Winter and her girlfriend, Halsey. Winter has never seen the New River Gorge Bridge, and Halsey has never tasted ramps, which should be against the law for any self-respecting West Virginian. Her parents were more citified, I suppose, having moved across the river to Harper's Ferry from Baltimore.

  Hours later, we meet the ladies at the Richwood Ramp Festival, and the four of us find a local diner in the midst of everything in the downtown that Winter deems *quaint*. I squint at that word, take in my surroundings, reckon I can see why she'd call it that, though it seems plain and normal enough to me.

  The diner, like most of the town during the festival, is heavy with the oniony-garlicky scent of ramps, and I think we'll never get this smell off our skin. My mouth waters just the same, and I give my attention to the orange page of daily specials listing a dozen ramp-heavy offerings.

  Our food arrives, and we dig into our meals, sampling bites from each other's plates, becoming a part of the chatter and clatter of the hometown diner. Halsey shovels an impressive forkful of ramp casserole into her little mouth that seems too small for her round face, and her eyes roll back in her head as she moans. "Where in the world have you been all my life, little ramp?" she says, digging in her fork again. "Sausage, cheese, rice, and *ramps!* Who knew that's the recipe for heaven on a fork?"

  Winter grins, and I'm struck again by how white her teeth appear against her red lipstick and midnight skin. Her dress is the same color red as her lipstick, and I think her striking beauty is too precious for a man, so it's good she's found a woman who can appreciate it proper.

Romie elbows me and smiles. "Whatcha thinking?" she says, and my face warms.

I lean back, drape my arm around her, and stick out my chest. "I'm thinking how special I must be."

Halsey pauses between bites to gape at my arrogance.

Winter never misses a beat. "Special?" she asks in her lilting accent. "Oh, like when-you-rode-the-short-bus special. Yes, I can see that."

We all laugh, then Romie says. "What do you really mean, *special?*"

"A feller would have to be special to sit here amongst three gorgeous ladies. Shoot, I'm looking forward to strolling the streets with y'all, let everybody in town see how important I really am."

Now it's Winter's turn to roll her eyes and groan, and we laugh again.

After we eat, we do just that, stroll through town, check out the festival booths and tents and storefronts, sip samples of local wine and taste sweet treats, in spite of none of us having room in our bellies for extra bites of anything.

I bestow upon Halsey the virtues of a well-made ramp salsa, and the two of us are taste-testing samples of the levels of heat we can stand, when I notice Romie and Winter off to themselves at the next booth, deep in intense conversation. People are milling around them as they stand close, not quite arguing, but not appearing to talk friendly, either. Romie's face shows consternation, and when they both turn to look at me, I know it's me they're discussing, and my gut sinks. It ain't the habanero ramp salsa that makes me feel ill.

Halsey is paying for her purchase, and I touch her arm. "I'm gonna catch up with the ladies over here at the flower booth." I motion to where the two women stand, see Winter hug my wife, Romie swipe at her eyes.

When I reach my wife's side, she's smiling like nothing in the world could be wrong. As soon as she's a few yards from Winter, I touch her elbow and lean to her ear. "What's going on?"

She bats her eyelashes. "Nothing, why?"

My jaw clenches. "That's not true. I saw you and Winter arguing, and you were crying."

She paws at the air. "Aw, that was nothing. A little girl talk. I was feeling a little bit emotional. We aren't mad or anything. Winter likes playing shrink is all . . . sometimes she touches my heartstrings."

I'm confused and say as much, and Romie gives a little laugh, as though I'm being silly.

"It's all good." Her smile is genuine enough, but I detect some kind of worry.

"You'd tell me if there was something wrong?" I ask. "We promised each other, no more secrets."

She searches my face, then glances away before facing me again. "No more secrets. We'll talk about it later. You'll see it's not a thing that has to do with you and me. We were talking about Missy."

I feel myself unclench. Girl talk, after all. I kiss Romie's forehead, and she briefly rests her head against my chest, then she turns and points to the rainbow of blooming plants decorating tiers of shelving in the flower-and-plant tent.

We walk through the rows—evidently, we have to look at every single item the festival has to offer—and Romie pauses to pick up a red geranium and sniff its petals. "Most people don't like the smell of geraniums," she says, "but I've always loved them. These, and the smell of tomato vines. They smell like . . . home."

I wonder at this word from her lips, *home*. I've never heard her say such a thing, and for a second my heart feels like it might bust. My Romie, my Runaway Romie, talking about something that smells like home. As soon as we get back to Stump Branch, I'm gonna put pots of geraniums all over our front porch and back deck and plant a whole garden full of tomato vines. I take the geranium from her hand and carry it to the register.

An hour or so later, I sit on a bench in the shade, babysitting the geranium as the ladies cross the street arm-in-arm to browse yet another shop, where I imagine they'll sniff the same candles and soaps they've smelled in the last half-dozen booths and shops we've visited, then probably again exit the door with nothing.

Two teenage dudes head down the sidewalk in my direction, and I see they're watching the ladies as they walk across the road. The guy wearing a baseball cap backwards sneers and speaks out of the side of his mouth to his friend, loudly enough for anyone around to hear. "Know what the only thing is worse than a bunch of dykes?" He nods toward Romie, Halsey, and Winter.

"Nah, what?" His shorter friend peers at him through thick lenses, as if this is a legitimate question.

"Two white dykes sucking up to a nigger dyke."

Before I can stop myself, I lurch to my feet, the geranium tumbling to the sidewalk. "What did you say?" My face is so close to the taller teen's that I feel his breath on my cheeks.

"Whuuuuut?" he drawls. "I was only joshing. A man like you can take a joke, can't you?"

He steps back, and I step right up against him again, point my finger between his eyes. "You disgust me. I came here with those three women, and one of them is my *wife!* I will clean your clock if I hear you say one more foul word about any of them." I shove my chest against him hard enough to knock him back a step.

He sneers again and holds up his hands, and it's then I remember there are two of them, and they are little more than overgrown children. I whip my head around to see the other guy, whose eyes look like bug

eyes now about to burst right through his thick eyeglasses. He holds his
hands out and shakes his head as if he's scared to death. This ain't his
fight. I turn back to baseball-cap jerk, grab his jacket to hold him still,
and when he snorts a laugh, white-hot heat lights up my head, and I
draw back my fist, ready to knock him into next month.

Fingers gingerly tap my cocked elbow, and I glance back to see
the bug-eyed kid. "Mister, he didn't mean nothing. He's just got a big
mouth, is all. He's sorry. Really. We're both sorry." His lip trembles, and I
drop my fist, but I don't let go of the taller guy's jacket.

The taller kid nods. "Look, man, I didn't know. Sorry 'bout your
wife." I release hold of his jacket, and when he shakes his head, there's
still that curl to his lip that makes me want to punch him even more.
"I don't want no trouble outta you." He takes a step to the side, but he
remains facing me as he walks past me at an angle, his hands still up in
the air. I wonder if I'm doing the right thing, letting him pass, or if he
deserves the pounding I'd like to give him. He's too young to hit, and I'd
likely go to jail if I punched him. I take a deep breath and blow it out,
but the anger is still there. Who is raising that kid, I wonder. What made
him say such a thing unless he learned it at home?

The two reach the bench where I sat, and it's then I notice the
geranium in its busted pot, dirt spilled around it. The guy in the baseball
cap glances down at the geranium and finds the root ball with toe of his
boot, sending it sideways under the bench. He snorts a laugh. "Whoops!"
I fist my hands and move toward them, and the two break into a run,
laughing nervously and shoving each other as they jostle their way
through the crowded street.

"Assholes." I take a deep breath and drop to one knee, scoop the
broken plant as best as I can into what's left of the pot, and dump the
whole mess into the green metal garbage can standing beside the bench.

By the time I've calmed down, hustled to the plant tent, and
scored an even bigger geranium, Romie, Winter, and Halsey come out
of a store and head toward me. It's all I can do not to run toward them,

put my arms around their shoulders, protect them from—from who? A couple of rowdy kids? From the whole crazy world? Yeah, that's what I want to protect them from, from this whole bigoted, sexist, mean, and angry world.

Romie's holding a white paper bag, calling my bluff about not buying anything. She's followed by Winter and Halsey holding hands. She looks at the geranium, and I know she can tell it's a lot bigger than the one I held when she left, and she grins the silliest smile. It's amazing how my wife's smile takes the meanness right outta me.

Romie and Halsey are both wearing cutoff shorts and t-shirts, and I can't help but compare how much prettier my wife looks than Halsey, who is still quite attractive with her fair skin, freckled nose, and reddish-blonde hair. Romie is still slender, though she's filled out now with more womanly curves, no longer the same Bony Romie she was in high school. If she wasn't my wife, I'd sure enough ask her out right here and now.

She catches my gaze, and her face lights up as she crosses the street toward me, grinning even broader now. "What?" I ask.

She shrugs. "Just that expression on your face. You look . . . I dunno. Happy." She bends down and lightly kisses me. "Happier than I've seen you in a long time. You and your pet geranium that has somehow grown larger under your impeccable care."

I laugh, knowing she is right, and I think *she* is happier than I have seen *her* in a long while, too. I wonder if we've a right to this happiness. I take her face in my hands and kiss her more fiercely than is proper for public display. When I release her, she sucks in a breath, and I decide we've paid enough penance through grief and sadness to cover a lifetime of sins. We deserve this happy moment. This one and every single one that follows.

*

The four of us leave Richwood and spend the late afternoon evening ambling through Summersville, walking the wooden boardwalk and stairs that lead down under our nation's longest steel-arch bridge. The ladies stroll ahead, fingering the rhododendron, white pine, and wild roses, while I kneel to check out the craftsmanship of the smooth turn of the pathway, how the deck boards are cut and pieced together to make a curve, instead of a boxy angle. I wonder if I could have done the same on Jimbo's ramp, decide this here kind of work takes a lot of practice, while I hope to never build a wheelchair ramp again in my lifetime.

I catch up to the women as we near the river, and I breathe in deeply, smelling the frothy-wet scent of the rapids. My chest puffs a bit when I tell Winter and Halsey that Daddy worked here for about six months as a welder on the New River Gorge Bridge, when the mines were on strike. It awes me to crane my neck and picture him walking along the catwalk and the incredible arch that spans the whitewater rushing before us. Taking in the natural beauty of these gorgeous mountains makes me wonder how a man could bring himself to intentionally tear one apart. Though I mined underground, the surface was mostly undamaged, and I consider again the layers of harm and wonder . . . how deep is too deep?

Later, we visit the Summersville Dam and stroll the enormous lake's manmade beach. Halsey wants to hike into the woods before it gets dark, and we find one of the trails leading from the lot where we parked. At the base of the trail, a young couple about our age takes a seat on a wooden bench as their baby begins to cry; a plaintive whimpering that strikes me as so different from that of Paisley Grace's desperate howl.

The mother drapes a receiving blanket across her shoulder, fumbles beneath it a moment before the baby's daddy hands off the whimpering bundle. The woman easily maneuvers the baby beneath the blanket, and she catches my gaze as I realize she's lifting breast to mouth, feeding her child beneath the cover.

My face gets hot, and I quickly turn away, see Romie give the young mother the sweetest smile. Romie's hand snakes down and rests low on her belly a moment, before it falls empty to her side. I think of Jimbo and his phantom pains, wonder if Romie feels the same itch of absence where her babies once lived.

"You two coming?" Halsey calls from where she and Winter stand, where the trail disappears deep into the woods.

The four of us take our time walking up the trail through the wooded gorge, not in any hurry to leave this wild, wonderful paradise. As we climb higher, I breathe deep the scent of the hemlocks replacing the cottonwood willows hovering closer to the riverbed. No one but God Himself could create a place so beautiful.

Winter plucks a sprig of pink dogwood and tucks it into Halsey's hair, and I do the same with a white serviceberry blossom. I tell Halsey how Daddy and I used to walk the woods behind our house in Stump Branch, tying long strips of red polyester that Momma would cut for us to tie to the serviceberry trees when they'd bloom.

"Why would you do that? And why red polyester?" she asks.

Romie speaks up from her quiet reverie. "Polyester ribbons won't fade in the sunlight. The serviceberries don't ripen until after the trees are so full of leaves that you can't see the berries. You'll never find them in the woods after the blossoms fall off. The birds'll eat the berries before you can pick them, unless you tie the red ribbons to help you locate the trees again."

I slip an arm around my wife's waist. "Romie makes one fine serviceberry pie," I say. "It's well worth traipsing the woods and tying ribbons to trees just to have a taste."

Winter rubs her belly. "This talk of pie is making me hungry again. Where's that place y'all talked about taking us for dinner?"

Halsey mock-punches Winter's arm. "If I ate as much as you do, I'd be as big as a house." Of the three ladies, she is the only one with a little extra padding, and I wonder if it's a battle she fights to not get too big.

We head back down the trail toward the parking lot, and when Halsey trips yet again over a root or a rock, I reach out to catch her. "I think we ought to change your name to *Autumn*, so y'all can be Winter and Autumn," I say.

Winter deadpans me. "Why Autumn? Why not Spring?"

I give her a serious look. "No, she's definitely an Autumn, because she *falls* all the time."

Romie breaks into a fit of giggles that she can't seem to stop, and soon the four of us are laughing more at her giddiness than at the joke, laughing so hard we have to wipe our eyes.

We're settled at a wooden picnic table on the deck at Smokey's on the Gorge, finding it hard to browse the menu when our eyes are constantly drawn to the incredible view of the river so many miles below us, swaddled between the deepening spring green of the mountains. The air chills a bit as the sun goes down, and the firepits dotting the deck seem to mirror the fiery sunset in the distance. At our table, I help Romie slide her arms into my old gray hoodie, as our waiter, whose nametag reads *Jack*, approaches for our order.

We pore over the wine list, applying every drop of knowledge we learned at the vineyard and in my course at the university. Finally, Winter selects a bottle of wine for the table, but Romie asks for hot tea to warm her insides, instead of a wineglass. It surprises me, knowing how she enjoys West-Virginia-made wines, but I don't say anything, order a few appetizers and water all around to tide us over. "We'll order dinner in a minute, Jack."

"No problem," he says. "Take your time. Live in the moment."

It seems an odd thing to say, but perfect, just the same. *Live in the moment.*

Winter and Halsey excuse themselves to find the ladies room, and I take advantage of our moment alone to pull Romie's back against my chest, hold her close, and breathe the outdoorsy scent of her hair as we stare out at the splendor of these still-standing mountains and the deep gorge between them.

"Live in the moment," she says, mirroring my own reflection on our waiter's words. She tilts her face toward mine. "I have something to tell you," she says. "But promise you'll keep it a secret." She watches me in that rock-hard stare of hers until I promise, and I know there will be gravity in what comes next. She uncrosses my arms from around her, places my hands over her belly. "I'm pregnant." She's still watching my face, and I open my mouth to speak, but my throat is seized so tight I can't make a sound.

I softly cup her belly, imagining the life that grows here: This life that is both mine and hers, a perfect genetic spiral made by—and from—the two of us. I slide my hands to her shoulders, turn her toward me, kiss her so passionately my love says all the words my mouth cannot speak.

CHAPTER THIRTEEN

ROMIE

We are barely in the Jeep and I've yet to buckle up when Jasper starts with the questions I knew were on the way.

"How far along are you?"

"Sixteen weeks."

"How are you feeling?"

"I feel fine, honey."

"Does Winter know? Missy?"

I take his hand in both of mine and squeeze it as he turns to me. "No. No one knows but you. Well . . . you and Doctor Gloria."

"Doc—you've already seen the doctor? What did she say?"

I nod and give him the most reassuring smile I know how to give. "She says everything is fine, Jasper. It's real good."

"Why didn't you tell me sooner?" His eyes search mine, dart back and forth like he's trying to remember everything that's happened in the last four months. "I could have made things easier for you."

I pat his hand. "I wanted to make sure," I say. "I wanted to hear a heartbeat." I blink away the water filling my eyes. "Besides," I say, then suck in a deep breath, make my words a prayer, "she says this pregnancy is different from the other two—that all pregnancies are different—and there's no reason for me to think anything will go wrong." I squeeze his hand. "She reviewed all my medical records from before we moved to Carolina and the ones from Greensboro, said there's no clinical reason for my prior—for the miscarriages. My ultrasound is good. My labs are excellent. She says we have every reason to expect a successful delivery."

Jasper hitches a broken breath, and I realize he's holding back a sob.

"Oh, honey." I hold out my arms, and he holds me as tightly as the console between us will allow.

When he finally releases me, I clasp both of his hands. "I feel *good* about this, Jasper. I really do. I want you to feel good about it, too." I shrug. "I'm not as worried this time as I was before. And I haven't been as sick this time."

"No morning sickness?" he asks.

"Only a couple of days earlier on. It's been weeks ago." I tilt back my head, glance above. "I believe—I *have* to believe—that our baby," I pat the spot low on my belly, "*this* baby—is going to be just fine."

"Dear God," Jasper says, squeezing his eyes shut, "please let it be so. Amen."

"Amen," I say. "It will be. I just know it."

He clears his throat, straightens, lets go of my hands, and buckles his seatbelt. He starts the Jeep, then leans over to kiss me once more before he pulls out of the parking spot. "So . . . does Winter know? Or Missy?"

"No, honey. I already told you. Only Doctor Gloria and you."

He steals a glance at me as he pulls onto the highway. "So that's not what you and Winter were talking about? You both looked at me at the same time, and it felt like you were talking about me." He glances at me again. "You promised, no more secrets."

"It wasn't about you, really. Well, it was in a way, I suppose, but not like you think." This isn't the time or place I wanted to tell him. Yeah, we promised *no more secrets*. I close my eyes for a moment, consider what telling him will mean for all of us. Winter is right: I'm past-due telling him what happened.

"Jasper, you have to promise you won't tell Jimbo. No matter what, this stays here, between us."

He brakes to a stop at the traffic light and turns to face me head-on. "Jimbo? What's Jimbo got to do with anything?" He glances at my belly, then searches my eyes.

"I told you, it's about Missy."

"And me? You said it's about me, too."

I let out a sigh. This is even more complicated than I imagined it would be. The light turns, and we're moving forward again. At least it's a long drive, so we'll have plenty of time to talk. I just don't know how to begin.

"Romie?" Jasper says, prompting me to say more.

"I don't know how to say it right, so I'll just say it." My mouth feels dry. "When Missy and I were in junior high, we hitched a ride, got in a truck with some boys. College boys. They took us to a cabin up in the woods, and they tried to rape us. Tried to rape *me*. I got away and ran all the way to Missy's house." I rub my face, as if I can scrub away the memory. I let out a shuddering huff. "Missy wasn't so lucky."

"Wasn't so . . . you mean . . . ."

"Missy was raped." The words come out a hoarse whisper.

Jasper sucks in a long breath, blows it out in a slow whoosh of air. "And Jimbo doesn't know?"

"No. No one knows except us. And Big Mike and Nick. And Winter."

"Big Mike and Nick? The college boys? You know their *names?* Why haven't you and Missy called the police? Rape is a felony!" His voice grows louder as he talks. "And Winter? You told Winter, but you didn't tell *me?*" He thumps the steering wheel with the heel of his hand.

"I didn't mean to tell her. It just . . . it just came out. You know she's always psychoanalyzing me. Psychoanalyzing everyone. Don't worry. She's not going to tell a soul. I trust her."

His nostrils flare. "Not going to tell a soul? What's with the secret? There are two rapists out there running around, and you and Missy and now Winter are giving them free reign—free hands—to do it again!"

Of all the emotions I thought Jasper would have, being angry with me wasn't one of them. "This isn't my fault! Stop yelling at me like it's my fault!" My throat is tight, and I lower the window, put my face toward the night air. I take a deep breath, swallow the chill down into my chest.

Jasper touches my knee. "Romie, I'm sorry. Honey, really." His voice is soft. "Don't get upset. We don't want you feeling stressed right now. It's not good for the baby. I didn't—I'm not blaming you for what happened."

"You're just blaming me for not telling everyone about it." My voice is weak and whiny, and I hate that I'm sniveling. "Until you've been there, until you've been in that situation, you have no right to judge us."

He's quiet for a moment. "You're right," he whispers. All the same, his hands have a death-grip on the steering wheel, and I know if the light inside the Jeep were brighter, I'd see that his face is red and his knuckles are white.

When I have my emotions under control enough to talk without crying, I speak again, and I'm part proud and part disheartened that my voice sounds cold in my ears. "This is Missy's decision, not mine. She said I gave up my right to say anything the minute I ran from the cabin and left her behind. And she's right."

"My God. Sweetie." Jasper rubs my thigh, slides his hand up and around my shoulder, pulls me toward him and kisses the top of my head. He holds me there as he drives, and I let him. He sniffs deeply. "I'm so glad you ran."

We've driven a few more miles before I tell him how it happened, how Big Mike chased me while Nick stood guard over Missy, and how it was Big Mike who did that awful thing to Missy, not Nick. I confess for the first time that I don't know if Nick was still in the tiny cabin when it happened, or if he stood outside. I never asked Missy, and she never told.

"Do you think the ra—that what happened has anything to do with Missy's drug use?"

"Absolutely. I know for a fact it does."

"She tell you that?"

"Uh-huh. She started using after she saw him again."

"Saw him? She *saw* the guy who did that to her?"

"Big Mike, yes."

"He's running around Stump Branch somewhere, and she's not going to call the law on him? What's his last name? I'll find that s.o.b. and kill him myself!"

Now it's my turn to soothe Jasper instead of him calming me. "It wasn't Stump Branch where she saw him. It was up around Huntington somewhere."

In the light from the dashboard, his face scrunches. "Where? Where exactly did she see him?"

"Around Huntington," I repeat. "At some convenience store somewhere around there. She said . . . she said he was with a woman and two kids. A wife, I guess. He was wearing scrubs."

"Scrubs! A man like that ain't fit to be a nurse."

"Or a doctor." My breath sounds ragged when I let it out. "Lots of people wear scrubs, though. He could be a hospital orderly. Or work in an old folks' home or do home health. He could even be a med student or instructor at Marshall." I press the heels of my hands against my eyes. "I don't know what to think. Sometimes I think Missy is right, not dredging up the past. He could be a good person now, a good husband and good daddy with kids. Accusing him might ruin his innocent family. Maybe he learned from his mistake."

"Raping somebody ain't a mistake, Romie."

The air whooshes out of me. "You ain't telling me anything I don't already know."

He's quiet for several miles, and I feel the day's energy running out of me. I've nearly nodded off when he speaks again.

"You say she saw him when we were in Greensboro?"

"Yeah."

"Then it wasn't loneliness that caused her to start taking pills. It was seeing that man."

I think about this for a minute and what he might be trying to say, when he explains.

"It's not our fault. Us moving away, you not hanging around with her all the time, and Jimbo working double shifts to take up my slack. That wasn't the reason she started using, after all." He lets out an *umphf*. "And Jimbo already told me he sold those Oxys we gave him to Weasel, so we had nothing to do with her getting them. Weasel would have sold those pills in a couple days or less. We didn't head to North Carolina for a few months after."

It feels like he's lifted something off me, something heavy I didn't know I carried. I imagine it lifted off him, as well.

Jasper rubs my leg, his hand warm against my chilly skin. I lean my head against him and let my heavy eyelids rest. As I start to doze, Jasper kisses my head and whispers into my hair. "I'm so glad you ran, Romie."

It's like I've been pardoned from a crime. I'm not sure if I'm imagining or dreaming when I hear Momma's voice in my head, saying, "I'm glad you ran, too, baby."

Three weeks have passed, and Jasper still isn't satisfied until he sits by my side during an ultrasound and sees our baby and hears the heartbeat for himself. I'm not due to see Dr. Gloria for another week yet, but my boss, Dr. Green, is tenderhearted to my pleading, so he takes me to the office suite next to ours every few weeks to see his radiologist friend, and we take a peek at my baby. Dr. Green knows my miscarriage history, and I think he's almost as concerned as I am, though he says he's doing this to ease *my* mind.

"Can you tell what it is?" Jasper asks Donna, the ultrasound tech.

She's quiet for a moment, rolling the cold doppler wand low across my gel-coated abdomen. She looks at me for permission, and I move my head in what I hope is a near-imperceptible *No*. Though I feel good about this pregnancy, I don't want Jasper to get his hopes any higher than they already are by knowing the baby's sex right now.

Donna stares at the screen, pretends to squint, though I know squinting won't make anything appear or disappear on the black-and-white screen. "I can't tell. The baby is small yet. Not too small, mind you. Perfect size for your gestational period. Just small enough and positioned so that I can't see the sex."

Jasper nods, and while he's watching the screen, Donna winks at me. We both know I'm carrying a boy.

Donna pulls out several tissues from a box on her ultrasound trolley, begins to wipe the gel from my belly as the printer spits out a string of pictures. "Everything looks perfect." She slides her stool a few feet over, cracks the door to the exam room and calls down the hallway. "Doctor Green?"

Dr. Green must have been hovering right outside the room, as he pulls open the door and Donna's hand drops from the knob. "Oh!" she says, grinning, and I yank down my shirt self-consciously. "Want to give your opinion?" Donna hands him the strip of black-and-white screenshots she's printed and smiles.

He peers closely and purses his lips as he examines each picture. "Placenta looks good," he mutters. He turns to Donna. "Movement?"

"A little wiggle worm," she says.

He turns his attention back to the pictures, slowly sliding the strip through his hands, studying each screenshot intently. He nods, then beams at us. "Looks fantastic! Barring any changes or concerns, we'll let Doctor Gloria Samuel take over the ultrasounds from here on out. Agreed?"

"Yes, sir!" Jasper says.

Dr. Green's head bobs, and he hands the photo strip to Donna. He beams at me, and I sense that he's proud of me. He nods once more, then slips out the tiny room without another word.

After I'm dressed again and we've left the medical arts building, we decide we're getting hungry. It's finally stopped raining for the first time in three days, and though it's early evening, the sun has peeked out, and it seems like a good sign. We pick up a carryout pizza at Alfredo's for dinner, and when we're again on the road, Jasper turns to me. "You ready to tell Jimbo and Missy the good news?"

Jasper's done a fine job of keeping my pregnancy secret from everyone except Redd, as he claimed Redd needed to know. Jasper insisted Redd give him time off to come with me to each of my appointments. I know he's afraid I'll get bad news, and he wants to be there for me this time if, God forbid, it happens again.

I put my hands over the swelling that seems to have appeared from nowhere this past week. "If we don't tell them, they're gonna figure it out any day now. Look at this little baby bump. I've put on three pounds in the last week."

Jasper *pshhaws* me. "Three pounds in a week. Shoot, I ate a three-pound cheeseburger for lunch today." He rubs his belly. "No one's said a word about my burger bump."

I grin and shake my head. "You're an idiot, Mister Grodin."

"What say we run this pizza on over to their place, make a party of it?"

I like the idea, and I fish my phone out of my purse. "Let me call to make sure they're home first. Don't want to get up there and find out they're gone. Now that Jimbo's driving again, seems he finds any excuse to make a run into town."

"Good idea."

I'm scrolling my recent contacts when Jasper's cell plays John Mellencamp. "Conjure the devil," he says. "Get that, would you?" He hands his phone to me so he can focus on the road.

I press the speakerphone key. "This is Mister Grodin's *sexetary*. How may I help you?"

Jasper chuckles, then Jimbo's panicked voice slices the air. "Put

Jasper on!"

I lift the phone closer to Jasper's face. "Jimbo," Jasper says. "I'm here, buddy."

"Can Romie hear? Take me off the speakerphone. Now!"

I bristle at his insinuation that I shouldn't hear what he has to say, and I move to take the phone off speaker, but Jasper shakes his head.

"It's just me now. Go ahead."

"I need you here. Right now!" He sounds panicked.

I close my eyes. Missy must be stoned again.

"Okay, we were just calling to say we're on the way. We were gonna bring—"

"Jasper," Jimbo's voice catches, and it's then I know he's crying. "I did it."

My body must know the gravity of what has happened before my brain puts two and two together, because a chill races across me, and I shudder.

"I shot Weasel," Jimbo says in a pitiful voice I hardly recognize. "I killed him, Jasper. I killed Weasel." Jimbo breaks into a howl that makes the hair on my neck rise.

"Okay, buddy. Okay," Jasper says, but I know he knows that it's not okay, that nothing will ever be okay for Jimbo again. "Take a deep breath and stay calm." Even as he says this, he floors the gas pedal, and we're taking turns faster than is probably safe. I hold on to the overhead grab bar, but I don't say a word.

"Are you sure he's . . . dead?"

"He's *dead!* I'm *certain* he's dead!" Jimbo is breathing hard into the phone, creating a whooshing sound my own breathing tries to match.

"Have you called 9-1-1?"

Jasper is answered by a whimper.

"Jimbo. Jimbo, are you with me?"

"Yes. I mean, no. No, I haven't called anybody but you."

"Okay, we're on the way, hang on tight."

I think he's about to hang up, and I make a baby-rocking motion with my arms. Jasper nods.

"Hey, buddy? Where's Missy and Paisley Grace?"

"Missy's here in the yard with Weasel. The baby's in her bedroom." He lets out another wail. "Oh, God. Oh, God, Jasper. I killed him *dead*. What have I done?"

My mind is racing, and I speak before I realize Jimbo will know I can hear what he's said. "Where in the yard?" I imagine Weasel's body lying splayed by the road with Missy standing over him.

"I covered him. I put a tarp over him. Hurry. Please, please, *hurry*."

I grip the grab bar tighter as Jasper wheels off the highway onto the single-lane country road that leads up the mountain to Jimbo and Missy's house. I hear the pizza on the back seat crash to the floor, but I don't bother turning around.

"We're turning up the hill now, Jimbo. Almost there," Jasper says. "Almost there."

"Okay. Okay. I'll be waiting."

He hangs up, and I place Jasper's phone into the console. I pick up mine and turn to Jasper. "You want me to call 911, or do we wait until we get there?"

Jasper's lips are in a straight line, and he runs a hand through his hair. "No. Not yet. Let's check on Missy and the baby, see what happened first. Weasel ain't gonna get any deader if we hold off a minute."

I blow out a long breath.

Jasper again rakes his hair with his fingers. "I can't even believe I said those words . . . that we're having this conversation. This is crazy."

"It's terrible. And terrifying."

He lets off the gas and turns to me. "Want me to take you home? This is a lot to deal with. I don't want you to get upset and stressed out. You know . . . for the baby."

"It's a little late not to get upset and stressed out." I reach for his hand and squeeze it in both of mine. "I really want to be with *you* right now. And I want to make sure Paisley Grace is okay, and Missy. I'd be freaking out if I were home while this is going on. When the police arrive . . . ." I imagine cop cars all over the yard, officers swooping in, arresting Jimbo; and Missy too stoned or too distraught to care for the baby; and Paisley Grace's screeching wails keeping anyone from holding her close and caring for her. No, I have to be there. This time, I won't leave Missy alone.

"Ohhhh," Jasper says on a breath. "This is gonna be bad. So very, very bad."

No matter how we imagined it, seeing it is worse.

As we round the bend and top out on the wooded knoll, Jimbo's truck sits on the side of the road about two-hundred yards from their home, a copse of trees partially shielding it from view of his house. From the road, there's a clear view of the front and side of their split-level, of Weasel's blue Camaro parked in the lower branch of the Y-shaped driveway, the part leading to Missy's salon.

"Why is Jimbo's truck here?" I ask.

"He must have seen Weasel's car and parked here, then crutch-walked to the house to sneak up on him," Jasper says.

As Jasper drive's closer, I see that Weasel's safety-glass windshield is crackled into a million sparkling pieces, and it's sagging limply toward the Camaro's interior. There's a large empty hole directly over the steering wheel. A blue tarp nearly matching his car is spread on the ground several yards from the driver's side door, and Missy's on her knees beside it. One corner is pulled back, revealing, I'm guessing, Weasel's face. Baby Paisley Grace is lying on the ground an arm's reach away, and even from this distance, I see her little fists and feet flailing in the air.

Jimbo appears from the back of the house, and he turns and limps toward the house again, then pivots awkwardly and lopes back again toward Weasel's car, using an odd-looking cane for balance. He either hears or sees us, and he stops, then stumbles toward our Jeep as we pull into the upper part of the driveway, his free arm pumping the air.

"That's a gun," Jasper says, his arm flying out in front of me, as if he can protect me if Jimbo were to shoot. He lowers the window. "Stop!" he shouts. "Put that gun down!"

Jimbo stops, and there's a wildness that has lit fire inside him that I have never seen before. His eyes—his entire face—is red and crazed. "I would *never* hurt you! Neither of you! *Never!*" He lifts the gun he holds by the barrel end, flings it toward the hardtop road, and it spins end over end until it thuds and bounces and finally spats harmlessly in his muddy yard. He's wobbly, and he wavers for a moment, hops a time or two, then regains his balance, but looks unsteady in stance and state.

"Wait here," Jasper says to me, and he opens the door and steps out, closing it behind him.

He's got both hands held in front of him, and I can't tell if he's planning to catch Jimbo, hug him, or intercept him, though without the gun, Jimbo looks helpless. His face crumbles, and a low-throated moan turns into a wail as Jimbo's head drops and his shoulders quake.

"Here, here, now." Jasper's voice coming through the window is soft, soothing, and tears spring to my eyes. He slowly steps up to Jimbo, and Jimbo leans into him as Jasper holds him close, pats his back as he sobs.

I quietly open the passenger door and climb out, step gingerly through the water-slogged grass, trying not to fall or saturate my shoes. I round the back of the Jeep, making sure to keep the car between me and Jimbo until I can be sure he won't do something else crazy.

I hate this. I hate the way I'm afraid of one of my oldest—my dearest—friends, hate that it has come to this. When I reach the back of the Jeep, I see Missy and hear staccato shrieks from Paisley Grace, and I forget to be afraid. I round the driver's side, walk right past Jasper and Jimbo, and make a weak-legged jog toward the baby.

Missy has flung the blue tarp to uncover Weasel's legs, and it appears she's giving him a pat down.

"What are you doing?" I ask as I near her.

She never looks up, but digs deep into Weasel's pocket, where she pulls out a roll of bills, shoves it into her jeans, then searches his other pockets. "Getting my money back."

I bend and scoop up Paisley Grace. The footie pajamas she's wearing are soaked on the back where she's been lying on the ground, and I slide her inside my jacket to warm her, hold her close against my chest, and gently bounce her. "Shhhh. Shhhh, It's okay, sweet one," I whisper into her ear. Then I turn back to Missy. "Missy, get up from there."

She pulls on the tarp until Weasel is completely covered. When she stands, her jeans are muddy from the knees down, and her hands and shirt are bloodstained. Without giving me a passing glance, she heads right for the Camaro, yanks open the door, and leans inside.

"Get out of there! Missy!" My shouting brings another screech from the baby.

Missy keeps searching, but for what I don't know.

"It's a crime scene, Missy. You don't want your fingerprints all over everything!" She slides into the car, and for a moment, I think she's planning to drive away. Then she climbs out, holding a wrinkled and worn paper bag in one hand, and a half-dozen or so plastic baggies filled with pills and who knows what else in the other. "Put that back!" I yell at her.

A lazy half-smile that in no way fits this situation spreads across her tear-streaked face, and it's then that I realize she's absolutely stoned. She holds up the bags. "He ain't gonna need these. Don't want 'em to go to waste."

Behind me, Jimbo is still sobbing and wailing. I can't deal with this craziness, and I turn and head back toward the Jeep with Paisley Grace. "Jasper," I say as I pass by him. "We've got to call 9-1-1 before someone else does."

Jimbo turns to me, wide-eyed. "Wait. We can move him. Get rid of the car. Nobody has to know."

Jasper gapes at his best friend since childhood, and it's a moment before he manages to speak. He puts a hand on Jimbo's shoulder. "You're in shock, buddy. Looky here," he says and waves a hand across the yard. "There's no covering up what's happened here." Jasper rakes his hair again. "What *did* happen here, anyway?"

Jimbo turns and surveys the scene, and it's almost as if he's seeing it for the first time. He shakes his head, and it's a full minute before he talks. "I saw his car in the driveway. I *told* him!" He hiccups a breath. "I've *told* him a hunnerd times to stay away from here. I warned him and warned him and warned him." He searches Jasper's face. "You know that. You know I warned him."

Jasper stays quiet.

"I just—I shot out his windshield. I wanted him to know I was serious, that I ain't playing." He slowly shakes his head as if he's dazed, and I think he must be in shock. "He came running out of the house, screaming at me. I wasn't gonna shoot him. I swear it. It was nowhere in my mind to shoot him. I only wanted to scare him. But then . . . ." He looks out over the yard, maybe seeing it play out again, and his voice grows rough. "Then here comes Missy behind him." Jimbo's face crumbles as he speaks, and he smacks at his upper arm. "She's got a rubber tourniquet hanging from her arm! Weasel was shooting her up! My wife! Little Paisley Grace's momma!"

Jimbo sniffs deeply, then his lips curl back. "I shot the sonofabitch. Killed him *dead*." It's as if he realizes what he's saying, and all the anger in him pours out at once, and he drops to his knees on the muddy ground and rocks back and forth as he howls.

Jasper leans over him, a hand on his back, then looks up at me. "I think he's in shock. Go in the house and get him a blanket, but don't touch anything."

"What are we gonna do?" Jimbo wails. "We have to clean this up!"

Jasper grips Jimbo's shoulder. "Any minute a car will drive up or down this road, and we've all had it. Missy's covered in mud and blood, and Paisley Grace hasn't stopped crying since we pulled up."

"She's always crying," Jimbo's voice is whiny and weak, defeated. He turns then to find Missy, sees she's moping toward the salon door, half-dragging her feet, the paper bag and the baggies dangling from her hands. Jimbo lurches to his feet, tries to run toward her, but loses his footing and falls face first. He digs at the saturated ground, trying to stand, before he screams like a wounded animal.

Jasper rushes to his side, but Jimbo shoves him backward. "Stop her!" he says, pointing a mud-covered hand toward Missy. "Take them pills away from her!"

Jasper bolts into a run, and he grabs Missy by the wrists, shakes her hands until she drops all she's holding. She strikes out at him, swinging wildly and weakly, missing him with every attempted blow. She falls to the ground, and when she reaches for the paper bag, Jasper picks her up by the waist and holds onto her as she kicks and screams for him to let her go. He turns his head toward me just long enough to shout, "Call 9-1-1. *Now!*"

Not one, but three, police cars arrive, along with a first-responder fire truck, followed by an ambulance. A short time later, a forensics van shows up, and behind that, a white van that I recognize as the coroner's. Red, blue, and yellow lights slash through the dusk, rhythmically splashing across the house, the yard, and our vehicles, strobing and smearing until my head begins to throb. Nauseous, I bend and rest my hands on my knees.

"Ma'am?" a tall, thin paramedic asks. "Are you okay?"

I squint and wave a hand toward the lights. "They're blinding me.

Can't you turn them off?"

The state trooper—his name badge reads *Garrett*—standing near her shoulder nods, then circles his hand over his head as if he's twirling a lasso. "Cut the lights!" One by one, the flashing lights on the county and state vehicles are turned off, though their headlights stay lit.

The lack of lighting does little to soothe my headache. "Can I get an Advil or something?" I ask the paramedic. "My head is killing me."

She eyes me a moment. "Are you on anything else?"

I shake my head. "No. I don't do drugs." I follow her gaze toward where Missy sits on the back edge of the ambulance, another paramedic and a statey attending her. "Yeah, just her. She's on God only knows what. Oxy, probably. Maybe he-heroin." I nearly choke on the word. "There was a tourniquet. . .."

She presses her lips together but doesn't speak.

"I'm pregnant," I say, and despite everything going on around me, something in my chest lightens. "I should tell you that. Ibuprofen's safe though, right?"

The critical look on her face softens. "Yes, it's safe in a small dose. I'll give you two 200-milligram tablets. Start with just one for now. If your head is still hurting in thirty minutes, you can take the other one."

"Thank you."

The blond-haired trooper who has been interviewing Jasper at the corner of the house walks away, heads toward his car, where Jimbo sits handcuffed in the back. Jasper walks to me, nods respectfully at the paramedic, then his forehead creases when she offers me a small bottle of water and shakes two brown tablets out of a small packet into her gloved hands.

"You okay?" He touches my arm, then looks toward the woman. "Is she okay?"

I nod and lift the bottle to my lips.

The paramedic eyes him before answering. "She'll be fine. Likely just a stress headache."

Jasper slides an arm around me. "They want us down at the station, Romie. We'll have to give formal statements."

"What about Missy and the baby?" I ask.

As if in answer, the trooper at the back of the ambulance helps Missy stand, then he turns her around, handcuffs her, and leads her to the squad car behind the one holding Jasper.

"What about Paisley Grace?" Jasper asks before I can form the words. "The baby," he clarifies.

We all look to the first-responder fire truck, where a burly firefighter's massive hands seem to shrink Paisley Grace as he holds her blanket-wrapped body to his chest. For now, she has stopped crying, but I wonder how quickly he'll pass her off once she starts screaming again.

"Can she ride with us?" I ask Trooper Garrett, who hasn't left the paramedic's side.

"No ma'am, I'm afraid not," he says. "Child Protective Services is on the way."

"No, you don't understand," Jasper says. "We're her godparents. We help tend to her when . . . we help them out when they need it. They don't have any family 'round here."

"You can ask Jimbo," I say. "Or Missy. Ask them, and they'll tell you it's okay for us to take her." A hand is put on top of Missy's head, and she's guided into the back of a squad car. I see Jimbo turned in his seat, looking behind him, watching it happen, watching his wife being arrested.

The trooper follows my stare, then looks back at me with a hardened expression. He puts his hands on his hips. "We'll sort all this out down at the station. For now, protocol says that CPS has to take her." Then his voice softens. "If you want," he says, "you can go inside and put together a diaper bag and a few clothes for her. And some bottles with formula."

This last is more than I can take. I stifle a sob and drop my pounding head into my hands, as if holding onto it tightly will keep it from exploding into a million pieces.

It's nearly two in the morning when Jasper and I finally drag ourselves up the steps and into our home. It seems we've answered a million questions about Jimbo, about Missy, about Weasel, about the baby, and about ourselves. We filled out paperwork, writing down references, our incomes, trying to guestimate our living expenses so we can appease CPS and get temporary custody of Paisley Grace. The social worker said it helps that I'm a nursing student and Jasper and I are both employed. She said it looks good on us that our house is paid for. We swore oaths before a messy-haired magistrate who appeared worn out with cases like this one, a fine sheen of sweat glistening on her dark forehead as if listening to our stories was hard labor—and I reckon it was, a heavy weight she lifts each time people like us open our mouths.

People like us. I can't believe what has become of us, of our best friends, of their sweet little baby girl.

We hope to hear tomorrow—*today*—that we can go back to pick up Paisley Grace. For tonight, what's left of it, she'll stay with a foster family, and I can only pray it's someone who will be good to her.

Pray. It registers with me that a week ago, I'd never considered praying for a thing, didn't believe it mattered, but now I can't imagine doing anything else.

I grab a couple bottles of water from the refrigerator and head toward the bedroom. We are mud-streaked and need showers, but neither of us have the energy. We're physically spent and emotionally sapped. "Let's just throw a sheet over the comforter and grab a blanket," I say. "I don't want to climb into our clean bed like this."

Jasper nods and heads toward the linen closet. His cell phone rings, and we both stare as it vibrates against the nightstand. It rings again, and neither of us want him to answer it, want to know what fresh new tragedy waits at the other end.

He places the linens on the bed and answers his cell. "Yes, this is him," he says. "Me. Jasper Grodin." His jaw grows slack as he listens, and his expression is part confusion, part amusement. "Okay, yes. I'll be right there."

"What?" I say as he slides his phone into his jeans pocket.

"You ain't gonna believe this. They're letting Missy go. She's out. We need to go get her and the baby."

"She's *out*? I thought they were pressing charges. Did she post bail? How?"

"I don't know. All I know is that they need me to come get her."

"I'm going with you."

"No, sweetie. You stay here. Get in the bed. You need your rest." He pulls me to him, kisses the top of my head, and the weight of his arms around my shoulders tells me he's exhausted.

"I'll rest in the Jeep," I say. "You're worn out, too, and I can't have you falling asleep at the wheel." He's too tired to argue, proving my point.

We're quiet most of the way into town, but as we near the station, Jasper speaks. "I don't know why they didn't keep her. It would be the best thing for her, you know. Help her dry out."

"Mm-hmm." I'm too tired to talk anymore.

"You know she's gonna get home and dig out some more pills or something. Hell, the police didn't even go into the house! What kind of investigation is that?"

I shrug. "Maybe they went inside after we left."

"Doubt it," he says. His voice is tight and gruff, more than just tired. His jaw muscle flexes. "I don't even want to see her. I'm so mad at her I could wring her sorry neck!"

I think about this a minute, realize I should probably be angry, too, but I'm too tired to be mad. Besides, Jasper is furious enough for the both of us. He thumps his hand hard against the steering wheel, startling me.

"You know Jimbo wouldn't have laid a hand on Weasel, if Missy hadn't called that piece of trash to come up there."

"How do you know she called?"

"You think Weasel would just show up with a needle and heroin? Out of the blue?" He shakes his head. "No. No way. She's called him. This is her fault. Just like it's her fault that Paisley Grace is in the shape she's in. That selfish woman defiled the very blood of that baby girl, and God only knows how long that little girl'll pay the price for her momma's sins."

I'm quiet for a moment, study on his words before I speak softly. "You know it's an addiction, Jasper. You know how it works; you've got enough medical background to know that opioids aren't something you can kick just because you want to. She's been trying." I swallow hard and repeat both her and Jimbo's words, likely their mantra. "She's been trying *real* hard."

He grunts, and I realize he's just blowing off steam, saying these things to me so he can get them out of his head, so he won't say them to Missy.

We drive into the station lot and Jasper pulls into a parking space. I'm surprised to see how many civilian cars are here at this ungodly hour. He places a hand on my knee. "Look, I know we're worn to a nub, but I think we should bring Missy and Paisley Grace home with us. I don't want her back in that house until one of us can go up there and take a good look around, see if we can find where she hides her stash."

I'm too tired to argue, so I nod. He's right, anyway.

I start to reach for the door handle, but he covers my hand with his own. "You stay in here. This might take a bit. There might be more papers to fill out or something. Lean back the seat and try to sleep." He pushes my hair away from my face and kisses me softly. "I have a feeling we won't be getting much rest this weekend."

*

Deep into dreaming, I hear babies crying, and the sound chills me. In my dream, I'm frightened by the falling babies—though I've never been afraid of them before. I search all around me, but I don't see them. I try to run, but the high-pitched wailing surrounds me, and I can't get away from it.

I awake to Jasper shaking me. "Romie. *Romie.* Can't you hear that?"

I blink and try to orient myself. I'm at home in my bed, though the crying babies—or *baby*—is still squalling. It takes me another second or two to realize it's Paisley Grace who I'm hearing, and she's here in our house. Startled, I sit up, though my brain is still cobwebby.

"I can't go in and check on her myself," Jasper says. "I don't know if Missy is dressed and whatnot. Seems like the baby's been crying for a full five minutes." He must see that I'm not fully awake, and he rubs my arm. "I'm sorry, sweetie. I know you're exhausted. I'd go in there, but it's not proper. Missy could be naked or something. I just don't know."

I swing my feet over the side of the bed, and they thump the floor like lead blocks. "S'okay," I mumble. I traipse down the short hallway, across the living room and kitchen, into the longer hallway that leads to two spare bedrooms, one of which is erupting with shrieks. I knock, realize there's no way Missy could hear me over the caterwauling, and open the door a bit, peek around it. Missy's eyes are shut, and she is holding Paisley Grace against her chest, one hand on the back of the baby's head, gently bouncing as she sits on the edge of the bed. In the full daylight breaking around the window blinds, I see the purplish circles around her eyes and swelling from a morning of crying.

"You look as tired as I feel," I say, and her eyelids flutter open. She looks weak, weaker than I recall ever seeing her. Though it's only been about four days since we sat in her salon and dished gossip and gushed over Paisley Grace's new summer wardrobe, Missy looks like a different person. Her lush auburn curls are fuzzy, and she looks like she's lost a good ten pounds—not that she had any extra to lose. How can a person decompensate so quickly? Go downhill like a sled on ice in a matter of days?

For the first time, I see her not just as a best friend, but like a nurse assesses a patient: she is pale beyond her usual fair skin, and her lips are almost gray. Her back is hunched so far over that her elbows are grazing her legs as she bounces. "You're *peak-ed*," I whisper. "Here," I say, reaching for the baby. "Let me take her a minute."

When Paisley Grace is in my arms, Missy almost melts into the mattress. I hum in the baby's ear, breathe deep of her baby-lotion fragrance, rock her gently in my arms. Her cries slow to a whimper, and I am thankful that whatever foster parent watched her those last hours kept her clean and dry. I balance the baby, and with a free hand, I pull the covers up over my friend. "You rest. It's been a hard night."

"And morning," she mumbles. "What time is it?"

I glance at my wrist out of habit, realize I'm not wearing a watch. "Not sure. I'd guess around nine or ten. We didn't get to bed until what? Four or five?"

Missy snakes a hand out from under the blanket, pats the bed beside her. "Here. You two lie down."

I consider this a moment as I make shushing sounds in the baby's ear.

"She sometimes sleeps better between me and Jimbo." A deep breath whooshes out. "Guess she'll have to get over that, won't she."

I round the bed, slide down the covers, and lay Paisley Grace beside her momma. If it'll keep the baby quiet so the four of us can get a little more sleep, it's worth it, so I crawl in bed and cover us. I roll to face the baby and Missy, fight the urge to curl around the tiny bundle, hold her tightly against me as if she were my own. Instead, I slide a hand beneath the covers, cup it low over my belly where my own child rests inside me. Paisley Grace puts a tiny fist in her mouth and hushes.

I don't remember shutting my eyes when Missy's voice causes them to open again.

"Are you going to ask me?" she says softly.

"What?" I whisper, not wanting to rouse Paisley Grace now that she's quieted.

"About the heroin." Her voice is tired, flat.

I don't want to have this conversation, not now, maybe not ever. But if she needs to talk, I reckon I need to listen. "I figure you'll tell me, if you want me to know."

She huffs a wry laugh. "Since when has me wanting you to know something ever stopped you from prying?"

Our eyes meet across the little lump between us, and we offer tired grins to each other. I ponder over what little things and what big things, over the years, we have done to hurt one another.

Missy inhales deeply, as if fortifying herself for what she's about to say. "I stopped the methadone the day after they weaned off Paisley Grace." She gently strokes a tiny tear from the baby's cheek with a finger. "I dunno. I guess I figured if this little bitty baby was strong enough to kick, so was I." She's quiet for a moment. "Except I wasn't."

I want to reach out a hand to her, to let her know it's okay, but I think of Jasper's words, about how she "defiled the blood" of Baby Paisley Grace, and I know it's not okay. It'll never be okay.

"I blamed you," she says, and I blink hard at her words. I don't know how I feel about her admission, or what to say in this silence that lengthens between us.

"I blamed Jimbo, too," she finally says. "Even blamed this sweet, innocent, little baby." She tenderly smooths hair from Paisley Grace's forehead. "But sitting in that holding tank, smelling the stink of piss and sweat, doubled over with stomach cramps and dry heaves. . . well, there was no denying it. This is nobody's fault but mine. Even what Jimbo did . . . it was my fault."

The words are out of me before I can stop them, voicing Jasper's suspicion of how it all went down. "Did you call him?" When her face goes blank, I explain. "Weasel. Did you call Weasel to bring those drugs to you?"

She grimaces and nods almost imperceptibly. "I wanted some Oxy. But when he got there, I told him no. I told him I changed my mind about it, didn't want to feed that beast, but I told him I'd like some Xannies, or Percs, or even a Valium. Just something mild to take the edge off." She reaches across the baby and touches my arm. "Understand: I was grinding my teeth, and the diarrhea was disgusting," she says, clenching her teeth as she speaks. "You have no idea how that kind of painful need—that kind of *desperation*—feels. It's God-awful." She sniffs long and deep, rubs at her running nose. "The heroin was his idea. I said no at first, but he said it was the best thing. 'A cure,' he called it. Romie, I hurt so bad I was clenching my gut. I couldn't—I *didn't*—I didn't say no a second time."

She snivels and shivers, and I watch the watermark of one of her tears on the pillowcase grow, unable to take in the pain in her eyes.

"I am going into rehab," she says. "Inpatient rehab this time. Thirty days."

I fully face her now. This is exactly what she needs. "Yes, Missy. Yes." My throat tightens as I try not to cry.

"It's the only way the judge would let me come home. I have to check in on Monday—tomorrow, I guess. She said she'd put out a warrant and have me arrested if I don't show up." She fishes in the bed for my hand, takes it in hers and squeezes. "Romie, I need you to take care of Paisley Grace. Would you do that for me? You and Jasper?"

I don't even breathe before I answer. "Yes. Yes, of course."

Missy's swallow is so loud I hear it. "You'll be a better mother to her than I am, anyway."

"Don't you—don't you *dare* say that, Missy. Don't ever say that. Look at her." I pull my hand away from Missy's, gently stroke the baby's plump, pink cheek, notice how quickly the downy hair on her skin is disappearing. "She's beautiful. She's healthy. She's getting stronger every day." I move my hand to Missy's cheek now, make her look me in the eyes, make her take in the truth behind my words. "You've done this for her. You brought her into this world, and you've fed her, clothed her, and taken care of her when all the odds were against you. Against you, against her, and against Jimbo, too. You three have had a time of it."

Missy rolls onto her back, cries and squeezes shut her eyes, but she doesn't speak until she gets herself under control. "One more thing," she says, and I feel myself brace for what's next. "I want you to take her to church."

I puzzle a moment at her words. "Church? She's just a baby. What good's that gonna do?"

"I want her to start church early. Maybe if I'd gone to church regular, if me and Jimbo'd gone regular, maybe we wouldn't be in this kinda shape." She turns in the bed to fully face me, touches my shoulder with a fingertip. "Maybe you and Jasper need to go regular, too."

I consider this a moment, recall Sundays and Wednesday nights in church with my momma and daddy. I think of going with my momaw, and of having to pay the preacher rent on my parents' graves—still having to pay rent for them to lie in the ground outside the church. I believe in God, believe in Jesus and the Holy Ghost, too, but I have trouble believing in church. "What's got you thinking along this line, Missy. It doesn't sound at all like you."

She searches my face. "She prayed with me. Prayed *for* me."

"Who?" I can't follow her train of thought, wonder if drugs have done this to her.

"The social worker at the jail. She told me that God already knew that I was going to do drugs when I was born, even before I was born. That He already knew I'd go from Oxy to heroin, and that Jimbo would—that he'd . . .." She sniffs loud and long, somehow manages to calm herself. "God knew all that even before He let me and Jimbo get born! See Romie? He let His only Son die for me, even though He knew

I'd mess up, and even though He knows I'm gonna mess up again and again and again." She grins now, then chuckles. "She said God gives us grace. And when she said that, I plain out got the giggles. I couldn't stop laughing, and it almost made her mad, I could tell. But then I told her how my baby's name is Grace, and how He really did give me Grace in baby form.

"She started laughing, too, Romie, and then once we got it out of our system and got settled, she prayed for me. And soon I was praying right along with her. I was thanking God for giving me real grace and Baby Grace, and I was thanking Him for forgiving me for everything I've done and everything I'm gonna mess up and do next." Her eyes shimmer, and my own begin to water.

"See, Romie, He already knows everything. And He forgives me *anyway*." She smiles at me. "That's the purest kind of love there is," she whispers.

Missy puts her hand on my cheek and wipes my now-damp face. "I want Paisley Grace to know that kind of love. I want you and Jasper to know it, too. And Jimbo. I really, really, *really* want Jimbo to know it."

I swallow loose the tight feeling in my throat. "When you get out of rehab, let's plan a Sunday, and all of us will go to church together."

She flops onto her back and stares at the ceiling, and her words come out strangled. "If ever I do get out of rehab. For good, I mean."

"You *will!* Inpatient rehab is exactly what you need. It's intensive, and it'll work. When you get out, this sweet little girl will be ready for you to hold her in your arms again." And then I say what is unlikely, but a heartfelt prayer, nonetheless. "And Jimbo will be back home before you know it. You'll be clean, this sweet little baby will be healthy, and the three of you can put this nightmare behind you."

Missy's stare is gaunt, haunted. "Jimbo won't be coming home for many years, if ever."

"You don't know that. These were extenuating circumstances," I say with more confidence than I feel. "Don't go convicting him before he's even been tried."

"The paramedic. The one who was in the back of the ambulance with me and the state trooper—I can't remember their names. She told the trooper she had seen Jimbo and Weasel down at the 7-Eleven in the parking lot. Said Jimbo shouted in front of God and everybody that he was gonna kill Weasel. Said Jimbo was reaching in behind him for a shotgun when Weasel took off in his car. She said probably a dozen people or more seen and heard it all. She said she had her little son with her, and that's the only reason she tore outta there instead of stopping to call the law. That trooper wrote down everything she said." Missy snivels and wipes her nose on the back of her hand. "He said that sounds like pre-meditation."

I turn, squinting against the light from the window and grope for the box of tissues on the nightstand. I hand a couple to Missy, then pull one and dab at my own eyes.

"That paramedic went so far as to say that, maybe if she'd reported it, she might could have saved Weasel's life—'cept she kept calling him, 'that boy,' and 'that young man,' making him sound all innocent. Hell, he's older than we are, and he sure ain't innocent."

I don't say anything, trying to envision Jimbo and Weasel in an argument at 7-Eleven, and I wonder when it happened.

"Jimbo's been vocal about it, about killing Weasel," Missy says, "that's for certain. But I never really thought he had it in him. I heard him say the same thing about Weasel to Darius a while back, and I know he's probably told everybody else he's come across. He had a lot of hate for that man."

I don't tell her that his hate was justified. I don't tell her that Jimbo had warned Weasel many times to stay off his property, and that even Jasper had flung a board at him and told him to stay away. I don't tell her that her own phone call to Weasel put this entire dreadful happening into motion. I don't tell her because the sorrow in her eyes tells me she already knows.

Paisley Grace wakes us, wakes me, at least, wiggling and crying, her tight little fist bumping against my face. I rise on an elbow, try to gather my thoughts, and when everything comes back to me, I drop my head back onto the pillow. She's insistent, though, and when the odor of ammonia reaches my nose, I'm fully awake, and I sit up, knowing she needs a fresh diaper.

Missy finally rouses a bit, squinting at me in the full sunlight escaping the window blinds. "She must be starving," she says. "I don't know when she last ate."

"I've got her," I say. "You rest."

Missy ignores me, sits up in the bed, and turns to fully face me. "You would make an excellent mother, Romie. It really is a shame what all you've been through." She pats my hand, squeezes it, and I stare at hers, the wonder of her words sinking into me.

"We shall soon see."

She cocks her head, not understanding.

"We were going to tell y'all yesterday evening before everything happened. I'm pregnant."

Her eyes grow wide now, and she reaches across Paisley Grace and pulls me to her, hugging me tightly over the crying bundle beneath us. "Oh, Romie! I'm so happy for you! Truly I am!"

When she releases me, I see the shimmer in her eyes, know that she means what she says. I think I will remember this moment forever. I reach out and hug her again, bringing a full-on shriek from Paisley Grace. I can't help but laugh. "Okay, little doll," I say, scooping her up. "Let's get you changed and get some breakfast in that little belly."

"Did you hear that, Punkin? Auntie Romie is gonna give you a baby sister!"

I'm surprised that the heaviness around us seems to have lifted, and I laugh at her words. "Did you hear what you just said? It doesn't even make sense. Auntie's gonna give you a sister? You *must* be exhausted."

"Hey!" Jasper's voice comes through the wall. "The chief chef is gonna have breakfast, er, *dinner*, on the table in ten. Get a move on!"

"Perfect timing," Missy says. "You gotta love that man."

Again I wonder at her comment, but I push the nagging doubt from my mind, pleased to have this moment of lightness—dare I consider it *happiness?*—among us.

After we've changed the baby, finished our eggs, bacon, and toast, and I've started a second pot of coffee for caffeinated fortification, Missy sidles up next to me at the kitchen sink. "Can I borrow the Grand Cherokee?"

It takes me a split-second to wrap my head around her question.

"I need to go home and pack up for rehab," she says. "I'm hoping you'll watch Paisley Grace for me. There's a few things I need to take care of before I go in."

I can't explain the uneasiness that keeps me from speaking, and when my belly tightens, I blame it on too much coffee, mentally scolding myself for drinking two full cups while pregnant. "I can come help you," I say. "We can bring the baby."

Missy pulls the dishtowel from my shoulder, takes a plate from the drainer, and wipes it dry. "Thank you, but I just need a minute alone." She softly touches my arm. "You understand. A lot has happened." Then she huffs. "A whole lot."

"Sure. Okay. Yeah. If you're sure you don't want help?"

"I've gotta pay a couple bills, cancel my salon appointments, clean out the fridge—I'll bring the milk and anything that'll spoil back to y'all when I come." Her voice seems too sweet and too bright, almost pleasant, for the drudging tasks she has ahead of her during this awful time.

I nod. "Why don't you bring your appointment book to me, and I'll make the calls tomorrow."

"You sure? You're not working?"

"Me and Jasper already planned last night that I'd take a few days off . . . you know, we figured we'd need to get the baby settled in, work out a schedule with our jobs, get ahold of your sitter . . . that kind of thing."

"Oh, yeah, that makes sense." She stares at me for a moment, and her gaze is thoughtful, even tender. I marvel at this side of her that I've rarely seen lately, and how she's been curiously pleasant all morning, given what she's facing.

She folds the towel and hangs it over the lip of the sink, then smooths her rumpled blouse. "Well, if you've got things under control here, I'll head on across the mountain and go home. I can't wait to get a hot shower."

Jasper walks into the kitchen, fresh-smelling and damp-haired from his own shower. "I laid out a clean towel for you," he says to Missy.

"Thanks, but I'm going home for a bit. I need to pack and take care of some bills and things before I go into rehab tomorrow." She smiles at him. "I hope y'all will drive me out there in the morning. I know it's a ways, but I don't want to leave my car there for a whole month."

Though we've already discussed this, his eyes widen. "A month of rehab."

"*Inpatient* rehab," I say. "It's the best thing." I want him to encourage her.

"No, yeah. You're right."

Missy touches his forearm, then wraps her fingers around it and squeezes. "Romie said y'all will take care of Paisley Grace. That's okay, right?"

He blinks. "Yeah. Yes, of course!" He looks toward the baby carrier where she sits quietly for a change, sucking on the ear of a plush bunny.

Missy slides her arms around Jasper, gives him a hug, holds him till he frowns and shoots me an awkward look. "I don't know what I'd do without you two," she says as she finally releases him. She looks toward Paisley Grace. "You have it lucky, little girl, to have these two people in your life. They are the best godparents a little girl could ever have."

She smiles at me so genuinely that my eyes begin to puddle.

"Now you be good for them while I'm gone." She steps to the carrier, bends down, and caresses the baby's face. "I'm going to go away for a while, little love. Mommy is going to get better—*be* better, just for you. Everything I do from this moment on, I will do for you, because I love you, Paisley Grace. I love you with all my heart."

CHAPTER FOURTEEN

JASPER

I step around the toddler play-table, dodge the wild-haired Barbie doll and the Thomas the Tank Engine stuffed plush on the floor, and carry my coffee cup to the dining nook table. The newspaper is still folded where I laid it, but the date stares back at me, and I wonder if Romie realized when she awoke that today marks three years since Missy died.

Sometimes I think of her last words to Paisley Grace, and I ponder yet again if we should have known, if we should have understood that when she spoke them, it was her forever goodbye. Romie doesn't think so. Romie believes she intended to come back, to go into rehab, to get better for Paisley Grace. Romie says it was just too much for Missy, going into that empty house alone, knowing the baby would be a grown woman before her daddy got out of prison.

When hours had passed and Missy hadn't returned, Romie called to check on her, to remind her to bring to us all the diapers and formula she had on hand for the baby. But she didn't answer. Romie tried again about twenty minutes later, thinking maybe Missy had been in the shower.

I knew before I ever pulled my rattle-trap truck into their driveway what I might find, though I expected to find her stoned, not dead. She was already chill to the touch when I got there.

It was her boots that got to me. Though we were full into May, a pair of Missy's winter boots sat cockeyed beside the bed where she laid, arms angled at her sides, her mouth and eyes open. On her stomach lay a small, waxy envelope, empty. But it was the plastic baggie protruding from one of her boots that finally caught my eye, and when I lifted it out, it held another of the waxed envelopes, this one still holding three blackish-brown rocks. For a moment, I thought it was coal, and I couldn't make sense of why she'd hide it there. Then I realized it for what it was. Heroin.

I thought of my own old mining boots, and of the money I'd stowed inside one of them back in the little house at Etter's. If the cops had searched Missy's house—and I still don't know if they ever did—they didn't find Missy's hiding place in her winter boots.

I stood and gently drew a hand over Missy's face, closing her eyes. I sobbed as I thought of Romie doing the same thing for my daddy, realizing for the first time the awful depth of sadness she must have felt that day. After a moment, I gathered myself enough to know I should call the police, and I briefly thought I should hide her boots, put them back in the closet where she'd no doubt kept them. But they were gonna know what killed her. Without question, they would know anyway. They might as well see for themselves. And shame on them for not finding that heroin first.

It was then I looked around for the tourniquet Jimbo had mentioned—*had it been only a day ago? It seemed like months*—the tourniquet that had dangled from Missy's arm. But there was no tourniquet, no needle, no spoon. I noticed then the darkness at the corner of Missy's mouth where she'd drooled. She'd *eaten* it. She'd chewed up God-only-knows how many of those little black rocks, those lumps of killer coal.

Still today, I wonder if she knew when she left this very room, our kitchen, when she said those final words to her tiny daughter, if she had planned to overdose. *Pre-meditated.* The same word used when Jimbo got 25-to-life.

I think I should go see him today; this day that must be awful for him. I don't go visit him as much as I used to at first, and I get the feeling he doesn't want me to come. His hardness frightens me, gives me nightmares even, though not for myself, because we're securely separated as he's held behind a thick plexiglass window when I visit. It frightens me for him, for who he's become, for who he will finally end up being one day. He's bulked out and muscled now, and there are two green-blue teardrops—prison tattoos—at the corner of his eye. First there was one, and I believed it was for Weasel, because he killed him. But a year later when the second one appeared, I wondered if it was in memory of Missy, maybe because he felt he'd killed her somehow with his actions, which isn't at all true, or if he's killed someone else while in prison. I tried to ignore it, stare instead at the brown of his eyes, but it was like a gnat at the corner of my eye, irritating and itchy. Jimbo tapped the tattoo with a finger, made sure I saw it. I gave the tiniest nod I could, so he'd know I'd seen it. I never asked about it, in part because our conversations are recorded and I didn't want him to further incriminate himself, but mostly because I don't want to know why it's there.

I sometimes wonder how a man can come to the point of killing another, and then I think of that day in Richwood, when, without the bravery—let's call it what it was—of that bug-eyed kid who touched my cocked arm, I may have pounded that smart-alecky boy into the dirt, the boy who said those hateful things about Romie and Winter and Autumn. I know for certain that I was furious enough to put a serious hurting on him, but I like to think I wouldn't have killed him. I think too of Big Mike and Nick, and what they did to Romie and Missy. I've still never told Jimbo what I know—*not mine to tell*, as Romie said. I think that if I'd have told him, together me and him woulda killed those two deader than doornails, and I'd be sitting in prison beside him. Bad things happen when you're that enraged. And that kind of hot anger simmers all over Jimbo now. He's got so much rage you can smell it on him.

It surprises me the rare times when Jimbo laughs anymore. Sometimes it's several months in between, and I'm grateful to the point of giddy when it happens, when I see for a split-second the lighthearted Jimbo he used to be. His smile isn't the same boyish smile he wore even as a grown man—it's more of a panicked sneer these days, like that of a wild horse whose first bit is being yanked on. Sometimes I lay awake at night imagining what new thing has put it there.

A squeal, followed by a fit of giggles, pulls me from these dark thoughts, and I look up from my nearly empty coffee mug toward the sound of fat little feet rapidly padding toward me across the polished wooden floor. "C'mere, little man," I say, scooping Jacob off the floor before he falls headlong, still top-heavy as he's learning to run.

Romie appears behind him, dressed in maternity scrubs with her hair in a towel, holding Paisley Grace on her hip. Romie deposits the toddler at my feet, where she grabs at my leg and pulls herself up, she, too, still unsteady at times. She's been walking for almost a year now, though she oftentimes fell and nearly always had a scratch, or a bump, or a bruise from her frequent tumbles. (We used to halfheartedly joke that *Grace* was a poor choice for her middle name.) I imagine it'll be no time until Jacob outpaces her, but it seems he has helped encourage her development in many small ways.

"Da," she says. "Da-*da!*" She raises one arm to me, her pudgy little fist opening and closing, demanding I hold her, too. I lift her onto my knee, bouncing both babes, feeling pleased that she now weighs more than Jacob. *Da-da.* At first, I tried to stop her from calling me that name, but Romie said to let her say it. Jimbo did, after all, sign the legal papers for us to adopt Paisley Grace, and shortly after he'd been transferred to max security, he told us to never bring her to see him again. Said he wanted her to think of me as her daddy, though I know it killed him deep inside to say that. Romie still mails pictures of Paisley Grace to him about every other week or so, though he never mentions them, and he refuses to let Romie visit him anymore. I told him it wasn't fair to her, because she lost Missy, too, and Missy was her very best friend. I told him that he is the only brother Romie has ever had, and he's taking that away from her, too.

Still, he refuses. He says it's because Romie reminds him too much of Missy, but Romie says it's because she won't leave without praying for him, and it makes him grumpy because he's under conviction to get saved. I pray every day that she's right, and that he'll someday accept what forgiveness God offers him, as I think it's his guilt that's making him so flint-hard against everyone and everything.

"You're soon gonna need to sprout another knee," Romie says now, rubbing her beach ball of a belly. She's over seven months along now, and the baby girl inside her is doing fine, Dr. Gloria says.

I nod. "We're both gonna wish we had more arms, too, when we've got three little ones running around here." I kiss Jacob on the top of his head. "You're gonna have to start using the potty chair like your big sister," I say to him. "I can't deal again with two of you in diapers." The thought makes me grimace.

Romie reaches for my mug, carries it to the kitchen where I hear her refill it, then pour a little splash in a cup for herself. "You be sure to get a headcount today at work, and text me with the number, you hear?" she says. "Becky's gonna watch the babes an extra hour or so this evening, until one of us gets home, so I can finish up the shopping. I want to make sure we have enough burgers and dogs to feed everyone Saturday."

She's referring to the graduation party she insists on throwing for me. She's proud as a momma hen that I'll walk the stage and get my bachelors diploma. We've already decided I'll go for my master's, and Redd is all for it, too. Environmental Policy and Management. It's the perfect match for everything I believe and know, and what I've learned has already helped me write a grant that awarded Blue Gold Wind Energy three-hundred K to help expand the wind farm. It's a drop in the bucket of Redd's grand plan, but when he received the award notice, he kissed me square on the forehead, so he's all a-go for my education, now.

I put the kiddos on the floor, and Paisley Grace squawks when Jacob picks up her Barbie, then she waddles toward him, picks up his Thomas plush, and offers it in trade. We could learn a lot from these babes.

Romie pulls out the chair across from me, backs into it, her belly keeping her several inches from the table. My, but she is gorgeous when she's pregnant. Glowing, *radiant* is the word that comes to mind. I open my mouth to tell her, but she's already nattering on about things she'll add to her grocery-store run for the party; napkins, extra ice, and more things I expect she'll forget by the time she gets there.

I unfold the paper as she talks, and the headline stuns me. *CHEMICAL SPILL POISONS GHENY RIVER: Hundreds of Thousands Without Water.* I suck in a breath.

"What is it?" Romie asks.

I look at her, but I can't speak.

"No! No! No!" Jacob shouts, and I gape at him, wondering how he has learned to read my thoughts as well as Romie does. "Mine!" he says, and Romie turns to him as he yanks his Thomas toy from Paisley Grace's hands, falling on his diaper-padded bottom in the process.

"He said a new word!" Romie says. "*Mine!* That's great, Jakey!"

He turns to her, confused, hugging his stuffed toy to his chest.

Romie beams at me, then her smile falters. "What is it?" she asks again. "What's wrong?"

I read the headline to her, and her mouth opens. It's a moment before she speaks. "Keep reading."

My mouth is dry, and I pull a sip of coffee, then begin. "At 7:14 a.m. yesterday, a leak was detected at the Gheny River Chemical Plant, allowing approximately 10,000 gallons of 4-methylcyclohexane methanol"—I pause, pleased at how easily the word rolled off my tongue, evidence of my studies—"that's MCHM," I say and glance at Romie, then continue, "allowing approximately 10,000 gallons of 4-methylcyclohexane methanol to pour into the Gheny River, just upriver from the Gheny County Municipal Water intake. This intake system provides water for over 300,000 people."

I let out a low whistle. "At 6:00 p.m., the Office of the Governor issued a 'Do Not Use' order. The West Virginia Department of Health and Human Resources immediately contacted the Center for Disease

Control in Atlanta, Georgia, about the chemical release and requested assistance in testing the levels of MCHM, as well as any other chemicals that may have spilled into the Gheny River and subsequently the Gheny County water supply."

I pause and look at Romie, see how ghostly white her face has blanched. She's slowly shaking her head, and her hands are holding her belly, as if she's protecting the life inside from the poison. "You okay?" I ask.

"That's upriver . . . what? Two, two-and-a-half hours? The Gheny flows into Nubbins Ridge River, and that splits down into Stump Branch." She hoists herself from the chair, walks into the kitchen, where I hear her open the pantry door. "Two cases of bottled and a gallon jug," she calls to me. "We need to stop on the way to work and pick up what water we can, while we can still get it. Can you bathe and shower in chemical-tainted water? You can't, can you."

My gut sinks. I already know where this is gonna lead. We won't be able to drink our water—not that we're drinking it anyway, though we do bathe in it. I can't recall learning anything about what MCHM will do to the skin, though I can't imagine it would be good for it, especially the tender baby skin of our young'uns.

I already know by Romie's tone what's next. She will want to leave here. My Runaway Romie.

I watch Paisley Grace and Jacob playing on the floor. I stare again at the hateful headline on the front page of the paper. We are seven weeks from Romie's due date. I think of Daddy and how he wanted us moved away from what he called "this poisoned land," and I wonder how quickly Romie will say that we have to up and leave here, what I will say to Redd, and where we will run to now. I clench my jaw, decide there's no way I'm leaving this time. This here's home.

". . . you listening to me?" Romie says.

I look up to see her standing with one hand on her belly, the other against the wall. "What?"

Romie shakes her head. "I said, you gotta see what you can do here. You know important people now, people at MSHA and the Environmental Services Division." She waves a hand through the air. "Make some calls today. See what you can find out. Redd will want to help out, too, I'll bet. There's gotta be something we can do. Start a petition or something." She puts a finger to her chin. "No, that probably won't help right now, but maybe later.

"I'll call my ladies' group at the church, and we can get a prayer chain going and start a donation drop-off center in the fellowship hall. I'll call the offices in the medical park and reach out to the hospital purchasing director, start collecting cases and gallon jugs of water. We can call the grocery stores around here, see if we can get some contributions. It'll be a tax write-off for them, yeah?" She pulls the towel from her head, slings it across her shoulder, and runs her fingers through her damp hair, tousling it around her shoulders. "Tell Redd you want one of his big trailers. We'll see how quickly we can fill it, and we'll haul water up there Sunday or Monday, make a donation." She nods in agreement with herself. "Those folks are gonna need our help."

I stare at her, marveling at her strength, at her wisdom, at this woman she's become. When did it happen?

"Jasper?" she says. "You with me?" She snaps her fingers toward me, as if I'm in a daze.

Maybe I am. "I—I just thought . . . I figured you'd want to leave here."

She stares at me, studies me a moment, until Paisley Grace toddles back into the room, holding her Barbie doll upside down, chewing on its feet. "Leave?" she says, glancing at me before she awkwardly picks up our daughter, lifts her onto her hip.

I shrug, still feeling confused, but proud, and a little afraid to believe what is happening here. "You know. Like when we moved to North Carolina to . . . to get away from . . . so we'd be safe. And then we moved to Etter's when . . . you know . . . I just figured you'd want to go."

Her small smile is sad and thoughtful. She sits again, this time in the chair next to me, reaches out and offers me her hand. I take it in mine and squeeze, rubbing my thumb across her fingers.

"This is our *home*, Jasper." Her gaze flits around the dining nook, out toward the living room, and back to me. "We have to protect this place, this land." She squeezes my hand, and her voice grows softer, thoughtful. "One day I want Jacob and Paisley and this here baby to walk through the woods with us. I want them to bite into the skin of a wild purple plum. I want them to pick serviceberries so we can make us a pie."

The knot in my throat nearly chokes me, but I manage to swallow around it. I rise partway from my chair, hold my wife's face in my hands, kiss her deeply. "I love you more than the mountains and twice as long," I say, and I mean every word of it.

Romie rests her palm on my cheek and smiles the most beautiful smile this world has ever seen. "We're bound to this land by blood," she says. "We're not going anywhere." She bounces Paisley Grace on her knee, then she leans down and plants a kiss on the top of the toddler's curly red head. "Besides," she says to our daughter, "not everybody tucks tail and runs."

***

AUTHOR'S NOTES

If you or someone you know suffers from opioid addiction, *stop reading this now*, and call 1-866-312-4647 or visit *www.Addictions.com* for help.

*

Mountaintop removal mining companies continue their rapacious destruction of Appalachia and other regions of America, destroying ancient mountains that will never be replaced; ruining rivers, streams, wildlife, and habitats, and damaging entire communities and the lives of those who live there. Please visit *www.ilovemountains.org* or *www.appvoices.org* for more information and to learn what you can do to help.

*

The fictional Gheny River chemical spill is modeled after the actual 2014 West Virginia chemical spill that affected over 300,000 people, causing over 600 victims across nine counties to seek medical attention for poisoning and chemical burns. Freedom Industries, Inc.'s (chemical plant's) absentee owner Gary Southern was fined $20,000 and sentenced to thirty days in prison for the spill which dumped approximately 10,000 gallons of 4-methylcyclohexane methanol into the Elk River just above the county's municipal water intake.

ACKNOWLEDGEMENTS

My deepest gratitude will always be to my dear husband, Randy; our precious son, Jacob; my mother Nilene Browning; and superb sibs Gary Browning and Becky Gray, for their never-ending encouragement, support, and love. I hope to always return it tenfold.

Unending appreciation and admiration belong to my steadfast mentors, Stewart O'Nan, Les Standiford, Leslie Pietrzyk, Marlin Barton, Robert Olmstead, Susan Tekulve, and Edward Falco, whose instruction, advice, and fine examples helped shape much of this work.

I gratefully acknowledge my amazing Redhawk Publications team; Patty Thompson, Robert Canipe, and Tim Peeler, who encourage, uplift, and inspire me to keep writing.

I'm thankful to my support and critique crews: Joe and Robin Fenwick, Cheryl Russell, Kristina Cooper Atkins, Micki Browning, Vinod Busjeet, Wikki Krawczyk, Jennifer Mondello, Yolande Clark-Jackson, Karin Gillespie, Karin Salisbury, Doreen Leone, Cat Pleska, Rachel Lanier Bragg, Eric Giroux, Mark Vickers, Graham Morse, Alec Osthoff, Liat Faver, Donna Girouard, Leigh Raper, Luis Castill, Rosie Sophia, Bob Dolan, David Allan Kelly, Caitlin Coutant, Sally Luce, Ginger Allison, Pamela Akins, Nancy Angles Grant, and Vicki Mahood. Thank you for sludging through the trenches with me.

Special thanks to Jeremy Wright for sharing your clinical orthopedic expertise and critiquing Jimbo's trauma, and to Johnny Holcomb for teaching me about wind energy and turbines and how they can help save our planet.

I'm grateful to the Converse University Low-Residency MFA Program (especially you, Rick Mulkey!), and Eckerd College's Writers in Paradise for providing me with lifelong writing tribes and a safe place to learn and grow on so many levels.

Lastly, I've written this story in loving memory of my dearly beloved daddy, Willis Gratton Browning, who was my inexhaustible, cheerleading Iron Man, and who inspired and appreciated Killdozer; and my granddaddy, Gaston Burrell Walker, the first coal miner I ever loved.

DISCUSSION GUIDE

There are no right or wrong answer to these questions; there is only your thoughtful opinion to be shared with others in your group, book club, or classroom. The author and her publisher hope these questions will encourage lively, respectful discussion of this work.

1. This novel is narrated by alternating viewpoints (Romie's and Jasper's). How does this inform, or misinform, the characters' viewpoints of what happens? How does it inform you, as the reader? Were the two narrators trustworthy and dependable, or unreliable?

2. Romie assumes much of Paw's care during his terminal illness, taking him to doctors' appointments, feeding him, and cleaning him, though both she and Jasper work full-time. Is her responsibility reflective of a socially perceived "woman's role" in parental caregiving? Have you seen or experienced this dynamic in your own family?

3. Both Paw and Jasper express a sense of pride and honor in their work as underground coal miners. Does this change with their introduction to mountaintop removal (MTR) mining, and if so, how?

4. How does the harrowing scene with Jasper and the rabbits reflect Romie's warning of how "damage done to the land" negatively impacts all who live on it?

5. As a child, Romie admired Missy and emulated her. How— and when—did this change? Are any of Romie's own actions responsible for this change?

6. If Jasper feels "at home" living at Etter Vineyards, why do you think he acts out and steals the wine barrels? Why does he keep his actions secret from Romie? Why is Willie so angry at Jasper over the theft and not as upset with Eric?

7. Jasper refers to his wife as "Runaway Romie." Is his description fair, and if it is, why do you believe Romie wants to run from any sign of trouble? Do Jasper's actions support Romie's avoidance of problems, and if so, is that a form of protection, or of co-dependence?

8. Does Romie feel worse, or relieved, when she learns that Missy saw Big Mike? Do you think each of the women make a right, or a wrong, decision in not reporting the man to the police? Why, or why not?

9. Romie expresses her dislike of Preacher. Why do you think she has a distrust of preachers and/or religion? Does that change throughout the story, and if so, what caused the change?

10. What responsibility, if any, do Romie, Jasper, and Jimbo have for Missy's drug addiction? Did Missy receive the support she needed from them in fighting her addiction?

11. Jasper is angered over a teenage boy's sexist and racist comment and almost hits him. Why do you believe Jasper's anger surfaces so rapidly and violently?

12. Does Jasper have any responsibility in Jimbo's actions toward Weasel? Discuss why or why not.

13. Romie desperately wants a baby, and Jasper wants a real homeplace in which to raise his family. How do the (sometimes poor) decisions they make change them? How do the ways in which they achieve their desires affect them?

14. How does Romie's (initially covert) environmentalism change her relationship with her coal-mining husband? Does her influence change Jasper's relationship to the land, or does his first-hand experience with coal mining and land excavation change his opinion on how we affect the land and how the land affects us?

15. What are *your* thoughts on what we mean to the land and what the land means to us? Has this novel changed your opinion in any way?

16. Do you find class structure or classism in this novel? If so, where, and how is it depicted?

17. If you could hear this same story from another character's point of view, which would it be, and why?

A final note . . .

Authors need readers—and *reviewers*. If you like this novel, please recommend it to a friend, and please take a moment to review it on social media. Even a quick, "I liked it!" on websites like Amazon, Goodreads, Facebook, Library Thing (or all of these!) can make a big difference in a book's (and the author's and publisher's) success.

We greatly appreciate your consideration and hope you'll check out other work by this author, as well as our other authors and poets at Redhawk Publications.

ABOUT THE AUTHOR

Rhonda Browning White gleefully resides in Hickory, NC. She received the 2019 Press 53 Award for Short Fiction for her short-story collection, *The Lightness of Water and Other Stories*. Her work appears in *The Ignatian Literary Magazine, Entropy, Prime Number Magazine, Pine Mountain Sand & Gravel, Qu Literary Journal, Hospital Drive, HeartWood Literary Review, Bellevue Literary Review, Steel Toe Review, Ploughshares Writing Lessons, Tiny Text, New Pages, South85 Journal, The Skinny Poetry Journal, WV Executive, Mountain Echoes, Gambit, Justus Roux, Bluestone Review*, and in the anthologies *Appalachia (Un)Broken, Ice Cream Secrets, Appalachia's Last Stand*, and *Mountain Voices*. Four of her stories have been nominated for Pushcart Prizes; alas, she is still a Pushcart bridesmaid. Her blog *"Read. Write. Live!"* is found at _www. RhondaBrowningWhite.com._ She has an MFA in Creative Writing from Converse College in Spartanburg, SC, and was awarded the Sterling Watson Fellowship and the Les Standiford Scholarship from Eckerd College's Writers in Paradise.

Rhonda Browning White is available as a guest lecturer, workshop leader, and book club speaker, virtually or in person. You may contact her at _RBrowningWhite@gmail.com_ to schedule.